The Indigo Solution

PSYCHIC SOLUTIONS, MYSTERY #1

PATRICIA RICE

Book View Café

Author's Note

I HAVE BEEN WRITING ROMANCE FOR FORTY YEARS—MY HOW TIME flies when having fun! And then the plague happened. Isolated for over a year, I needed a challenge to keep from going stir crazy. I took a story that might have been my usual contemporary romance with a psychic twist, added a mystery, allowed a host of interesting characters to insert themselves, and let the story take its own path.

I'm not sure what genre the result might be called, but I hope it's as entertaining for you as it was for me!

For those of you just finding me—my original Magical Malcolm series was built on the premise of an 18th-century world where the characters had no explanation for the curious abilities of my Druidic-descended Malcolms— although my scientific Ives did their best to analyze them.

Here in the 21st-century world, we still cannot explain how our sense of smell can evoke memories and emotions or how some people see numbers as colors and a host of other interesting idiosyncrasies. *My* particular peculiarity is the ability to spill words faster than my fingers can type, with the unfortunate result that it takes me weeks to clean up the mess. We all have our superpowers.

The point of this meandering prose is—we are all as different as pebbles on a beach. We may have certain surface resemblances, but our granular makeup is unique. Each of us is individual, a product of genetics and environment. We may like to categorize by race, gender, religion, or psychic ability, but that's just a classification, not a person.

So, please, do not try to categorize my eccentric characters. They developed in their own environments, with their own peculiar genetic makeups (and in the case of my Malcolms, that can be very peculiar indeed), and I am not making any statements when they do their own things. I can't tell why I spill words any more than I can explain why this particular bunch of insular Malcolms turned out the way they did.

Please do not attempt to insert your reality into my Malcolm fantasy— they'll set your hair on fire. That's just how it is. Enter my world, and you accept it as is.

Hugs to all my wonderful readers willing to do so!

AND FOR WHAT IT'S WORTH—AFTERTHOUGHT DOES NOT EXIST IN real life. Unable to travel during the plague, I couldn't go back to the Carolinas and explore to find the perfect setting, so I've made it up. Yes, I based some of the more eye-opening statistics and realities on actual South Carolina counties. Vague memories provided the setting. The location, however, is entirely fictional to suit my plot. Just imagine someplace a witchy family in the 1600s might settle and go from there. . .

Prologue

GIVEN THE SPEED HIS LOVINGLY RESTORED XKE COULD TRAVEL, Afterthought, South Carolina was less than an hour's drive from Damon Jackson's Savannah office. Roaring down the rural two-lane, Jax glimpsed a brick-pillared welcome sign hidden behind an untrimmed crape myrtle and slowed to a crawl to avoid speed traps. This assignment was far beneath his skills, but he carried out each mission as if the world depended on it, as in fact, it had upon occasion. This wasn't one of them.

Except for his time in service, Jax had lived in the South all his life. The muddy pond and stand of ancient trees after the welcome sign, the county seat's neat streets, ornamented with ancient, shiny-leaved magnolias, didn't charm him. The flowerpots beneath the Victorian lampposts left him unimpressed. His focus was on finding the firm's young ward and prying her out of grasping hands.

He scanned the brick shops—none more than three stories. The church steeple towered a floor higher than the courthouse's cupola. The lack of a Wal-Mart or Piggly-Wiggly wasn't unusual. Like so many other small towns, Afterthought was lost to the faded glory of the Civil War.

With his top down, he could hear sixties music pumping from the Oldies' Café. A Siamese cat licked its paws in the sun of a shop window. Glancing at the cat, Jax almost missed the sign beneath a gabled overhang, but he braked at the glitter of a crystal ball in the big plate window. PSYCHIC SOLU-

TIONS AGENCY written in gold lettering adorned a small black plaque dangling over the sidewalk.

He gave the Malcolms credit for being a class above MADAME THERESAS TAROT READING, which was the usual front for unimaginative flakes and con artists. He glanced in the window as he rolled past, but the sun was too bright against the glass to see inside.

Jax parallel-parked the XKE in front of Hank's Hardware. Climbing out, he strode past a stand of tomato seedlings back to the *agency*. The cat had disappeared. Jax shrugged off the stares from behind windows up and down the street. All small towns had built-in neighborhood watches. If the kid was here, everyone in town knew it. She couldn't hide.

Even though the door was already open, a bell rang as he stepped inside. Momentarily blinded from the sun and the dozens of spinning crystals and whirligigs, he had to wait until his eyes adjusted before noticing the curvaceous female behind the counter in the back.

He blinked again to be certain his vision was clear.

Medusa was his first reaction—except riotous orange curls replaced snakes. Her stony gaze, however, ought to have frozen him to the floor. Women did not generally react to him as if he were Public Enemy Number One.

Although, admittedly, her plush mouth had difficulty forming a disapproving line, and the crystalline blue of her eyes resembled the cloudless sky more than ice. Interesting, but irrelevant.

She had no way of knowing who he was. How did he deserve that glare?

"Mavis Malcolm?" he inquired, asserting his authority with his tone.

He couldn't tell if the tight line of her mouth curved in amusement or disapproval. Her lips appeared to be a dark rose color that clashed with her orange halter top. He was trying too hard to see what the top concealed when the crystals over his head began to chatter. He shut the door on the rising breeze. His first mistake.

He was large and the space was small and cluttered, but that didn't cause his impression of confinement. The knowing glare in Medusa's eyes had him twitching like a prisoner—a sensation he was particularly unattached to.

Jax belatedly realized that he'd arrived in his paint-splattered camouflage and not his usual suit. The Stockton team training exercises resembled war zones.

"Hmmnn?" a disembodied voice asked from behind the counter.

"The Magician? It seems so," Medusa replied. "Best warn the others."

The voice had sounded human, and her reply indicated human, but logic prevailed. Jax towered over his diminutive nemesis to check behind the counter. A Siamese cat gracefully climbed from a basket on the floor, shooting him a disgruntled look as it slipped behind the curtains. "Talk to cats often?"

Closer inspection of his human target revealed orange short shorts and more curves than justified by her slight stature. When he looked up again, amusement tweaked her smile. He hadn't expected the front for a psychic con game to be quite so. . . *interesting*.

He didn't need *interesting* mucking with his mind.

Her eyes laughed. They weren't crystal but blue flecked with silver and green. "I expected better of a Magician," she said, nonsensically. "A little *presto chango* would be good. *Let there be light* would be asking a little much. But talking cats?"

Momentarily befuddled by her scent of ylang-ylang and multi-colored eyes, Jax had to rethink his plan to intimidate his opponent into handing over the child. He'd imagined someone older and savvier, not an obvious flake.

Before he could formulate a suitable action, the door flew open again. An equally diminutive—but much stouter—woman swept in, accompanied by a golden retriever. "I came as soon as I heard the Magician had arrived." The cat followed her in, looking smug, and vanished behind the counter again.

Jax cocked his head to study the new arrival. The flowing red caftan and silver chignon pinned with astrological hairclips formed a stereotype of the charlatan he'd expected. Relieved that he didn't have to terrorize the cat-eyed flake, he focused his attention on the newcomer. "Mavis?"

The charlatan narrowed her eyes and dramatically swung the flowing arms of her gown. "Begone, heathen, spread your enlightenment elsewhere," she intoned, adding more prosaically, "You could start with the mayor."

Behind him, the Medusa snorted but said nothing.

Unruffled, Jax regarded the new arrival. He disliked the deceptive asshole part of law work, but he could handle it—up until the time he throttled his prey. "I do not know any magician. I am Loretta Post's guardian, and I have it on good authority that she is here or on her way here."

"Post?" The older woman looked at him with incredulity. "Do you see a Rolls Royce out there that she could have arrived in? The only fancy car on the street is yours. I can't imagine a wealthy Post would *walk* into town."

"But they might arrive by bus, especially if they're only ten," he countered.

The woman muttered something that had the retriever growling. Jax had the greatest respect for animal teeth and no desire to harm a dog. He could, if he must, but now that he was out of the military, he preferred non-violent confrontation.

"I should have introduced myself. My apologies." He reached for his jacket pocket and realized he was still in the sweat-soaked polo and camouflage pants he'd been wearing when he'd received the call about Loretta. He dug for his billfold instead. "I'm Jax Jackson of Stockton and Stockton out of Savannah." He located a slightly mangled business card and handed it over.

"This says Damon Jackson." The charlatan didn't look mollified. "As in *demon*."

"Named after my grandfather, which is why I prefer Jax." He turned to give another card to the Medusa behind the counter—but she'd vanished.

Hadn't he heard her snorting not five seconds ago?

Seeing the sway of the curtains behind the counter, Jax cursed. He'd been so focused on the woman he thought was the culprit, that Medusa had escaped—probably with his runaway ward. Propping his hands on the old-fashioned wooden counter, he vaulted over the top and raced through the storage room to the open door of the back exit.

One

ONE HOUR EARLIER:

ARETHA FRANKLIN'S "RESPECT" BELLOWED FROM THE OLDIES Café. Whistling her theme song to ward off developing premonitions of trouble ahead, Evie Malcolm bounced down the post office steps, shoving a suspiciously official-looking notice into her back pocket. The April day was too lovely to succumb to paranoia.

"Gertie's ex must be back in town," she told the golden retriever sniffing the scrumptious odor of simmering gumbo. The café owner and her ex were from New Orleans, but Gertie never cooked Creole unless he was in town.

Observation—her means of survival.

Honey snuffled and trotted on, leading her past the café and the empty lot Mavis had been filling with azaleas for years—without permission from the absentee owner. Evie suspected her mother buried charms and talismans beneath each plant for reasons known only to her. A good witch never told.

At this hour, traffic was light. The Harley roaring down Main Street could be heard three counties over. Evie glanced up expectantly—sure enough, the mayor's son was on his way out of town again. She glanced toward city hall—serious black cloud hovering.

The official city notice burned a hole in her pocket. The mayor had a murky aura these days, but tax notices came from the county courthouse, didn't they?

"If Tobias is mad at his dad again, trouble is brewing." The mayor's son had a young soul, but he was usually one of the good guys.

Honey yipped, not because she understood, but because she had food for brains, and they were nearing home. "I could find out what's brewing if people would simply give me a little respect," she told the dog.

Respect wasn't happening. Evie had lived here all her life, and people thought they knew her. They didn't, really, but she understood their limitations.

Despite the small-town mindset, she loved her home of Afterthought, South Carolina. Once a farm town for sharecroppers, it was now the county seat and a tourist destination for city dwellers. The sun sparkling off the windows of the Victorian brick shops and the colorful pots of ivy geraniums decorating the old-fashioned lampposts depicted a fantasy of serenity that big cities didn't offer.

But it was a fantasy, she knew. She saw the dark undercurrents others couldn't.

Orange curls bobbing against her sunglasses, Evie danced to the tune of Aretha down the brick sidewalk. Outside her mother's shop, Evie let the golden retriever pause to admire the Siamese cat lounging on the window sill.

The entire *county* population didn't amount to more than five thousand people—a great place for growing up, a lousy place to find a job.

Correction, a great place for finding jobs like dog walking, a lousy place to apply her real talents. At a hundred pounds, Evie wasn't cut out for more than poodle-walking. And ghost-hunting, although that wasn't precisely a booming business. With a sigh, she tugged her mother's retriever into the Psychic Solutions Agency and Gift Shoppe.

Honey yipped a happy greeting at the plump woman inside.

Garbed in a flowing multi-colored caftan, Mavis Malcolm glanced up from the tarot cards spread on the counter, her misty blue eyes an exact match for Evie's. "There's a turbulence in the air, dear," she reported. "The Magician approaches."

The mayor's murky aura and Tobias's angry departure had already warned her of approaching trouble. Evie glanced at the tarot spread on the counter to better interpret her mother's warning. The card showing Hermes lay smack in the middle—the *Magician*, emblem of new adventure and bringing light out of darkness. Also a troublemaker. *Not* what she needed.

"Maybe the Magician is His Honor, the Right Royal Mayor Blockhead, and he's sold the town for a nuclear dump." She handed over the envelope from the post office. "If he can condemn an entire trailer park, then he's probably declared this neighborhood a disaster zone."

The trailer park condemnation still rankled. Mavis had to sell her double-wide and move in above the shop. The mayor and his council had been granted eminent domain for a pharmacy, which the town badly needed. Somehow, the deal had been bungled and now the homes of dozens of seniors had been reduced to a parking lot used mainly by officials at the county courthouse.

"That boy is bad, I'll grant, but he's a jester, not a Magician." With her graying hair pinned up in a business-like chignon, Mavis slit open the envelope and frowned. She tucked the notice into her pocket without further edification.

"We're not busy." Mavis emerged from behind the counter to take Honey's leash for her morning coffee break. "Lock up after me, and maybe the Magician will pass through without stopping."

"Not busy" was a chronic problem for an agency marketing tarot reading along with ghost busting, animal psychiatry, clairvoyance, and a colorful array of crystals and gewgaws. The gewgaws kept them in groceries. Still, Mavis's premonitions had to be taken seriously. She was good at what she did. Black clouds over city hall and the arrival of a dealer in change were potentially more ominous than lack of business.

Hair prickled on Evie's arms, and she frowned. She was sensitive to the temporal disturbances caused by spirits crossing through the veil, but even though Afterthought's downtown dated to the Civil War, it boasted very few ghosts. Evie had laid most of the local spirits to rest over the years. She probably just needed to put a sweater on.

She waved her mother off, flicked on the television for a weather report, and didn't lock the door as suggested.

"Mrowr?" Psycat, the Siamese, sat up in the window and tilted his head questioningly.

"Magician, from the tarot deck." Flipping to the cable weather map, Evie saw no storms on the horizon. "He explores the world in order to master it. Very powerful card."

"Chainnnnch." Psy snarled, expressing his disapproval. Ever since Evie's vet cousin had experimented with teaching the cat to communicate, the Siamese had had an opinion on everything, or maybe she was hearing her own thoughts. The cat leaped from the window to stalk the store's perimeter.

"Without change, there is no progress," Evie countered, flicking off the TV.

"To whom are you speaking?" a polite voice asked from the open doorway.

Damn, that's what she got for talking to cats. *Scare off the clients, why don't you, Evie?*

Plastering on a smile, she studied the visitor blocking the sunny day. Goose bumps chased up and down her arms. Black clouds, magicians, and now this.

A serious child with wide blue eyes concealed behind black-framed Harry Potter glasses waited for a reply. The child wasn't the problem.

The apparitions sticking to her warned the turbulence had arrived.

"I talk to myself a lot," Evie replied.

Ghosts usually stayed with *places,* not people. Either the spirits or the child possessed some powerful voodoo. She didn't dare drift into the dangerous subconscious state she needed to fully read auras until she understood the situation. "What can I do for you today?"

Wearing her mousy-brown hair in fraying braids, the sturdy child entered the shop with a heavy backpack and glanced around in curiosity. Studying a photo of a haunted antebellum mansion Evie had cured last year, she answered politely. "I am looking for Evangeline Malcolm."

"Who's asking?"

"That's a defensive response," the child said in a tone far too mature for her—ten, eleven?—years.

Beneath the counter, Psy snorted knowingly. Evie nudged the cat with her toe. She had reasons for being defensive.

The child produced a manila envelope from her backpack and laid it on the counter. "My name is Loretta Post. Evangeline is my guardian."

Evie choked on her tongue. The turbulence had definitely landed. Skirting around the insane idea of anyone appointing ADHD-afflicted *her* as guardian, she settled on the impossible. "Post? A Post hasn't deigned to cross the boundaries of Afterthought in. . ." She paused to think about it. "Since great-grandmother Letitia Malcolm ran off with. . ." She squinted, trying to call up the family lines.

"Evan Post, my great-great-grandfather."

"Whatever. Posts don't make Malcolms guardians of their children. They barely acknowledge our existence. Besides, lawyers would be involved. Where are your parents now?"

Looking like a small adult dealing with a dense child, Loretta slid the envelope toward Evie. "Lawyers *are* involved. They say my parents are dead and I know they're not. That's why I had to come alone. Lawyers want my money."

Ahhh, the poor kid. The first stage of grief was denial, and this was a major case if she'd ever seen one. She wanted to hug Loretta's skinny shoulders in sympathy, but the shadows clinging to her sagged with despair. Not promising.

"How did they die?" She added hastily— "Or not die."

"They *said* my parents died in a boating accident." Loretta studied the crystal ball on the counter while choosing her story.

Evie appreciated her efforts. Malcolms learned to fudge the truth early and effectively, if only to live in semi-harmony with their neighbors. Evie waited for the rest of the lie.

"But I know they were coming here to Afterthought. They told me so."

"Their ghosts told you?"

Loretta glared over the top of her glasses. "My *parents* told me. Over the phone. *Before* they supposedly died."

That part of the story needed a little work. "Posts don't come to Afterthought," Evie reminded her.

"They do if they want to sell land," Loretta countered. "Posts own half the town."

"You learned that online, didn't you? The county assessment records are all on the internet these days."

"The point *is*," Loretta insisted, "they weren't on their yacht like the lawyers said. The lawyers are lying. Do you think they could be hiding my parents in a cabin in the woods until they hand over all their money?"

"That's one possibility, I suppose." So was putting them on a rocket to outer space. Probability and possibility did not necessarily equate. And judging by those shadows. . . How could she possibly make the kid accept that her parents might be ghosts? Evie's parenting skills were on a par with her credit record—not so good. "But you gotta understand—I can't look into your story without making a few phone calls to check things out. What's the name of your school?"

Loretta picked up her backpack with an expression of disgust. "You can't call them," she said flatly. "You can't call *anyone.*"

Evie felt an icy shudder of premonition and opened her inner eye to Loretta's aura. "Why?"

"Because the lawyers are trying to kill me."

Loretta's aura flared the clear blue of truth.

Two

THAT DID IT. EVIE DIDN'T LIKE PRYING, BUT THERE WASN'T ANY way she was letting that declaration go unchallenged.

"Lawyers do not—" she started to say to cover the blank look that would appear while she concentrated on the child's aura. "—oh, my," she murmured a moment later instead of whatever she'd meant to say. "An Indigo child."

Evie wondered if all Indigos carried their own ghosts with them. Sad ones. Frightened ones. Weary ghosts who hadn't learned to communicate. Please, please, don't let those poor, pleading shadows be the child's parents.

Evie had *heard* about Indigo children, but she'd never met one. All she knew was that they were supposed to be old souls who were easily identified by their higher than average confidence and sensitivity to the world, occasionally to the point of being disruptive—and disobedient.

Loretta's aura spilled a spectrum of purples, lavenders, and blues, the colors of communication, clarity, and intuition, currently muddy with half-truths. A child's aura should be barely visible, but Loretta's— definitely favored the psychic Malcolm side of the family. Which might explain the ghosts. Malcolm sensitivity was a magnet for trouble.

"An Indigo? Is that an example of a psychic solution?" Loretta asked when Evie didn't elaborate.

Evie squeezed the bridge of her nose and tried to organize her leapfrog-ging thoughts. School counselors had urged her mother to give her Ritalin, but sometimes dealing in extra perceptions simply resulted in solving too many puzzles at once. Spacey thinking had its purpose. "If you're an Indigo child, you should have your own psychic solutions."

"My parents say there are no such things as psychics, only frauds who are too lazy to earn an honest living." The statement sounded like a challenge she hoped Evie could refute.

"Those same reliable, trustworthy parents who named a near stranger as your guardian?" Evie wasn't much on explaining herself to non-believers, and she was just a tad irritable at being taken for a fool. Even the people in town who *knew* she was intuitive often thought she was stupid. Or a bubble off normal. Which was why she got no respect.

But right now, logic ruled. The odds of a stuffy, rich Post leaving their child in the hands of a poor and flaky Malcolm were considerably worse than those of this week's lottery.

"My parents met Evangeline at one of our family reunions." Loretta set her chin stubbornly, sticking to her preposterous story.

Indigo children were fighters, Evie remembered, the warriors who carved a path for future Crystal peacemakers—another phenomenon she had yet to meet in Afterthought, where peace meant the Shepherds' hounds were locked inside the barn for the night.

Family reunion? That had been a decade ago. . . The Malcolms were a very large family, and she had some difficulty believing any Posts had been there. If she remembered rightly, she'd been busy looking for ghosts at the time and hadn't paid much attention to the adults. So that statement was pretty much a solid lie.

Focus, Evie. On something like—where the heck were the kid's parents? With dread, she finally opened the envelope and studied the lawyer jargon on a half dozen legal-sized pages of heavy-duty stationery. If the kid had forged this, she was good.

Psy leaped to the counter and pawed at the envelope before curling up and waiting expectantly.

Ignoring the cat, Evie found her name first and stared at it in disbelief. Not just Evangeline Malcolm, but Evangeline Serena Malcolm *Carstairs*. Not that anyone acknowledged her long-gone father anymore. Malcolm women favored their maiden names even when married, and definitely when widowed or divorced. The divorce rate was pretty high.

She scanned the document until she located Loretta's name—Loretta

Aurora Post. She didn't recognize the letterhead from the law firm of Stockton and Stockton out of Savannah, but she didn't hang out with lawyers, unless credit collectors counted.

"Yo, lady, still with me?" Loretta asked, tapping the counter. "It's all right there."

Evie checked the signature—John and Tiffany Post.

Stroking the smirking Siamese, Loretta watched Evie from the corner of her eye. Evie didn't need to read auras to know the kid was quivering with fear and doubt behind that mask of indifference. Why—and how—had a child that young found her way here?

The thought of losing parents at such a delicate age tugged at Evie's soft heartstrings, but still, she couldn't fall for a con this blatant. The mayor would throw them out of town if the agency got written up one more time by journalists poking fun at their woo-woo methods. Throw in a little child endangerment. . . Turbulence of nuclear proportions.

"This is impossible," Evie argued, shoving the papers back into the envelope. "No one asked me to be a guardian. Shouldn't I have signed these somewhere?"

"*You're* Evangeline?" Loretta asked with what sounded like a squeak of despair. "I expected someone. . . bigger."

Ouch. She couldn't even get respect from a kid. "Five-two is a perfectly normal height," she retorted, pushing the envelope across the counter. Of course, she'd had to take years of self-defense courses to prove that. "My great aunt is an Evangeline. Someone must have mixed us up. She married centuries ago and goes by Brindle these days, not Malcolm."

"Centuries?" Loretta's huge blue-pansy eyes grew wide with doubt and anxiety.

With a sigh, Evie took pity on the brat. "In a manner of speaking. Great-Aunt Evangeline is a Civil War re-enactor. She got married on the battlefield. She lives in Atlanta now." And used her middle name of Valerie because it sounded like Valkyrie, but that wasn't relevant.

"She doesn't work for Psychic Solutions, then," Loretta concluded in relief. "The Evangeline Malcolm I want works here. That must be you."

Yeah, that had to be her, Evangeline Serena. Leave it to her clairvoyant mother to call her hyperactive, attention-deprived daughter serene.

"I only put Psychic Solutions on my resume to sound official. I'm an independent contractor." As in, dog walker, tarot reader, and ghost buster.

Try putting that on a credit application and see what happened. "And I still think you have the wrong person. Why would your parents leave you with someone they've met only once?' Not that she remembered meeting them at all, which made this even more preposterous.

"Maybe because they feared they would be kidnapped and wanted a psychic to find them?"

Psychics only found kidnappers on TV. That statement required explanation.

Belatedly locking the door as Mavis had advised, Evie ushered her newly discovered "cousin" up the stairs to the apartment her mother had carved out of their attic storage room.

She filched a microwave pizza from the freezer, zapped it, and stuck it in front of Loretta. "All right, convince me not to call Stockton and Stockton and tell them I've found you."

Loretta's bangs were so long, they nearly concealed her eyes. Not until she'd finished chewing her first bite did she answer. "My guardian should have control of my millions, not the lawyers. They don't want you to know that."

Millions? Nuking another pizza, Evie leaned against her mother's bright yellow kitchen wall and tried to envision *millions.* She couldn't even envision a hundred dollars all in one place. A million kittens might populate Charleston. A million. . .

"Yo, Earth to Evangeline, you still here?"

Uh uh, she was in la-la land and liking it far better than her crazed reality. "Keep talking," she told the kid. She wasn't a material girl, but the potential of millions. . . Of course, sorting lie from fact was the problem here. She knew she was being played, but she didn't own a cell phone and couldn't leave the kid to run home and do a quick Google search for the kids' parents. Luring the obstinate brat to her home seemed sketchy.

"The lawyers stuck me in this creepy all-girls boarding school where they teach *equestrian skills*," Loretta said with a scorn that could have blistered the pizza without need of a microwave.

"Most girls your age would sell their souls for a chance to ride horses." Evie relinquished dreams of traveling to Machu Picchu and Stonehenge on *millions* and returned to the extremely interesting moment.

Loretta transferred her evil pixie scorn to Evie. "Most girls my age wear *pink* and giggle about boys. Gag me."

Said the glasses-wearing nerd in black and brown. The kid definitely marched to a different drummer. Evie had no problem with that. "I forgot I was talking to an Indigo, sorry. Do you visit your parents on an astral plane?"

"What?" Loretta regarded her with suspicion.

Well, so much for expecting a Post to think *really* far out of the box. "Look, I don't know how else to put this. We don't know each other."

Evie settled at the table with her pizza so she was on a level with the kid. "I don't remember your parents from among a kazillion other people at the only reunion I ever attended. I was only sixteen and your mother probably wasn't even pregnant with you yet. You must have dozens of relatives more suitable to take you in. So why are you here?"

For a moment, big blue eyes puddled up and steamed Loretta's lenses. She stopped to clean them off on her napkin. "You're a Malcolm. You work for a place called Psychic Solutions."

"So does my mother and half my family at one time or another. I just happened to be the one behind the counter today." The only one not better occupied with a real job, but Evie didn't mention that. She could get a job any time she liked. Holding them was another story. She whistled Aretha under her breath.

"You're the Malcolm who talks to ghosts," her pint-sized guest said with certainty. "I read it online. You convinced Mabel Ashcroft's granddaddy's ghost to stop uprooting the mock oranges."

One of her more successful cases, but as far as Evie was aware, the story was *not* online. Mabel refused to let anyone talk about it, or she'd have to explain *why* her granddaddy's ghost was digging up bushes. "How did you learn that?"

The kid returned to her pizza with a shrug. "I ask questions. Mabel's gardener has kids, and they talk."

"Facebook," Evie said with a sigh. "Unbelievable. The world doesn't need psychics. We've got Facebook and Google to answer all, and YouTube to show it."

"*Anyway,*" Loretta continued with a long-suffering sigh, "my parents wanted you to teach me how to use my latent talents."

Evie spluttered and almost choked on her pizza. Coughing, she reached for her ice tea. "Latent talents?"

"I'm psychic," Loretta informed her coldly. "May I have another pizza?"

This would be a good time for a fairy godmother to fly by, or one of her interfering relatives, or even her know-it-all older sister Gracie. Gracie was a teacher. She knew kids. Evie talked to *ghosts*, not kids. And so far, Loretta's ghosts had only learned to manifest, not talk.

"I thought you just told me that your parents thought all psychics are frauds." She got up, rummaged in the freezer again, and found a Haagen-Dazs chocolate bar. Loretta brightened considerably. So, there was a real kid behind the glasses somewhere.

"I lied," Loretta replied. "I was testing you."

Three

SLIPPING OUT THE BACK EXIT, EVIE SIGHED OVER THE IMAGE OF bronzed and sculpted Camouflage Man. Unfortunately, it didn't take a mind reader to know he liked to hunt.

After hearing Loretta's terrifying story of *accidents* that had endangered life and limb, Evie still didn't have a firm grip on what was lie and what was truth. She just knew the child and her ghosts needed help. When she'd heard the angry voice downstairs, she'd told the kid to take the fire escape and hide before she'd gone downstairs to check out the new arrival. Good thing, too, the Magician had an angry aura—never a good sign.

Having heard Loretta scramble down the fire escape, Evie didn't stick around to hear who the Magician claimed to be. Instead, to divert him from her mother and give Loretta time to hide, Evie dashed out the back, deliberately leaving the door open so he would follow. She had twenty-five years of experience in dealing with skeptics, enough to know that men were incredibly dense, single-minded, and easily led astray.

Although, when coupled with Loretta's fears of a killer, the intimidating bodybuilder could easily be a hired thug. His square shoulders had stretched

19

his black knit to its limits, and his pecs would suit a superhero emblem. She favored the Hulk.

And he was chasing after *her*. Evie could hear his boots pounding the pavement of the back alley. The fence should deter him. Shoving Loretta's documents more securely into the back of her shorts, she ducked through the narrow break in the wooden planks behind Hank's and darted across the parking lot to the tree-lined residential street behind it.

When her mother had entered the shop, Evie had taken advantage of the Magician's distraction to examine his aura. His was a narrow band of deep dark red—an angry, aggressive color. Men like that could have violent or easily aroused tempers, but his aura was so compressed as to be more opaque than transparent, making it impossible to read all the hues. Was he or was he not a killer? He certainly wasn't a warm fuzzy parental model.

It was her task to sort out the truth and decide what to do about those guardianship documents. Loretta wasn't lying about being afraid. Unfortunately, she was lying about a lot of other things. It remained to be seen if the Hulk was a liar, too.

Despite all evidence to the contrary, Evie was *exactly* what the child needed to solve this dilemma. Maybe the kid really was psychic. She was part Malcolm, after all.

Beside Great-Aunt Val's house, Evie grabbed a familiar low branch on the pine tree. She had grown up here and called this house her own now. She could play hide-and-seek in the old Victorian all day if she chose, but she preferred not to have superhot-hero trashing the place. She simply needed to give Loretta time to escape. The kid seemed smart enough to accomplish that.

Flinging the guardianship papers through the open living room window and behind her couch with the rest of her mail, Evie clambered up the tree. With practiced expertise, she swung over to the porch roof. She wasn't invisible. She only meant to distract and take a minute to think things through, so she settled down to watch the Hulk lookalike racing down the street. He'd not been able to fit through the fence and had taken the long route around—not lacking in intelligence then.

His head loomed higher than the overgrown gardenia guarding her front yard. He scanned the Victorian like a sniper hunting prey—as if he *knew* this was her place. Evie couldn't have hidden from that sharp gaze if she tried.

So she didn't waste time trying. Her idiosyncrasies had insured that she suffered years of childhood bullying. In retaliation, she had developed many means of creative survival. She was quite good at leveling the odds. Unfortunately, this guy's military buzz cut and menacing attitude had a chilling effect on her anticipated fun. He meant business. *Bummer.*

The instant GI Joe spotted her on the porch roof, he stalked past her gardenia, onto her property. *Trespassing.* Evie chose the ploy designed to deter her most dangerous opponents. She emitted the ear-piercing high C she'd perfected, one loud enough to alert her neighbors and accurate enough to reach a crescendo that set off car alarms. The mayor hated when she did that.

Her sharp-nosed nemesis merely crossed his arms and glared up at her, which ticked her off. Her operatic voice was a musical glory, to be treated with awe. Once she set it off, she knew she had nothing to fear. Nosy neighbors were already dialing 911. Sheriff Troy would arrive within minutes. She'd helped him find missing children over the years. He owed her.

In the meantime, Evie decided to teach the deaf mute below a little respect. She was damned tired of people thinking she was weak just because she was small-boned. She'd graduated with honors from her martial arts classes, but the element of surprise generally saved her from bruising.

Let's see how a Magician took an attack from a Hummingbird.

Evie launched herself feet-first off the roof, aiming for the wide target of the intruder's shoulders. With just the right trajectory, she could stagger him backward—before she hit the ground running, leaving the bully to the not-so-gentle mercies of her neighbors.

To her utter shock, muscled arms plucked her out of thin air before she could hit anything. None of her victims had ever moved that quickly or with such accuracy. Suspended well above the ground, Evie concluded she was too damned old for this trick.

He had arms like steel tree trunks. Pity she couldn't find boyfriends with muscles like his. On second thought, she resented being hauled around like a sack of flour. She continued her high-pitched keening.

Distraction and running hadn't worked. Time for Plan Three—physical assault. Not unskilled in dirty fighting, Evie debated gouging steel-gray eyes but lost her nerve. Since the Hulk was merely looking annoyed, she refrained from jabbing the carotid. Unfortunately, his high-and-tight cut hair was too short for yanking. Instead, she sank her thumbnails into the flesh beneath his square chin, but even his jaw was as hard as the carved bronze sculpture he resembled.

He scowled and waited for her to quit screaming, as if that would happen in his lifetime. Just because she was small didn't mean she could be man-handled by any stray killer. Evie wrapped one fist in his shirt and swung the other at his nose.

He turned his head, and her knuckles collided painfully with his broad cheekbone.

"What the hell did you do that for?" he demanded, tightening his grip on her waist.

Which meant she dangled six inches off the ground, pressed flat against what had to be military armor. Surely no human torso could be that hard all over. She purely didn't appreciate the position.

Did the jerk think he'd saved her from a fall? No one was that delusional. But on the off chance he was, she didn't break her knuckles again but raised the operatic scale. Another car alarm went off. And because she didn't like dangling, she aimed a knee at his groin.

Releasing her waist with one arm, he grabbed the back of her halter top, and picked her off him like an insect, jerking her far enough away to mess up her aim. She nearly broke her kneecap slamming it into his hip bone just as the sheriff's siren pulled up out front.

Her scream and the siren cut off at the same time. The silence was telling.

With satisfaction, Evie dug her thumbs into the pulse points of his elbows. "Hurry, Sheriff!" she yelled. That cry usually sent most bullies fleeing.

The Magician didn't even attempt to escape. Lowering her to the ground, he twisted his arms to grasp hers and nearly crushed the bones of her wrist.

"Yeah, hurry, Sheriff," he called laconically as the yard filled with people. "I want to press charges of assault and battery."

Sheriff Troy had his hands on his gun belt as he skirted the gardenia, but one look at Evie trapped by the Magician's fists, and he dropped his aggressive posture. "We've been wanting to hogtie her for decades. Never saw anyone actually do it, though."

"He's trespassing," Evie protested. "And if this isn't assault, what is? Look at him! He's a stone-cold killer with blood on his pants."

If she was really lucky, Troy would lock him up until she smuggled Loretta out of town. That hadn't been her original intention, but she wasn't letting a little kid anywhere near a man who would crush her like a bug. She'd taken down the biggest man in town with ease. This guy was superhero mate-rial—except for the lawyer/killer thing. Super-villain, then—if she believed Loretta. *That* was a problem.

The impassive stranger released his grip and stepped back. Evie rubbed circulation into her wrists and glared at him. Just because he was twice her breadth didn't mean he could intimidate her.

She made a career of tackling *ghosts*, for pity's sake. Dealing with unpredictable poltergeists registered high on her scare'o'meter.

He looked down at her as if she were a poodle climbing his leg. Evie kicked his shin.

Finally, he winced.

"I could probably charge him with terrorism for looking like that," the sheriff obliged, obviously enjoying her predicament. "But he's got a point. You just assaulted him."

"I'm protecting my property."

"I'm not damaging your property. I was defending myself," the Magician retorted, losing a little of his aloof façade, she noticed with satisfaction. Color flushed beneath the bronzed skin over his square cheekbones, and the grim set of his mouth brought out the dimple in his square cleft chin. Square all over, he was. Not quite six feet but broad everywhere—and muscled.

"He's trying to kill my cousin." Evie knew that was a rash accusation, but she needed to see what he was made of before she decided whether or not to believe him or Loretta.

"If by your cousin, you mean Loretta Post," GI Joe growled, "then she's a runaway, and I'm trying to return her to school."

Evie didn't possess a temper. She had enough flaws and didn't need another. Instead, when she got mad, she got incredibly focused. Unfortunately, that kind of furious concentration meant her conscious mind often checked out and her subconscious took over.

Which it did now. Her inner eye opened. A cold blue-red in his third chakra with a gray overlay had her shivering. Red flares of *lust* staggered her backward.

Evie swayed as her senses switched gears from expected violence to his suppressed passion.

The gorilla caught her before she toppled and plunked her down on the stairs as if she were a vaporous nitwit. "Bring her some water!" he shouted, apparently accustomed to giving orders.

Shaken back from her trance, puzzled by what she'd seen, Evie dismissed his he-man tactics in favor of studying what she'd sensed. No shadow indicated lies or danger—except from his fury. Or his lust. What the devil was this man?

"Scorpio," she finally muttered in disgust. "Intense."

As usual, a crowd had gathered. Now that the law had arrived, her neighbors felt safe enough to lean out their windows. At least, she wasn't in any danger of being murdered in front of an audience.

"Evie takes spells like that," Sheriff Troy explained to the frowning stranger. "She gets weird expressions, then goes kinda limp. She sometimes says crazy things, but so far, she hasn't hurt nothin' but people's feelings."

"Has she seen a doctor?" the Magician growled without a hint of sympathy.

Troy hitched the belt up over his paunchy belly and grinned. "Doc says she needs a healthy dose of Ritalin. Now, are you pressing charges or not? I gotta say, you being a stranger here and all, the judge ain't likely to do you any favors."

"That's cause the judge is my son and he's sweet on her mama," Mrs. Satterwhite called from her bedroom window next door.

Sighing in exasperation, Evie stretched her legs and admired one orange-painted toe peeking out of the hole in her tennis shoe. No respect, no respect at all. They talked over her head as if she were still a child instead of a grown woman who'd just single-handedly saved her cousin from. . .

Heck, she didn't know what she'd saved Loretta from. A Scorpio? One twice her weight? That ought to count.

"If you were attempting to protect my ward," a deep voice rumbled, intruding on her reverie, "then I'll thank you and not press charges."

He'd talked directly to *her* and not the sheriff. And he'd understood what she'd been doing! In surprise, Evie glanced up and immediately regretted doing so. She didn't want to see *laughter* in the eyes of a man who could make Hercules envious.

Call her crass, but from her petite standpoint, muscle-bound men were *not* objects of admiration. His shoulders alone were just way too obnoxious.

"If you're done screaming, Evie, I'm gonna get back to work." Troy tipped his hat. "Seeya in church?"

"If I'm not murdered in my sleep," she called back. "You know who to blame if I wake up dead."

Chuckling, the sheriff shooed the crowd from the yard—leaving her alone with a stranger.

"Evie?" the Magician asked with suspicion.

She should have been insulted earlier when he'd thought she was her mother. "*Evangeline* Malcolm," she clarified, wishing she could read minds as her cousin Priscilla did. He certainly glared at her with the stone-cold eyes of a killer.

"Where is Loretta?" he demanded.

"Probably halfway to Hong Kong by now. Are her parents really dead?"

He hesitated one beat too long for Evie's comfort.

Four

Jax crossed his arms and watched the colorful madwoman scowl. He didn't know what he'd said wrong—hell, for the sake of client confidentiality he hadn't said *anything*—but he waited with interest to see if she would jump him again. That was an experience he wouldn't mind repeating—somewhere a hell of a lot more private. Public spectacles weren't his beat.

His adversary's once perfectly respectable top had slid high up her belly. He politely tried not to stare at her gaping neckline, but her cleavage revealed an eyeful.

Everything about her screamed flaky charlatan—except her crystalline glare and refusal to back down. Or perhaps she was too stupid to understand he could break her in two and still take her remains to court.

When she waited him out, Jax had to drag his mind back to the moment. "I do not discuss the personal affairs of my client with strangers."

"I just introduced myself. Give me your name, and we won't be strangers." She didn't sit still to await his answer but yanked down her top, danced up the porch stairs, and pushed a porch swing, making it clear it would be easier to catch a grasshopper.

Which meant he needed to try a firmer tactic. "Jax Jackson, of Stockton and Stockton, Loretta's guardian." Hadn't she been there when he'd introduced himself earlier? He'd distinctly heard an impolite snort at the time.

"Fine, Mr. Jax Jackson. Loretta is my cousin. We trace our lineage back to my great-grandmother Letitia Post née Malcolm. And I must add, you're doing a damned poor job of taking care of her. She said she left Savannah *yesterday*."

At least she hadn't denied knowing the kid, so half his mission was accomplished. "The fact that I found her without aid of police proves I'm more than capable of keeping up with her. Now where is she?"

Yeah, yeah, he walked right into that one—if he could keep up with the kid, he'd know where she was. He shouldn't allow a grasshopper to distract him. Instead of waiting for the obvious retort, Jax stalked up the steps and entered the house. Rural houses were never locked. "Loretta!"

"You're trespassing. Legally, once you're inside, I can shoot you if I feel threatened," she warned with deceptive nonchalance, following him inside.

Grasshoppers probably didn't own guns. Pocket explosives and charlatans might. He hadn't made up his mind which she was. Since he'd come straight from a role-playing game with members of his firm, he wasn't armed, not by normal weapons anyway. That didn't slow him down.

Finding no obvious hiding place in the cluttered front room, he continued toward the kitchen.

Trailing him, *Evangeline* Malcolm swung onto the Formica counter so her eyes were on a level with his. Orange curls in her eyes, she sat there with her legs crossed like a capricious genie on a magic carpet. How could someone so small have legs so long? Had to be the short-shorts.

The scent of ylang-ylang mingled with hot tar after her stint on the roof. Jax would forevermore acquaint those smells with a half-naked woman straddling his hips before they'd even been introduced. No wonder his mind was in the gutter. He was normally much more focused.

"I'm a lawyer. Shoot me and half the state bar would line up to see you fry." The state bar in several states. He was licensed in most of the southeast. He scanned the kitchen for his missing client and nearly went cross-eyed.

A kaleidoscope would have been easier to search. Hot red, gold, and orange, striped curtains flapped in the breeze from the open window over the sink. The same theme ran through placemats, throw rugs, and dish towels. The walls were a deep, rich red, if he could see past plates painted in colorful roosters.

The cabinets were white and the countertop was battered green Formica, an oasis of sanity in her Day-Glo world, but not one his granite-and-stainless-steel upbringing could relate to. He checked the pantry and found no suspects crouched amid the canning jars—she *canned?*

Refusing to be distracted from his purpose, he looked for another door.

"She's gone," Evangeline said, swinging lithely from the counter and following. "You won't find her unless she wants to be found."

Given the size of this old house and the number of stairways the kid could run up and down, Jax was afraid that was true. Still, he wouldn't be doing his job if he didn't call her bluff and check. Besides, against his will, he was starting to enjoy himself. Out of his element, his inquiring mind demanded he explore the genie's jeweled cave.

He tried to concentrate on hiding places in the high-ceilinged back bedroom, but his attention was drawn to stacks of books, tarot card layouts, scattered CDs—"Puff the Magic Dragon"?—pillows in colors even Crayola didn't know about. The bedroom screamed sixties.

The genie smirked. He wanted to bottle her.

"Here's a rag, catch a few dust bunnies while you're down there. My aunt hasn't been home to clean her room in a while." She dropped a shirt in front of his nose as he checked under the old-fashioned tester bed. The wood floors creaked beneath his weight.

"You ought to nail these planks to get rid of the squeaks." Ignoring the tie-dyed rag, he stood and searched the wardrobe. The house was so old, it had no closets.

"What, and let thieves sneak up on me?" she mocked. "Next time we play hide and seek, I'll know where you are with every step you take."

Jax rubbed his nose and wondered if this was what it was like to have a headache—a nagging pain that wouldn't go away. "Look, the kid isn't even eleven. She's taking the death of her parents hard. She hates school. And she's playing you for a chump. Just tell me where she's at, and I'll address her concerns."

Provided the Malcolms weren't playing *him* for a chump. He'd know more about their business when Roark got back to him. For now, Jax erred on the side of reason. Or heeded the brain in his pants. Hard to tell after having his bones jumped and lovely ripe melons squashed against his chest. He would take this job more seriously if he was facing real danger.

Obviously, he didn't get out of the office often enough.

"Judging by your aura, I doubt you'll listen to her concerns." She threw open the door to a bathroom smaller than his walk-in closet.

Aura? Crossing his arms in exasperation, Jax propped his shoulder on the door jamb and scanned the pint-sized tub designed for his pint-sized tormentor. Or her missing aunt.

"If you're from Stockton and Stockton, Loretta thinks you're trying to kill her," she continued while his mind slid to naked genies in that tub.

The tub was aqua. As in, blue-green. The shower curtain was in both blue and green, stars *and* stripes. "Has your aunt ever considered a career in interior decorating?"

"Now that was just plain mean, not to mention an extremely poor diversionary tactic." She swung on her sneakered heel—she wore *Keds* for pity's sake—and stalked down the dark hall in what should have been an angry huff, except she was too cute to take seriously.

"What do people normally say when accused of being a killer?" he called after her. He'd be damned if he'd share that cluttered living room with her. He'd end up listening to Peter, Paul, and Mary and having his palm read.

Which reminded him—he hadn't searched the shop down the street. He suspected if he checked his text messages, Roark would have provided the family connection between the gray-haired eccentric at the shop and the ginger genie in here.

He removed his shoulder from the frame and debated between aiming for the front door or the upper story.

"She's not at the agency," his nemesis said calmly as he eyed the door she'd left open to the yard.

"Who, Loretta or the brilliant mind-reader who called me a magician?"

"That's my mother. She judged you rightly, didn't she? You stir trouble. Even I'm not likely to find Loretta if you continue turning the town inside out."

"And I should believe you, why?" Although, amazingly, he did. Jax studied that realization instead of walking out. Normally, he had good people instincts. He'd been jumped on, pummeled, kicked, nearly arrested, and otherwise made a fool of by this miniature Barbie. So why in all that was holy would he listen to the flake?

"Because Loretta trusts me and fears you," his tormentor responded without a hint of inflection, answering his internal question as well as his stated one.

Jax itched to push her buttons in the way he knew best, but he'd learned to resist temptation. Instead, he watched her flip a tarot card on the coffee

PATRICIA RICE

table and tried to get a grip on who she was and what she was hiding. It was his job to understand people, and he was damned good at it.

She grimaced and shuffled the deck. She wasn't even looking at him. *That's* what was bothering him—she wasn't the least bit worried. She *knew* he wouldn't find the kid, even if he tore the house apart.

Despite all the hysterical melodrama, the sarcasm, the cleavage exposure, the seemingly bubble-brained Evangeline Malcolm had *deliberately* plotted every single solitary step to give the devil child a chance to escape. She hadn't even objected to his searching the house, because it gave Loretta more time to get far, far away. *Damn.*

"You're a witch, you know that?" Jax shut the front door, threw a stack of Neil Diamond tapes out of a papa-san chair, and gingerly perched on the circular bamboo edge, praying the rickety basket wouldn't tilt and dump him on the floor. If the kid was upstairs, she'd have to come down sometime.

"So I've been told." Evangeline shrugged and settled cross-legged on a battered shag rug as if she had all the time in the world. "What's your excuse?"

"For what?" He scanned the room, searching for some clue that Loretta had been here.

"For being who you are. All my life, people have called me a witch, so fine, I act like one. Did people call you a robot?"

"I'm not a robot."

"You act as if you have a stick up your rump. You're a robot with suppressed anger issues."

That would be thanks to his adoptive father and boss, but that was his issue and not for public consumption. He owed Stephen Stockton too much to complain.

Even if the genie really was the kid's cousin—and it had to be a far distant relationship since her name wasn't on his short list of the kid's family—he still had to take Loretta back to school. Multi-millionairesses needed security.

"Witches don't listen to Neil Diamond," he countered, somewhat sense-lessly. Maybe the incense was affecting his brain. He searched for its source but could see no telltale smoke. His gaze fell on a crystal bowl of dried rose petals. Potpourri, not incense. From his experience with frauds, she simply didn't add up.

"My aunt's house, remember?" The popsicle-colored genie glared at the cards she'd laid out on the floor, picked up one that looked vaguely male, and

30

ground it beneath her sneaker heel. She gave it an extra slam for good measure, and Jax winced. He was pretty certain she was seeing him in that card.

"I prefer Tchaikovsky." She handed him a different deck from the one she'd laid out. "Shuffle, then lay out six on top, six underneath." She indicated the square black plastic table beside his chair.

"Your tastes run to the 1812 Overture?" he asked in sarcasm. Maybe she laced her potpourri with narcotics, but he couldn't see any sign of Loretta here. Or danger. As far as he knew, tarot cards didn't kill.

"I'm not normally violent." She disconcerted him by hitting close to the topic on his mind. "So, no, I don't need cannon to enjoy Russian passion."

She was talking about Tchaikovsky. Relieved, he threw the cards as instructed. The kid had run here for a reason. *Know Thy Enemy* was carved into his frontal lobe.

"But as Napoleon did the Russians in 1812," she continued, "people underestimate me." She flipped a thirteenth card onto the deck he'd laid out and sighed deep enough to pull her knit top tight across her breasts. "The planets hate me."

He studied the card she'd thrown. It was labeled *The Magician.* Glancing back at her, he saw her eyes widen and her pale eyebrows rise in shock.

Abruptly, she rose from the floor. "Do you believe in ghosts?"

Did the woman ever sit still?

"Of course not." Jax rested his weight on his feet to leverage out of the rickety chair, wondering what in hell had set her off.

"Then go back to Savannah and leave Loretta to me." She rummaged behind the couch and picked up a manila envelope from a stack of mail and magazines scattered beneath the open window. "This document proves that I'm her guardian."

With a snort of disbelief at the declaration and her filing system, Jax drew out the paper printed on Stockton letterhead. It looked amazingly genuine, which meant she must be a con artist of a far higher caliber than her online presence indicated.

He scanned the verbiage and the signatures in growing alarm. The document was dated after the one in the firm's file. If the papers were genuine, he should have a copy, and he didn't. But they looked damned real, and he'd have a hard time proving they weren't. The signatures were even notarized. He memorized the notary's name. If it was properly filed in court, *it would give her complete control of Loretta's fortune.*

His temper started to catch up with his thoughts, and he glared at Evangeline Malcolm, presumably the Evangeline Serena Malcolm Carstairs mentioned in the guardianship papers. "This looks purely mercenary to me. What does it have to do with ghosts?"

Five

EVIE COULDN'T IGNORE THE FRANTIC GHOST HOVERING JUST over the intense Scorpio's left shoulder. She crossed her arms and regarded Mr. Jax Jackson with her inner eye. She was starting to tune into his wavelength faster now. As before, his aura shot red-hot flares, but this time, she could connect the flares with his chakra. Finally, she had a better grasp of what she was dealing with—a literal-minded, ruthless control freak. No help for Loretta there.

An aura like that revealed intense focus and a buttload of passion—a character capable of killing or loving deeply. The dark shadows beneath indicated he'd already tried the killing. Soldiers killed, she realized. Still, she couldn't take chances with Loretta's life. Decision made.

"If you don't believe in ghosts, then we'll have to converse on levels you can understand." She said it with more assurance than was justified given he was a lawyer who could have her locked up for the better part of her life if those papers were fake. Stupidity wasn't one of her many flaws.

She forced her gaze not to drift past Jackson's steely eyes to the furious shade behind him. "That document should be sufficient to convince the judge that I'm Loretta's guardian. I want her school records transferred here. If you'll arrange for a clothing allowance, I'll see she's appropriately dressed for the public schools. I shouldn't need to touch what she calls her millions."

Although, if the distinctly male apparition urgently shaking his head behind Jackson's right shoulder was to be believed, Evie might have to recant that declaration in the near future.

Money might be necessary to escape a killer. What the heck did a dog walker know about killers? *Nada.*

Evie didn't want to believe Macho Man was the psycho Loretta feared, but the specter behind him seemed quite adamant about wanting *Jax* Jackson gone, which was a shame. She liked a good challenge and was starting to enjoy wearing his patience to a frazzle. Killers really ought to have muddier auras than his, shouldn't they? She'd have to introduce herself to one to find out.

"You need to go now," she told him firmly, collecting her scattered thoughts.

"You're seeing something in those cards that you actually believe?" he asked in incredulity, looking up from the papers she'd given him.

She jerked the documents from his grasp. Because his square frame blocked the front exit, she turned on her heel and headed for the kitchen. "If you won't leave, I will."

She might not have experience with lawyers, but she recognized Jackson's stubborn streak. Arguing with the man was futile. She jogged down the back steps and through the broken hedge into her neighbor's yard. If he intended to murder her, it would be in front of the town gossip.

To her disappointment, he didn't follow. The universe had never sent her a Magician before. She shivered. A man who could shine a light on darkness. . . Could lawyers do that?

Better question, did she really want to see what evil looked like?

She jogged down the alley behind the Main Street stores, pondering how to keep Loretta away from her lawyer guardian. The Fool couldn't deceive a Magician without help. But she wasn't an utter Fool. She popped in the back-door of the bookstore/stationery/business shop and left the guardianship papers for Remy to copy and hold onto until she returned.

Reaching the agency's loading door, Evie heard Mavis in the front. Mid-day clients didn't exist, and her mother didn't normally carry on conversations with Psy. Despite her veterinarian cousin's attempts, no one could have a reasonable discussion with a cat. Or her mother, for all that mattered. That probably meant Jackson had taken the street path to the shop. If he wanted to search the premises, she hoped he enjoyed getting around Mavis.

She couldn't cross the old pine boards of the storage room without the floor creaking. Since she didn't want her mother murdered by anyone but herself, Evie grabbed the store's secret weapon and lingered behind the curtains to study the situation.

Mavis didn't turn from her examination of the crystal ball on the counter, but she knew Evie was there. She always did—another annoying factor. "Mr. Jackson appears to have misplaced his ward, dear. Is it safe to tell him where to find the poor girl?"

With a sigh, Evie brushed past the gauze and into the sunlight flooding the shop. Magic Scorpio Jax Jackson leaned his broad shoulders against the wall between the front door and window, his muscled arms crossed over his football-player chest. The only physical point she'd give him was that he wasn't six feet tall and didn't loom over her.

He quirked one dark eyebrow and focused his steely gaze on her raised weapon.

"A barbecue fork?" he asked with disbelief.

"Stainless steel, better than a stiletto, totally legal, guaranteed to toss a side of ribs." Evie laid it on the shelf below the counter and answered her mother. "His aura is angry and stubborn but not that of a child molester. I have to reserve judgment on whether or not he's a killer since he's obviously military. His tarot verifies he's the Magician, and combined with his aura, that could be dangerous and powerful, but not necessarily malevolent."

"Then I can tell him—"

Evie vehemently shook her head. Mavis didn't finish but gazed at her questioningly.

"I need to communicate with the ghost warning me against him. The apparition vanished after Mr. Jackson left, and it's not with him now, which is very unusual. Spirits generally stay in one place, and this one never visited until he and Loretta showed up."

Jax rolled his eyes. "Give me a break, ladies. I'm not a naïve ten-year-old, and you can't convince me of your so-called paranormal abilities by talking nonsense."

Evie nailed him with her glare. "You want science? Neurology studies prove that a degenerative lack of cells in the area of the brain that affects compassion, coupled with narcissistic arrogance, produces serial killers. You have yet to show compassion for Loretta's plight, and your arrogance could topple walls."

"You're calling me a *serial killer*?" He glared at her in incredulity.

What little she could see of his tightly controlled aura flickered just enough to make Evie contemplate reaching for the barbecue fork. If she read him right, he was feeling guilt. Serial killers did not feel guilt. That didn't mean he wasn't a killer.

As if realizing he was losing control, he returned to robot lawyer mode. "You can't defraud Loretta of millions with your fairy tales. I have forensic investigators who will strip that guardianship document into its phony components for the courts. You don't stand a chance in hell. Let's get Loretta back in school where she belongs, okay?"

"Documents?" Mavis asked. "Is that what I'm seeing in my ball? I thought they were old deeds. They're yellowed and sitting on a desk, but I can't read them."

Psy leaped to the counter to peer into the ball, but he wasn't inclined to add his opinion. He curled up around the base of the crystal and protected it with his skinny body.

Unmoved, the I'm-too-sexy lawyer slipped on his expensive sunglasses and jiggled his car keys. His entire attitude said he wasn't going anywhere without Loretta.

Some other day, Evie might admire a man who could make a point without speaking. Right now, his refusal to listen was seriously crawling under her skin. She shot him a challenging glare. "There's a red velvet lampshade in Aunt Val's attic. Do you think if we put it on his head and wrapped a gold shawl around him, we could pass him off as a lamppost?"

Mavis looked worried. The lamppost's lips quirked upward. Good to know he had a sense of humor. He'd probably laugh maniacally while hacking her up with his chainsaw.

The lamppost checked his watch. "Closing in on lunchtime. Loretta probably likes chicken sandwiches. Want me to run next door and pick up some?"

"I promised Gracie I'd stop by for lunch," Mavis said worriedly. "Evie, does this mean you won't be able to cover for me?"

Jackson quit jingling his keys.

Better, much better. He was finally recognizing he wouldn't be leaving anytime soon without her cooperation. Respect, at last, however limited it might be. Evie propped her chin on her hand and batted her lashes outrageously. "I think we should split up. Mom, you go say hi to Gracie and Aster, remind them I'll be over to baby-sit tonight. Stop in and say hi to Pris and

Iddy while you're at it. I'll stay here and let Mr. Jackson guess which one of us has Loretta. It should be a lot of fun."

Jackson countered by clipping on an earpiece and keying a button on his watch. Mavis frowned in concern. Evie took a seat on the counter stool and spun it in circles. She hoped Loretta was hiding somewhere comfortable. Evie's chances of forcing Jackson to believe her before she saw the inside of a courtroom were right about even with convincing the Supreme Court that psychics exist.

"Roark?" Jackson apparently spoke into some invisible mic. "Loretta's in Afterthought. Send in the team, will you? We've got a couple of flakes who are holding her for ransom."

"Now that's an outright lie!" Mavis exclaimed. "You set that man straight right now. The very idea! I'll have you know Malcolms have been upright citizens for centuries. Our duty is to protect our children!"

Jackson barked a few more orders before signing off and gazing down at Mavis who now stood half a foot below his nose, waving a cinnamon broom at him.

"Better watch out, she's been known to whack people with it," Evie warned, still idly spinning. "Mom, if you can sweep the trash out, the energy in here would be much clearer."

"I'm getting lunch. When the brat shows up, send her next door to me, or my team will find her for you." Good as his word, lovely Jackson stalked out.

Well, she'd never liked military cuts. An unbelieving lawyer wouldn't give her any respect anyway.

Which was another good reason she'd never have a private investigator's license. She was damned good at what she did, but no one ever believed her.

"Oh, dear, you've made him angry. Perhaps I better not leave you alone." Mavis returned the broom to the wall.

"He's always angry, Mom. I'm guessing from the gray in his fourth chakra that he's suppressing some vital part of him, and he's likely to explode like a pressure cooker one of these days. It's not our job to worry about Jackson. Do you know where Loretta's hiding?"

"I don't even know who Loretta is, dear, but if it's the little girl with glasses, she's up on the widow's walk at the bank. It's not very safe up there."

Evie sighed and wished her twisted brain would come up with an easy solution. "Once his *team* shows up, she won't be safe anywhere. Loretta is a Malcolm, by way of the Savannah Posts. She says she's a millionaire and someone is trying to kill her. She gave some convincing examples of a few dangerous accidents involving dropping jardinières and tree branches—provided she's not lying. I don't suppose you know anywhere we can keep her until I work this out?"

"Do you think that's wise, dear?" Mavis frowned worriedly. "Shouldn't she be with her family?"

"Probably not until I talk to the ghost following her. Or following Jackson. Or both. Or at least find out who inherits her millions," Evie added gloomily. She'd watched enough mystery shows to know what happened to millionaires. Too bad Loretta's parents hadn't figured out that money couldn't buy life.

"Well, that's all right, then," Mavis agreed, "if you know what to do."

Mavis was probably the only mother in the world who wouldn't question ghosts or Loretta's millions. She lived in a fascinating realm of immediate concerns that dissipated the moment she expressed them.

"Why don't I have Bill run up and fetch the child and show her the old bank vault? They can have lunch in there," Mavis suggested, as if people ate lunch in bank vaults every day.

Ever since Mavis had told Bill Wright he was destined to be bank president, he had gratefully satisfied Mavis's eccentric requests. Until then, he'd been far too shy to apply for the job he now held.

"Loretta's already had pizza and ice cream, but the vault sounds good," Evie agreed. "Maybe I can find the spirit and talk to it without Loretta or Jackson present, although I'm thinking it won't be easy." Ghost-busting was much simpler than ghost-talking, but *c'est la vie.*

"I'll stay with Loretta until you're ready. Let Gracie know and don't take too long." Mavis walked out with a happy wave now that she had a direction.

Evie tried to decide whether being prescient like her mother or talking to dead people was easier, but it was an old argument to keep herself distracted, and she didn't get any further with it than before. Like Mavis, she needed direction.

Summoning ghosts wasn't easy. It would be more practical to surround Loretta with her own *team.* Evie debated dialing her cousin Idonea. Iddy got all the sexpot genes in the family. Raven hair, tall and slinky, she projected the common image of *witch.* Ideally, Iddy would hex Jax.

Unfortunately, Iddy had a perky personality, talked to animals, and was a vet. Still, she was good to have around.

Wondering what kind of team jumped when Macho Man called, Evie phoned Iddy.

"Heard you cornered a hunk this morning, Evio," Iddy answered. "Spill."

"The hunk is over at Gertie's café, courting food poisoning with chicken sandwiches. Want to take your latest experiment over and find out more?"

"About food poisoning or hunks? Because if I have a choice, I choose hunks. There's a dire dearth in this town."

"Tell me something I don't know. He's out to nail my hide to a court-room door, so have at him." Evie's nose twitched at the lie. She didn't want Iddy to have at Jackson until she'd had her chance. But she was nothing if not realistic. Sort of. In an existential sort of way. "I need to speak with the ghost he brought to town."

Vaguely, she wondered if Loretta's turbulence had brought multiple ghosts to town and if one had simply hooked up with the lawyer. She needed far more information than she currently possessed.

"Ooooo, a haunted hunk. Okay, but I don't think La Chusa is trained well enough to help. I'll try, though. Let me find someone to cover for me or the doggies will go hungry."

La Chusa was Iddy's latest experiment in animal communication. Psy had turned out to be a little too smart and independent for her cousin's purposes. Ravens were less self-involved and more trainable than cats. Evie tickled behind Psy's ear, and the Siamese smacked her fingers.

"If our target isn't at the café when you get there," Evie told her cousin, "he'll probably be over here with a lampshade on his head." She hung up, leaving Iddy chuckling.

Evie ran over her mental checklist of relatives again, looking for more *team* members. She'd rather not call on her aunts, if it could be avoided. They'd only annoy Mavis, and then there really would be turbulence in Afterthought. Flying cats and voodoo dolls and bonfires at midnight were not conducive to rational action. Sibling rivalry could be a fearsome thing, which was why she wasn't adding Gracie to her team, although she did phone her sister to say Mavis had gone to the bank and might not make lunch. Gracie's telekinesis wasn't any more useful than their mother's clairvoyance in this case.

Telepathy, though, would be extremely convenient. She left a voice message for her cousin Priscilla. Pris was impossible to reach most of the time, but eventually, she came through.

Unable to read crystal balls, Evie sat on the sill of the big front window and watched until she saw the tall, skinny figure of Bill Wright working his way around the cupola of the bank. She didn't know how diffident Bill would talk a nervous child off the roof, but she hoped Loretta was smart enough to know when she was cornered.

Sure enough, a moment later, the pair walked hand in hand through the doorway to the stairs. If Jackson was chowing down at the café counter, he wouldn't notice.

Wishing she had a ghost-busting vacuum like in the movies, Evie continued sitting in the window, opening herself up to the universe, and scanning the street outside with her third eye.

No apparitions appeared. Her sensitivities didn't tingle.

Damn. She'd have to tackle the ghosts the traditional way, which meant bringing Loretta and Jax together. Damn and double damn.

Six

Glancing impatiently at his watch, Jax felt someone take a seat to his right. He glanced up just as a lanky, raven-haired female took a seat two stools down. She carried a crow on her shoulder.

If he were a betting man, he'd wager this was another of Evie's con artist relations. Or the entire town was nuts.

Crow Woman had a classic Roman profile and a bronzed complexion. She was almost as tall as he was, and in another time and place, he might be interested. But the orange-haired firecracker had his attention. Jax swilled his coffee and waited.

The gnarled, cotton-haired old lady waiting the counter slid a saucer of water and a bowl of cereal and fruit in front of the new arrival. Crow Woman held the water saucer up to the bird on her shoulder and placed her to-go order while the bird drank. The crow bobbed a little to the oldies tune the sound system cranked out, then glared at Jax through beady eyes.

His phone beeped with a text that Roark had arrived and was setting up his equipment. His team should have been in Savannah, an hour away, but they were spooky at the best of times. They'd traced the kid for him and had probably tracked Jax just to prove they could.

He clicked his ear phone. "Start with the known addresses and spread out from there."

Apparently unwilling to wait for his treat to be offered, the crow hopped down to the cereal dish, tilting the bowl with its weight, and slopping the contents across the counter. It began pecking at the loose grains, approaching Jax's hamburger.

"E-mailed your report," Roark told him.

"Just give me the highlights." Jax picked up his burger before the bird considered it prey.

"Whole family is nuts," Roark reported, not confirming anything Jax hadn't already ascertained. "Perpetually bankrupt. Lived there since shortly after the Salem witchcraft trials if I'm reading in between the lines right. They've been sued as frauds—get this—for *centuries*. And they've never once been convicted. *Never*. Your Evangeline Serena Malcolm Carstairs has a spotty juvenile record, mostly pranks and complaints. Bit of a hothead, it seems."

Jax heard frank admiration in Roark's usually noncommittal voice. The *pranks* must have been of the rebellion-against-authority sort. His investigator had a penchant for organized anarchy, and Jax couldn't see Evie as a shoplifter. Definitely graffiti-on-the-water-tower type. Jump-on-the-bad-guy type, too. Huh, maybe *dump the water from the tower on the bad guy* if he thought about it.

He might need to pay a little more attention to his adversary.

"Red hair," Jax offered in explanation. "Let me know when you're set up." He clicked off.

Crow Woman leaned over to gather the scattered cereal and return it to the bowl. "If that's your friends in the utility truck, they're in the mayor's favorite parking spot. If you want to stay on his good side, you'd better have them move to the paid parking lot around the corner."

Jax didn't bother asking how she knew what vehicle his team drove. No mystery there. This was a small town. Everyone knew each other's vehicles. He nodded at the bird. "Health department doesn't mind crows?"

"Raven. They're a lot larger than crows." She held out her palm for the bird to pick at the cereal. "Watch his tail feathers when he flies off. They're shaped like a fan. A crow's is straight." She paid for her order, picked up the bag, and opened the door. Holding the bird on her wrist like a falcon, she commanded, "Tell Evie what we saw," and flung it skyward.

Evie. Evangeline. Jax's shoulders itched.

Now that he was facing the window, he watched *Raven* Woman wave to a familiar sturdy, gray-haired figure near the bank building across the road. The raven wasn't to be seen and neither of the women spoke. The black-haired beauty swayed on down the street in the opposite direction of the new age shop.

His phone beeped again. *Roark*. Impatiently, Jax clicked his headset. "What?"

"Reuben's been hijacked by a striped space cadet outside the perp's house. His eyes are crossing. What do you want me to do with her?"

Striped space cadet. Recalling Evie's mention of cousins, Jax rubbed the frown off his brow. "There's a whole tribe of them. Watch out for Raven Lady. You'll know her when you see her. Follow them, lock them in the van, whatever, until we find the girl."

"Raven Lady just arrived," Roark said with a distinct note of approval. "Can I keep this one?" He cut off before Jax could learn more.

Swearing to himself, Jax switched off the phone. A moment later, less-than-ethereal Evangeline Malcolm Carstairs appeared in the open doorway. Instead of entering, she leaned against the jamb, hip cocked jauntily, arms crossed. Positioned to watch him as well as the road, she appeared to be anticipating someone's arrival. She was short and rounded in all the right ways, but he'd bet a month's income that she'd look like her fireplug mother in twenty years or so.

That thought didn't faze him as it should.

Said mother now waited on the bank stairs across the street. Neither of them so much as waved at each other.

A moment later, a slight figure in black glasses emerged from the bank doors, and triumph surged. *Ha! At last.* Looked like he'd won this round. Jax's first instinct was to jump up and grab the kid.

His higher instincts recognized Evie's strategic position. She'd already outplayed him once. Better to calculate her next move. He stayed in place, finishing his burger. Once he focused on why the scene struck him as a little awry, he grimaced.

Evie hadn't said a single word since positioning herself in the doorway. She didn't hold a cell phone and Loretta didn't own one. She could not have communicated with Loretta. Still, he had the distinct feeling that Evie had manipulated this entire scene, that she'd known where Loretta had been hiding, and had ordered her out.

Tell Evie what we saw, Raven girl had ordered.

His skin itched, which indicated facts did not align. He knew that feeling too well.

In resignation, Jax called Roark back but got his partner, Reuben. "I don't want to believe it, but we've got trouble with a capital T."

"And it's not rhyming with pool?" Reuben was a music aficionado and had infected all of them with inane lyrics over the years. "Is that the mark walking toward you? Should we proceed?"

Jax hadn't wanted to call in his pair of anarchists. R&R barely acknowledged the existence of the law, and Jax's adoptive father would crap in his Armani if he found out he had set them on the loose. Hopefully, what Stephen didn't know wouldn't hurt him, because Jax was watching Loretta take the hand of Evie's mother, while Evie waited in the doorway for the two of them to arrive. And not one person out there was holding a cell phone to arrange this gathering.

He was counting on R&R locating hidden cameras and microphones to disprove this pretense of psychic tomfoolery. But if he was right, the setup was too elaborate for normal kidnappers and extortionists. He couldn't take any chances on Loretta's life or well-being. He'd suffer his father's scorn and another painful whack at his reputation before he'd let anything happen to a kid.

"Don't reveal yourselves," he told Roark. "Just stay close."

"They've already ID'd us," Roark reminded him. "We either go in or hide."

Shit. "Hide." He needed to get his hands on Loretta, without terrifying her. Then the guys could start tearing the town apart, if need be.

Evie watched him with all too transparent interest as Loretta entered with Mavis in tow. Jax stood up and wished he was wearing something a little more business-like than dirty camouflage as the pig-tailed, ten-year-old millionairess entered and frankly gave him a thorough once-over.

"Mavis says my lawyer is not a killer," Loretta informed Evie, but a question lingered in her voice.

"Mr. Jackson's aura is angry, not murderous," Evie reassured her, although Jax heard the amusement in her voice. "And Mavis is a clairvoyant who knows things she shouldn't. Her word is good."

Jax wasn't fond of being a target of humor, but at least he knew his ward was safe, for the moment. He needed to call and let the firm know, but the sudden stiffness of the genie in the sunlight warned him to wait. Instead of savoring her victory, she no longer seemed focused on this plane of existence. Her attention was riveted on an object over his shoulder. Her expression. . . was not quite right. It was akin to watching a bright child lose her sparkle and slump into unconsciousness.

He glanced over his shoulder, but even the waitress wasn't in sight.

Not speaking, Mavis held a finger to her lips and shooed Loretta to the stool Raven Woman had vacated.

Exasperated by this performance, Jax waited for ghostly sounds or blobs of gel to emanate from the ceiling. Maybe the pair worked with the café and the gewgaws on the shelves were positioned to rock ominously. He hoped for a better show than Evie just standing there, frozen. Her sexy halter top, shorts, and bare feet were too mundane to establish any woo-woo credentials, although the nimbus of sunset curls added a nice touch. She'd apparently shed her tattered Keds at the shop. Any other woman her petite size would be strutting around in high heels.

Her blank expression disappeared. She frowned and rubbed her temples. A pity she looked so damned adorable or he'd laugh aloud. Rather than conveying a medium speaking with the spirit world, she looked ready to throw a temper tantrum. Her scowl was even better than one of his.

Hearing a rattle behind him, Jax spun around in time to watch a water glass fly off a shelf. He instinctively flung himself in front of Loretta. The glass bounced off him, hit the counter, and landed on the floor, smashing into shards at their feet.

Loretta leaped from her stool and fled into Mavis's arms—which irritated Jax beyond reason. He was the obvious protector here, not a plump dumpling of a gray-haired witch. And the glass-shattering poltergeist trick was too old for words. Someone could have been hurt.

"See, he's trying to kill me," Loretta cried.

In two strides, Jax crossed the room, grabbed Evie by the waist, and hauled her off the floor. Caught off-guard, she didn't even kick his crotch this time but offered a peeved huff when he set her down on a stool.

The two grizzled patrons in a back booth showed interest but no particular shock.

"What did you do that for?" Evie swiped her nimbus of curls off her forehead, giving him a clearer view of the crystalline fury of her eyes.

"You're barefoot." He pointed out the obvious. "Where's the broom?"

"You want me to fly out on it?"

45

It took a moment before he realized that they had two different ideas of the uses for a broom. If he picked up a stick, she'd see it as a magic wand, while he'd fling it for a dog to fetch. They not only operated out of different sides of their brains but in alternate universes.

The realization was most illuminating.

The ancient waitress arrived with, presumably, a normal broom to sweep up the glass.

Loretta interrupted before he had to reply, directing her horror at the women. "Did you *see*? I don't know how he makes tree limbs fall or glasses fly, but he wants me dead."

He who? Was his ward as crazy as the women she'd run to? Or were the women persuading Loretta she was in danger?

Before he could question, the genie shrugged.

"Jax *protected* you. Glasses can't kill. No one here is trying to murder you. You have ghosts." Evangeline glanced at him, waiting for him to defy her.

Raising his eyebrows at this entertaining defense, Jax simply waited for the rest of the performance. He'd give her enough rope to hang herself with.

When he didn't object, Evie continued explaining, presumably for his benefit as well as for his skeptical ward. "You need to understand that ghosts are a life essence, a form of energy. A protoplasmic field doesn't normally have the ability to zip about as we do. It takes most of a ghost's energy just to materialize. If the ghost experienced a great deal of trauma or passion in dying, that energy might be triggered by the place of death or a person related to the phenomenon."

Loretta frowned. "You're saying you saw a *ghost* throw the glass and try to kill me?"

"No, I'm saying the spirit used all its energy following you and hasn't the ability to communicate more. Since you can't see it, I think it's trying to catch your attention. I don't believe your life is in danger."

Loretta looked rightfully dubious. "A ghost broke the glass to get my attention?"

"That, and in frustration from not being able to communicate. That might be the cause of the other accidents you told me about." Using her bare toes, Evangeline spun on the stool Jax had placed her on.

"Can you tell who the ghost is?" Loretta asked dubiously. "I don't know any dead people."

Unable to figure out her objective, Jax waited to see how the genie would reply.

"No, I can't. He seems adamant about disliking Mr. Jackson, but he can't express why. We'll let him gather his energy again and maybe we can hold a séance."

"Or use a Ouija board," Mavis suggested. "You're fairly good at wielding that, and it would take less energy."

"It will have to wait until this evening," Evie warned. "The others had to go back to work." She spun to glare at him. "Unless Mr. Jackson here has some notion of anyone who might hate him and be trying to reach him from beyond."

Jax rubbed his forehead. The women must have practiced this routine a thousand times to repeat it without sounding foolish. Or they were damned good actresses. "Contrary to popular thought, I am only a lawyer. I do not kill people. I want to be there for your performance."

His techie team would get to the bottom of this soon enough. Still, Jax didn't want to be the big bad wolf in Loretta's eyes. He knew the horrifying experience of being orphaned. It was the reason he'd taken this account. So he erred on the side of caution—he'd have to play along, until he'd reeled in the fish and had evidence.

He wouldn't be so easy on Evie and Mavis. For the first time in *centuries,* he would prove the Malcolms were criminal frauds.

~

"WHY CAN'T WE TALK TO THE GHOST NOW?" LORETTA ASKED, striving to keep the plea out of her voice as she sat cross-legged on Aunt Val's colorful carpet.

It had been a long afternoon of Jax Jackson hovering like a thundercloud while Loretta refused to speak to him. The only way Evie had been able to pry out Loretta's story so her lawyer could hear it was to ask questions about the incidents the child swore had endangered her life. Falling tree limbs and flowerpots dropping from balconies definitely sounded like poltergeist energy to Evie. Since the energy was evidently directed at Loretta, the child had every right to think she was a target.

The matter of John and Tiffany Post's deaths was a different tale entirely.

Jax had been even less communicative than Loretta. Evie was still contemplating rummaging for the lampshade.

In her experience, communication was vital—from both sides of the veil. Observation was what she did best, although people seldom appreciated that fact. It took skill to read auras. Pulling together all the puzzle pieces from everything she learned was her next best trait. Pulling facts from mule-headed subjects. . . not so much. Which was why she'd learned to study what her senses told her.

Focusing on the Ouija board set up at a card table, Evie let her teacher sister answer Loretta's demands.

"The planets will be in a better conjunction at eight," Gracie said soothingly. "It's almost time."

Evie could tell the poor kid needed a hug, but her own spirit was too agitated to provide calming elements.

Jax and his testosterone hovered like an evil presence over the estrogen-laden atmosphere of the Malcolm family gathering. Fortunately, he'd not called in the *team* both Pris and Iddy had checked out. For all Evie knew, though, the house was surrounded by kidnappers or cops. Psycat prowled as if sensing the tension.

A five-o'clock shadow darkened Jax's square jaw. He hadn't changed from his paint-splattered camouflage and bicep-revealing black T-shirt. He didn't belong in her front room. Just his body language screamed negativity and rejection. He'd taken one of her aunt's chrome dinette chairs from the kitchen, propped it against a wall as far from Evie as he could get, and straddled it as if he were watching a play unfold.

He was every authority figure Evie had ever despised—judgmental, narrow-minded, unimaginative. . . She had all the words written in her journal from adolescence.

And still she wanted to earn his approval. Probably some deep psychological need for the sperm donor who had been her father. She really needed to be focusing her befuddled mind. If she didn't talk to Loretta's spirits tonight, she'd blame it on Jax.

Ignoring Jax's hovering presence, sexy Idonea fed her raven from a cereal bowl. Pragmatic Gracie was on the phone with her daughter. Evie winced. She was supposed to be babysitting so her sister could attend a PTA meeting.

Priscilla drifted in with the wind. One never knew what Pris would be from one day to the next. Tonight, she'd streaked her mouse-brown hair with pink and blue and layered on purple eye shadow. She wore her vague, attuned-to-the-whispers-of-the-universe mien. For all Evie knew, Pris could be planting telepathic suggestions in Jax's mind to follow her home. Or she could be communicating with Martians.

Beneath that harmless candy-colored camouflage, Pris was pure menace.

Mavis passed around a tray of gingerbread and served coffee and tea. Evie didn't take either. Somehow, she needed to find her focus before the clock chimed eight. Instead of finding her center, she noted that Jackson didn't seem interested in I'm-too-sexy Iddy, mother-figure Gracie, or blissful Pris. The only person he scowled at was Evie. So nice to be the center of attention. *Not.*

What would happen if she couldn't speak with Loretta's ghosts? Would he grab the child and run?

Evie shifted in her uncomfortable chair at the card table as the clock on the mantel clicked closer to the hour.

Sitting on Evie's left, Iddy had settled the Siamese on her lap and the raven on her shoulder. On Evie's right, Pris admired the candlelight on the crystal ball—or her own colorful reflection. Sitting across from Evie, Gracie had a tarot spread out on the green vinyl. She was amusing herself flipping the cards without hands. She had her back to Jax so he couldn't see the silly trick, or Evie suspected he'd be checking for strings.

Mavis took a seat next to Loretta by the fireplace, protecting the child with her sturdy breadth. An Indigo child could be an open invitation to trouble. Evie had a suspicion it was Loretta's energy that fed the spirit following her. Spirits usually left Mavis alone.

When the mantel clock chimed, Mavis switched off the floor lamp. Taking a deep breath, Evie waited until the others had their fingers on the planchette before she leaned forward to add hers. She was always reluctant to use this form of communication since it opened a path to all spirits and not just the one she wanted. But surrounded by the various protections of her family, she was as shielded as she could be.

Jackson moved his chair forward to watch.

"Identify yourself," Evie called to the aura immediately coalescing over the board.

The planchette moved. Mavis usually jotted letters on a notepad as the arrow jerkily pointed them out on the Ouija board. Often, the spirits hesitated, and it was difficult to tell if they meant to point out a particular letter or not. Evie's mother had learned to circle the questionable responses. Without trying to read what was forming beneath her fingers, Evie concentrated on channeling. She closed her eyes, confident her family would catch any clue.

The sharp slam of the lawyer's chrome chair hitting the wall and Loretta's cry of startlement jerked Evie back to the moment.

Opening her eyes, she caught Pris's slide toward the floor, and Jackson's dive to catch her. Only then did she realize the room was illuminated by a blue light that didn't come from candles or electricity.

Seven

CURSING UNDER HIS BREATH, JAX DUMPED THE SPACED-OUT cousin on Evie's couch, into the competent hands of the gray-haired witch. The weird blue glow evaporated as quickly as it had formed. He snapped on the nearest lamp to ascertain that Loretta was safe.

He found the kid underneath the card table, examining it for rigged devices. He'd known the kid was smart. He had just feared the need for family might undermine her intelligence.

Before he crouched down to check for himself, he couldn't resist studying Evie. She was still seated at the table, but the way she wrapped her arms around herself spoke volumes he couldn't translate. Shouldn't even try, or he'd be caught up in this web of deceit. As he knew from experience, it was much too easy to allow emotions to overrule the brain.

Feeling uncomfortably large in the confined environment, surrounded by women, he got down on his knees to examine the table with Loretta.

Above their heads, the blond teacher spoke to no one in particular. "It could have said L-A-C-K-L-A-N or L-A-C-K-L-A-N-D or maybe it's two words, L-A-C-K space L-A-N-D."

Jax nearly knocked his head on the table at the name. His gaze caught Loretta's owl-eyed expression, and he made a face. "I don't suppose it could say *lack mind*?" he asked in an undertone.

Loretta smiled hesitantly and relief swelled. She was a sensible kid with a good brain, kind of like his baby sister, and he didn't want her hurt by all this mumbo-jumbo. He backed out from under the table.

"Lakeland," Evie murmured, now cradling the Siamese cat that had leaped from her cousin's lap to hers.

The genie looked exhausted, Jax realized. He hadn't noticed the dark circles beneath her eyes earlier. But redheads had translucent skin, so it was probably just the miserable light in here. Blowing out the sputtering candles, he looked around for another lamp.

"Lakeland?" With the crow still perched on her shoulder, the vet took Priscilla's pulse. "Isn't that the company that wants to buy Witch Hill?"

"Not Witch Hill—Lee's Forest," Mavis corrected. "The town council didn't like the family name."

The teacher hooted a soft laugh, but Evie didn't bother to smile, Jax noticed. These women would do a serious number on his head if he didn't escape soon. Afterthought might consider itself rural, but even at safe speeds, it was little more than an hour's drive back to his condo in suburban Savannah. It was time he put an end to their nonsense.

"This has been a lot of fun and games, ladies, but we haven't talked to any ghosts or solved any problems. It's time I returned Loretta to her school. They're expecting her." He'd take another look into Lakeland Development when he got back to the office. Standing, he held out his hand for Loretta.

She didn't take it. That could be problematic. He really didn't want to haul her out kicking and screaming. He glared at Evie. "You promised," he warned her.

She hadn't really, but she nodded absently and began doing that circling thing with her fingers on her temples. Jax had the urge to try his hand at massaging her neck, except he couldn't be completely certain he wouldn't throttle her.

"Loretta, I'm really not finding any dangerous spirits," Evie said cautiously.

"Did it tell you where to find my parents?" Loretta demanded. "Are they in this Lakeland place?"

Jax winced and waited for Evie or one of her family to say the fraudulent words that would encourage Loretta to continue searching for her supposedly missing parents.

Evie turned the icy shards of her gaze on him as if she knew what he was thinking. Jax nearly fell into their crystalline depths. Damn, he had to get out of here before the walls closed in.

"Did Loretta's parents own land around the lake?" she asked.

Caught off guard by a question that was much too pragmatic for the scene she'd set, Jax hesitated.

"The Posts claimed to own all of the pond and a portion of Witch Hill, down to the boat dock," the color-streaked brunette answered for him, apparently regaining consciousness.

She was right, but that was public knowledge and not any example of telepathy or whatever she was trying to prove with her fainting spell. Jax folded his arms and nodded at Evie's questioning look. Loretta's parents had owned half this town. Now Loretta did.

"The Jester is in charge," Mavis replied enigmatically, shuffling the tarot deck.

"We have more than one Jester in town, and the message I received wasn't from any of them." The spacey brunette stood up. She regarded Jax with absent-minded confusion and turned to Evie. "For what it's worth, all I caught was *Thieves.* I sensed a great deal of panic in the words."

"Male?" Evie asked, then tightened her arms around herself when Priscilla nodded and began gathering up her belongings.

"Dark hair, glasses?" Evie asked. Space cadet nodded.

"The Baker's mare is in labor. I have to go." Assured that her cousin had returned safely to her senses, the vet held out an arm for the raven. "La Chusa is showing me a man with dark hair and glasses, too, but raven spirit vision is limited."

"*Lechuza,* owl?" Jax asked, desperately attempting to stay on top of this exchange.

"*La* Chusa, collects soul of the dying." The vet smiled at his disbelief.

"The spirit's aura shows him as angry, anxious, and frustrated." Evie didn't rise from her seat, but Jax noticed she was regaining her color.

"My father wore glasses," Loretta announced. "Maybe he's being held prisoner and trying to reach me?"

Idonea and Priscilla dug in their purses for keys but didn't acknowledge the kid.

Jax clenched his fingers into fists and waited as Evie rubbed her forehead. He didn't hit women, but he'd pick up Loretta and carry her out if any of them tried to sink their talons into her.

"Lots of people wear glasses," Evie said reassuringly. "And our spirit vision isn't necessarily clear. You should never, *ever* take anyone's word for what they've seen or heard or felt. You have to question all the facts and look at every side for the truth. We can't even know for certain that we're all seeing or hearing the same spirit, or even the one who is following you."

Jax swallowed his surprise at this admission and waited for the ax to fall.

"Then what good are you?" the child cried angrily, wiping tears from her eyes. She stood up and headed for the hall. "You're supposed to be psychic and help me find my parents! I'll get my backpack and find a *real* guardian."

As Loretta stomped toward the back bedroom, Evie raised her bruised gaze to encompass her family and Jax. "The spirit showed many of the same colors in his aura as Loretta. I'm pretty sure it's her father following her, and that he's dead and trying to reach her."

"Poor baby," Mavis murmured, casting an anxious glance after the child.

"Of course he's dead," Jax grumbled, impatient with this act that had solved nothing. "We have the death certificates for both of them in our files. And don't try to tell me he wants to tell Loretta he loves her. John Post was a world-class myopic moron who never saw past his bitch of a wife to know he even had a kid."

Mavis clucked disapprovingly. "John was a bright little boy. He lost his mother young, so maybe his wife gave him something he needed."

Jax winced as he realized that John Post was the parent related to the mad Malcolms, not Tiffany.

He watched Evie's lips twist wryly and wondered what that meant but quashed his curiosity and stuck with the practical. "In either case, he's dead and can't help anyone. Are we all agreed that Loretta is better off at school?"

Evie rose to her bare feet and confronted him, practically toe to toe. He could look down and admire the sunset highlights of her hair, if she hadn't turned a threatening scowl to him instead. He was just a little too aware of her breasts practically brushing his chest to be comfortable.

"Where was John Post's body found?" she demanded with almost the same inflection of disparagement he'd just used.

"It wasn't. Loretta's parents were lost at sea last fall. Their yacht was found capsized in the Bermuda triangle. The court finally declared them dead before transferring Loretta into the firm's guardianship last month."

He watched in curiosity as the scowl slipped from Evie's pale face and her blue eyes grew vacant. He was starting to think she was epileptic. But she pulled out of her trance fast enough and swung around to speak with her family before they left.

"If the spirit here tonight was really John Post, I don't think he has the ability or strength to transport himself from the Caribbean," she told her audience. "He barely has the energy to push the planchette. It's amazing he even managed to drop dead tree limbs on Loretta."

Gracie tilted her head and looked interested. Priscilla and Iddy nodded in agreement. Mavis just waited expectantly.

"I think. . ." Evie didn't enlighten them but stopped speaking when Loretta reappeared in the doorway with her backpack. "I think Loretta needs family with her. Jax, I really believe I need to file those guardianship papers at the courthouse. Sorry."

In another life, he would have swiveled on his heel and put his fist through the plaster wall. His brief career in the military had taught him anger management.

In his current role of controlled respectability, he donned a stiff smile and nodded. "Fine. We can meet in front of a judge. Meanwhile, I'll move in here to supervise Loretta's welfare as provided in the court-approved guardianship."

That was how he knew if there were any spirits here, they were evil ones who'd planted that insane suggestion in his head. . .

He swirled and glared at Evie's supposedly telepathic cousin, but the vague brunette merely smiled and opened the door. "You'll be a lovely addition to the family." Priscilla strode into the night before anyone could throw things at her.

"On that note. . ." Iddy waved cheerfully. "Let us know when you need us, Eve!"

Eve, the ultimate temptress. Jax pinched the bridge of his nose and remembered Loretta's forlorn gaze.

This wasn't all about him. It was about a kid whose parents were dead and who needed reassurance that someone cared. He knew the painful reality of how that felt.

And heaven help him, the only ones even pretending to care were Evie and her demented family.

~

SIPPING HER HOT CHOCOLATE AND SWINGING HER STURDY school oxfords, Loretta sat at the counter, warily watching much as a dog watches for a crumb to fall from the table. Evie could have sworn she didn't possess an ounce of maternal instinct, but the forlorn Indigo child tugged at her heartstrings.

The Great White Lawyer was barking quiet orders into his phone as if everything had been decided, and it was all over but the farewells.

"You do realize that Loretta, as an Indigo child, is very possibly her father's channel from beyond the veil, not me?" Evie broke the uneasy silence that followed Jax's earlier proclamation of suing and moving in. Malcolms and lawyers weren't the best possible combination, in court or out.

"My father is not dead," Loretta said predictably. "Maybe I'm channeling his *thoughts*." She looked quite interested in this possibility.

"Maybe Loretta is like a radio frequency booster," Gracie suggested. "I don't think we've all had such strong reactions at once."

"It's probably not wise to repeat that experiment, then," Mavis countered. "Should a malevolent spirit be near, who knows what we would unleash?"

"If it's Great-Uncle Orbis, we'd all get drunk and burn the house down," Evie agreed, adding a smile of reassurance for Loretta, who still looked uncertain.

"Then don't you think it's wisest if I take Loretta back to school?" Jax asked, also predictably, as he snapped off his phone.

"No," all the Malcolms replied in unison.

Startled that she had such support, Loretta glanced at their determined faces, then turned to Jax. Knowing Loretta's manipulative streak, Evie put an end to whatever mischief she was conjuring.

"Loretta certainly needs to be in school, but she also needs answers to her questions. And if her father—" Evie cut off that thought at Loretta's frown and switched to "—if a spirit is trying to speak through her, she needs to be with people who can help her. We can't keep calling these poltergeist-like incidents *accidents*. She could be seriously harmed if the spirit misses his aim next time and drops a rock on her. I doubt seriously that skeptics like you will understand."

The doorbell rang. Jax smirked, peeled himself off the wall he'd been holding up, and went to answer it as if the house were his.

Evie liked to think of herself as laidback and easy-going, or at least easily distractible, but Jax was quickly becoming a needle under her skin. She followed him to the door with some hope of forestalling whatever he'd plotted.

She came to a halt at sight of a man so much taller and broader than Jax as to make Macho Man almost seem average. Especially since Jax had a normal buzz cut, and this dude sporting a natural tan had shaved his head bald and tattooed his temples with what appeared to be Egyptian hieroglyphics.

He handed Jax a suitcase and flashed a metal-adorned smile at Evie. "Good vibes, bébé. Keep the faith." He saluted her with a finger to a raised eyebrow sporting a steel ring, then swung on his heel with military precision and marched back into the spring darkness.

"You've just received the Titanium seal of approval. Where do I sleep? Upstairs, I assume?" Jax raised a questioning dark eyebrow and glanced at the stairs he'd yet to traverse.

The upstairs was Evie's sanctum—and storage rooms for three generations of junk. She'd temporarily placed Loretta in her aunt's room down here. This was never going to work.

"I'll put Loretta upstairs with me," she decided. "You can have Aunt Val's room." With Neil Diamond and the Monkees and lava lamps. In protecting herself, she'd found the perfect solution. If that room didn't drive him screaming into the streets, nothing would. "You'll be guarding the doors and keeping killers off the stairs."

Eight

BY MIDNIGHT, JAX HAD THE SIXTIES MUSEUM TUCKED OUT OF sight in the wardrobe and in a stack of boxes scavenged from the alley. He'd thrown in the colorful bedcover and shag rug as well. The four-poster was now stripped to barely acceptable blue sheets and the pine plank floor was bare. Remnants of old linoleum clung to the edges. The floor needed a good sanding and finish.

The 1940's vanity held his sleek laptop. He'd not discovered any wi-fi to hack but his cell had a powerful hotspot. In an emergency, he could call in his team and their equipment. But he'd rather leave them to their illegal exploration of databases that might provide any information on Lakeland Development.

Jax was merely the guardian the firm had assigned to Loretta. He'd not worked with the Posts or on any of their business dealings. *Lakeland* was a real estate project his father and the firm's partners were working on.

He had the firm's files on John Post open and was perusing the numbers and. . . *deeds*.

Didn't Mavis mention yellowing deeds on a desk?

"How did you fit all Aunt Val's stuff into those boxes?"

Jax jerked his head up to contemplate the genie in the doorway. Sadly, she wasn't wearing shorts and halter but an aqua robe and what appeared to be whale slippers. "In the military, I learned to pack tightly. Any more ghostly revelations?"

"I'm pretty sure John Post isn't buried in the Caribbean." She picked up the cat that had followed her in and placed it on her shoulder.

"Authorities found the yacht floating upside down with no signs of life aboard. Their car was in the parking lot at the Charleston harbor where they usually docked the yacht. Evidence is pretty conclusive."

"Circumstantial. Anyone could take the keys, drive the car, sail the yacht, jump on a waiting vessel, and abandon the yacht. They want you to *believe* the Posts are dead, and I believe they are, but why the elaborate ruse?"

"Why not believe they've been kidnapped as Loretta does?" Jax sat back in the too-small chair. When she talked logic, he listened, apparently.

"Loretta is trailing one spirit, possibly two. Who else would it be but her parents? I don't know if they're protecting her or their fortune, but they're definitely warning me against you." She studied the bare walls and his bed and shook her head. "Powerful magicians have better uses than interior decorating."

"I require order. If I'm stuck here for any length of time, I'll organize my space as needed. If you don't like it, I'll take Loretta and leave." He deliberately ignored her spirit talk. Perhaps he could train her to talk sense.

"Maybe the ghost is warning you'll organize my life." She looked weary but amused. "For lack of a better identification, I'll call him John. He's trying to type on your computer."

Jax swung around. The files he'd been looking at disappeared, replaced by a document index. The cursor hovered over a different file, and then the laptop went dark. The glass of water he'd been drinking flew off the vanity.

If the poltergeist was supposed to be John Post, he had a short fuse.

Interestingly, he recalled one of the partners talking about their client's temper. He refused to wonder if Evie was reading his mind or had other means of knowing about Loretta's father and had somehow performed the glass-throwing trick again.

"He's gone." She lifted her shoulder from the jamb. "You might try working with me sometime instead of against me. Could be interesting. You seem to have an affinity for ghosts."

She left him trying to retrieve his internet connection.

An affinity for ghosts, right. The only work he wanted to do with the psychic genie was in bed.

He could hear her rattling pots in the kitchen. Once satisfied he hadn't lost any of the firm's files, Jax shut the computer down and followed her.

"I don't believe in what I can't see." He looked around for a coffee machine and couldn't find one.

"Which would include God, viruses, and radio waves." She put the tea canister back on a shelf that didn't include anything marked *coffee*.

"Viruses can be detected by microscopes. Any number of devices detect radio waves. There is no such thing as a ghost detector. Energy can be measured and detected but can't be self-directed, as your ghosts claim to be."

"You, personally, can't *see* paranormal energy self-direct. I get that. I can see it, but I understand I'm rare. Doesn't mean it isn't possible for everyone to see paranormal energies once we develop the right device—except only people like me believe, and we're unlikely to invent anything."

Jax snorted his agreement to that very true statement.

She didn't let that stop her. "The shame is that you are suppressing a very powerful force which might work for the benefit of all. But you prefer to believe anything not in scientific texts doesn't exist, which I assume means souls and psychic phenomena. Go back and play with your computers. If I were you, I wouldn't believe in the internet. I can't see it."

She poured hot water into her teapot and carried it out.

Jax noted she didn't bother offering him any.

He didn't know why he felt insulted. Yes, he was accustomed to having women wait on him. But he knew how to take care of himself. He didn't want tea anyway.

He returned to his computer and ordered a coffeemaker and beans with expedited delivery. If he had any *force* at all, it was his intelligence. He knew how the internet worked, and it wasn't on spectral energy.

He returned to scanning the files of Post assets until he found the one that had crashed the system.

It was labeled Lakeland-Lee's Forest.

Carrying the Siamese cat called Psy, Loretta crept down the stairs in the dawn light. She had been told she had exceptional night vision and acute hearing, but she didn't need either to know the adults were sleeping. Jax snored and Evie didn't move. Loretta had thought her always-restless hostess dead until she'd detected breathing.

Until these past months, Loretta had thought she knew who to trust. The supposed death of her parents and the greed she saw in everyone who knew of her wealth had caused her to doubt her abilities. Once upon a time, she would have trusted an open soul like Evie. Now, she knew to worry about whether Evie was really on her side.

She didn't know a great deal about her money except that lawyers handled it, and other people wanted it—which made Jax equally worthy of suspicion.

She also knew Evie hadn't believed the fake guardianship papers, even though they were excellent forgeries. Most people would have taken them straight to the bank. Instead, Evie had scoffed and ignored potential wealth. She'd also fought for Loretta, so there was that.

Loretta poured some milk for herself and the cat.

"I need to decide, Kitty," she whispered, scratching the cat's head as she'd seen Evie do. "They may have shut down my credit card. I could test it at the cash machine at the bank. How far could I go on a thousand dollars?" She knew that was her credit limit.

The cat stopped to clean its whiskers.

"But Evie's family listens to me. Who else would do that?"

The cat purred *Meee* and leaped into Loretta's lap.

Loretta giggled at her imagination. Her mother would have smacked her if she'd said the cat had answered her question. The teachers would have sent her to a therapist. They already had once, when Loretta had told them the PE teacher had a disturbing bubble and touched the first graders inappropriately.

She didn't take PE, had only met the teacher once, and she should never have mentioned bubbles. The school had decided she was a troublemaker. The therapist had been unable to persuade her that she was imagining things. So Loretta had talked to all the kids until she'd convinced one of the little girls to tell her parents what the teacher had done. The result had been. . . unpleasant.

"Is it good or bad that I caused a teacher to lose her job?" she asked the cat. The first graders had happier bubbles now, she knew. The other teachers had taken to eyeing Loretta warily.

Smmarrrt the cat purred, before jumping down to nose the empty kitty dish, rattling the pan.

The snoring in the back room halted. Loretta didn't understand adults the way she understood little kids. She supposed she should study the situation a little longer before running again.

She liked it here. Evie's family didn't laugh at her or treat her like a freak.

Mr. Jackson, however, had a very strange bubble. So did those weird men sleeping in the van parked in the alley.

She climbed on a chair to reach a sweater hanging by the back door. Putting it on over her pajamas, she tugged it around her. "Want to go for a walk?"

Psy immediately joined her.

~

Determined to command respect from her unwanted house guest, Evie donned her best capris. Unfortunately, her only clean shirt seemed to be one with sparkly rainbows saying *Being Human is Complicated, Time to be a Unicorn*. Oh well, it covered her where it counted.

Most of the upper story of the sprawling Victorian was used to store *heirlooms* the family didn't want in their own houses. Only Evie's bedroom and a small guest room were habitable. She had partially cleared the small room for an office, but she'd not quite got around to figuring out what one did at a desk. Maybe she'd keep client files, should she ever have clients. She stopped to check on Loretta.

The fold-down futon couch in the office made a fine bed for a child. Evie frowned at the lump of covers. *There was no aura in that bed.* Loretta's indigo was so bright that she didn't need to concentrate to see it.

Panicking, she raced down the stairs, hoping to find the brat fixing herself breakfast.

The back door was open. Psy wasn't circling his bowl. Milk sat on the counter.

"Deep breath, Evie." She could hear the shower, so Jax hadn't stolen her. She needed to have a long talk with the kid—if she found her.

Sliding on flip-flops at the back door, Evie stepped into the early morning sunshine. It would be a scorcher later today, but it was good now.

Mrs. Satterwhite had bacon frying—she must have received her Social Security check. A delivery truck was unloading at the hardware—Hank's garden supplies were early. Her sensitivity to temporal disturbances picked up no new activity. All seemed normal. She crossed the yard to the back gate.

What wasn't normal was a white utility van parked in the alley behind Hank's. *R&R, Inc*? Never heard of them. Evie returned to the kitchen, found a sturdy carving knife and a small paring knife. Tucking the small one in her waistband and covering it with her shirt, she returned outside, brandishing the larger one.

As she approached the van, she could hear Loretta. The kid didn't precisely chatter, but she could be loquacious when called on.

Wouldn't kidnappers have gagged her and driven away?

Knife still in hand, Evie attempted to read auras through the van's panels, but they were unusually thick—or whatever tools it carried blocked the humans inside. Oh well. . .

She yanked open the driver's side door.

A hard arm wrapped around her waist and hauled her backward just as a. . . scimitar? . . . swung across the entry, barely missing her nose.

"Enough, already!" she screamed, smashing her head backward into Jax's nose. His muscled body and masculine scent—not nearly disguised by his recent shower—had imprinted on her memory. She didn't care if he'd just saved her from nose decapitation. She was done with being hauled around.

The bald, tattooed tanned guy from last night stuck his head out. "You have ta knock." He returned the blade to its hiding place.

Jax dropped her, presumably knowing her next step would be to aim for his shins. Hard to emasculate him when she was facing the wrong direction. The damned man smelled too good, and she hadn't had her tea yet.

"It's my alley, and I don't have to knock for trespassers or potential kidnappers." Evie glared at Hieroglyph. If he thought those tattoos were intimidating, he hadn't met any of her family. She yelled into the van, "Loretta, what's wrong with you? Don't you know better than to talk to strangers?"

Even the kid had apparently not been intimidated. Evie spun on her heel and glared at Jax. "Is this your weird idea of a security guard?"

The lawyer was wearing normal jeans this morning instead of camouflage. But the bicep-revealing T-shirt wasn't any better than yesterday's. Maybe he couldn't find shirts that fit better over that Hulk frame.

"They charge too much for parking around here, man." Hieroglyph answered before Jax could speak. "And look at how the kid sneaked right past both of you."

The back door of the van opened and Loretta hopped down. "Mr. Roark and Mr. Reuben showed me how to play Bubble Witch. It's better than chess."

Bubble Witch. Evie closed her eyes and held her tongue until she found an innocuous reply. "Pink hair and balloons?"

"Well, it's silly," Loretta admitted. "But it makes Mr. Reuben happy. And I knew they weren't kidnappers. They have twisted bubbles, but they're translucent."

All right, that left her gobsmacked, as her Brit cousins said.

Jax leaned into the van. "Install security and go home, guys. I'm not paying you to babysit."

"Hey, we're not charging for sleep hours, unless we have to pay for parking. Those meters are rigged." Hieroglyph sank into the driver's seat and the back doors slammed, presumably by the unseen Reuben. Which probably made the tattooed driver Roark. Reuben and Roark, *R&R, of course.*

Even without tea, Evie recognized the need to speak up. "Hold up there, boys. I want to know these twisted bubbles before they set up security on *my* house. And who gave *anyone* permission to set up security?" She tapped Jax on the shoulder and when he turned inquiringly, she shoved past him to lean into the van. "Out now, folks. Breakfast in fifteen. Use Jax's shower if you need it."

She grabbed Loretta's hand and marched back into the house. "If I were your mother, I'd send you to your room right now."

"I had a nanny. She told me she'd have daddy spank me. But he never did. I know when people are bad," Loretta finished reassuringly.

"Right, because translucent bubbles are good even if they're twisted." Evie pointed at the banquette seat in the breakfast nook. "Sit. Explain. Eggs or cereal?"

"Donuts." The kid climbed up on the bench and Psy immediately leaped into her lap.

"No donuts. Eggs or cereal, then explain." Evie was very *very* focused this morning. She hadn't been able to open her third eye to examine auras, but those two men glowed all on their own.

Nine

Reuben whistled from the back of the van. "That's one badass woman you found there, bro."

Reuben had degrees from Duke and MIT. But as the kid had noted, he had a twisted mind, if not whatever a bubble was.

"Her kitchen is out of Oz. If Bubble Witch is your thing, then get your crooked asses inside. You have effectively blown your covers to hell at the hands of a ten-year-old." Jax didn't wait for a reply but stomped back inside, furious with himself and the world.

He'd let a *kid* get past him. She could have run anywhere. Yeah, he was a lawyer and not a prison guard, but he should have known by now that Loretta was an escape artist.

He hadn't realized she wanted to escape Evie.

And she hadn't. She'd just been a normal kid exploring her territory. He'd have done the same.

He was never going to have kids. He didn't have time for daily heart attacks. At least his sister stayed where he put her.

He offered up another prayer of gratitude for the Stocktons. The rainy night when the police had taken his twelve-year-old self out of his parents' comfortable home and placed him and over-sensitive Ariel in a crowded, noisy foster home, with kids stacked to the ceilings, was indelibly engraved on his memory. The next day, when his father's boss and his wife had taken them in, he'd vowed never to be bad again. Stephen Stockton might be a royal pain in the ass, but he'd saved their lives. Ariel would never have survived the foster system.

Jax knew how Loretta felt, having her feet yanked out from under her with the loss of her parents. He'd deliberately been blocking that memory for years.

Evie was sliding French toast on Loretta's plate when he entered the kitchen. The kid poured a lake of syrup over it. *Normal* kid, Jax repeated. But even normal kids required routine maintenance.

The genie had accepted that fact without complaint or demands for money. His cynical radar didn't kick in, even though that behavior was beyond the boundaries of all he knew as normal.

He must be hungry.

"Mavis is bringing coffee from Gertie's. French toast for you? I don't do bacon." She waited, spatula raised.

Coffee? The mind-reading old witch was reading his mind—or she preferred coffee to her daughter's tea. Jax sat across from the kid on the old-fashioned banquette. "Coffee is good. French toast is fine, thank you. Do you not eat bacon or did you run out?"

"Can't afford bacon and no longer like it." She splatted more toast on the griddle.

"I'll buy groceries. It's not your job to feed everyone. I'll hire a cook."

Evie glared at him. "This is Afterthought, South Carolina, population 3237. We have a dearth of available labor force. Even Pris works in the city. You'd have to hire Gertie away from her café. I'm perfectly capable of cooking for Loretta. The rest of you will be gone shortly, right?"

"Not until I'm assured of Loretta's security." However in hell he managed that with a public school and insane people as her caretaker.

"His bubble is the size of a walnut," Loretta said cheerfully, addressing Evie. "But walnuts grow into big trees, don't they?"

"Ones that grow mistletoe." Evie flipped the toast, sounding much too gleeful. "Explain about bubbles, please."

Jax needed his coffee before he heard this.

Carrying duffels, Roark and Reuben entered, providing a welcome interruption.

He pointed at the room he'd used last night, belatedly recognizing it as a servant's room for the cook Evie didn't have.

Reuben was a tall, lean nerd—ebony, with a modest Afro pulled into a man bun and adorned with a finger bone. Instead of tattoo art, he had scarring on his cheekbones and forehead. Jax hadn't asked—none of them did personal. But he assumed Reuben was identifying his tribe, even though Reuben had been born in Miami to middle-class professors. Jax got that. Sometimes a man had to make a statement.

Out of respect, Jax had never made any rebellious statements that would get his autistic younger sister booted out of their adoptive home. He still wasn't entirely certain that *statements* hadn't got his biological father killed. Franklin Jackson had not been one to quietly ignore wrong-doing, which Jax already knew from experience could bring the roof down on him.

His goal was to get rich so he could keep Ariel safe, which also involved finding out exactly what had happened to his father—if only so it didn't happen to him.

Not glancing twice at his not-exactly-inconspicuous team, Evie served up a platter of French toast. "Twisted bubbles?" she reminded Loretta.

The front door opened and a golden retriever dashed in. Mavis followed more sedately with a drink carton of coffee cups.

Jax pondered his walnut-sized bubble and the contrast of Evie's circus of a kitchen with his sedate, stainless steel one. He resisted adding syrup to eggs and waited for coffee.

"Twisted doesn't mean bad," Loretta claimed, through a sticky sweet mouthful. "Just different."

Well, that was a little obvious. Jax breathed coffee fumes gratefully when Mavis set the box in front of him. It held four cups and Mavis took one of them. *She'd known his team was here?*

"Gertie said one of your friends prefers hazelnut. She marked that cup with an H." Mavis took her cup to a stool beside the central island butcher block—obviously not part of the original Victorian kitchen but probably a 60's renovation.

Gertie didn't know his team was here, did she? Or the whole damned town knew. Why not?

"Thanks, Mom. You want your usual?" Evie threw an egg on the griddle.

"That's fine, dear. Am I taking Loretta over to the school this morning? The auspices are good."

"We're learning about twisted bubbles first," Evie warned. "Loretta?"

The kid finished off her milk, leaving a white mustache on her upper lip —like any normal kid.

"People are all different," the kid said, sensibly. "And they change. Most people just have. . . invisible bubbles?" she asked hesitantly.

Of course, the kid had just been playing a game called *Bubble Witch*.

Evie nodded as if she understood. "I see auras. Most people have layers that fluctuate with mood. Sometimes they're too transparent to see. Something like that?"

"Maybe." Loretta seemed skeptical. "I see bubbles *inside* people. Some have big ones, sort of around their hearts, that grow when they laugh and get smaller when they cry. Those are the best teachers."

"The ones with empathic hearts are usually good souls," Mavis added helpfully. "That's a very interesting insight."

Jax drank half his coffee and kept his opinion to himself. Bubbles equated to *souls*? Rubbish.

Reuben stalked in, newly showered if not shaved. He was apparently aiming for respectable with only partially ripped jeans and his MIT T-shirt. Jax pointed at the seat beside him and handed him the hazelnut.

"Twisted bubble?" Evie encouraged. The petite genie set a plate stacked with French toast in front of the scary scarred Black guy without blinking an eyelash. "Fruit or syrup?"

Jax hadn't been offered that choice. Maybe walnuts didn't get fruit.

Or maybe she knew Reuben was gay and was insulting him. Who the hell knew?

Reuben requested fruit. Reuben had a twisted bubble. Jax waited.

"Have you ever blown bubbles?" Loretta asked. "Those great big ones we're not allowed to blow inside?"

"They twist into lovely shapes, dear." At the butcher block, Mavis dipped a strip of toast into the runny egg Evie slid in front of her. "They're pretty in the sunlight."

"Like that." Loretta nodded as if that made sense. "They twist and shrink and then grow and wind into shapes again. They're transparent and rainbow colored and pretty but not like the little round bubbles machines make."

Jax snorted. "You're rainbow colored, my friend," he murmured to Reuben.

Reuben grinned. "Shut up, smartass."

Loretta gifted them with a frown of scorn. "I don't know many people with bubbles like that. I need to learn about them."

"So twisted isn't bad, just different?"

Evie slid another platter of egg toast across from Jax just as Roark emerged, not looking any different than when he'd gone in. The bronzed, bald Cajun actually had a full head of extra-thick, curly hair but hated messing with it. He also owned an infinite supply of khakis and denim work shirts instead of a bodybuilder's usual tight shirts and jeans. He thought they made him look professional.

"Twisted is bad if it's not *transparent*," Loretta corrected. "But mostly, bad is small and dark."

Evie shot Jax a look from beneath a fair, upraised eyebrow. "Like a walnut?"

Loretta frowned. "Walnuts in their shells are green. Doesn't that mean they can open and grow?"

"Not once they reach the shriveled stage. That means they're dead meat." Evie grinned and set a platter of toast and fruit on the butcher block near her mother as the super-sized Cajun took a place next to Loretta's small frame.

"Huh. Dried up sponge maybe? We studied sponges this year. Anyway, lawyers almost always have black pit bubbles but Jax's is different. It's soft."

"Like a prune," Evie suggested. "Or a raisin."

"What da *hell* we talkin' 'bout, man?" Roark asked, digging into his breakfast.

"Bubble souls. Yours is fruity and twisted." Jax informed him, forking his toast.

"*I'm* fruity and twisted," Reuben corrected. "Jax here is a shriveled walnut."

Jax gave up on bubbles and returned to Mavis's question about school. As long as they were being ridiculous— "Since our Indigo child is saying she reads soul bubbles, does that mean it's safe to let her go to school because she recognizes bad guys?"

Loretta gave a long-suffering sigh. "I'm right here, *man*. Ask me."

"*Yay* for the kid," Evie called softly, scooping up strawberries.

"What does Evie's soul look like?" Jax asked.

"Big colorful bubble mostly. But it shrinks into a silver dagger sometimes. I don't know what that means yet. I've not seen that before, either."

~

EVIE DIDN'T HANG AROUND FOR DISCUSSIONS OF SILVER daggers, school, and who washed dishes. She had her dog-walking job to do—and an area she needed to investigate.

Thanks to her vet cousin, Afterthought had some of the best-trained animals in the state, maybe the country. Not that they were show dogs, but Iddy insisted on teaching animals how to take care of themselves.

Evie let the old Basset hound and mutt run loose when she reached her destination. They took off into the shrubbery while she sat on the branch of a low-limbed oak and studied the pond that gave the proposed Lakeland development its name. What did Loretta's parents want them to know about this mud puddle?

For one, she knew in spring it filled with run-off from thunderstorms. It dried up over summer. The pond had flooded after a hurricane last fall and been full most of the winter, but that wasn't a given. Since they hadn't had a big rain in weeks, it was shrinking again. It wasn't a recreational haven by any means.

There were a couple of rowboats stranded on the sides, so presumably people thought there were fish in it. She didn't fish but she thought a pond had to be stocked. Had someone stocked it at some point?

The terrain here was basically rolling red clay. It could be farmed, but this was Witch Hill, owned by her family over the centuries. Malcolms didn't farm, to her knowledge. There was an abandoned Civil War-era farmhouse farther up the hill but no barn—and a twentieth-century cottage on the far side of the hill that got rented out. And Jax thought Loretta owned this?

The dogs barked. Swinging her legs, Evie scanned the path from town. Seeing a familiar muscled figure jogging down the dusty road, she sighed and whistled for the dogs. She swung down and offered them treats when they came running. She hooked up their leashes and debated heading back into town. But just in case. . . she opened her inner eye and examined his walnut soul.

Still repressed and intense but not as angry as yesterday. Maybe he'd just needed to get away from his office for a few hours.

"How did you know I was up here?" she demanded when he was within range.

"I didn't. I wanted to take a look at the property." Jax shoved his hands into his pockets and examined the mud puddle. "Mosquito heaven."

Evie laughed. "Put that way, yep. Environmentalists say we have rare breeds of frogs and some kind of mice that can't be found anywhere else. I don't think they've studied the mosquitoes."

"Rare insects probably need rare mice to breed and are the only food the rare frogs will eat. And agricultural runoff is making them toxic or turning them into super-frogs." Jax scratched the mutt's head and regarded the gnarled oak she'd just been inhabiting.

So much for dressing respectably. He didn't even know she existed this morning. She should ponder her aptitude for dressing for invisibility. "Eye of newt and all that. My ancestors kept this land for a reason. You won't find much agricultural run-off since they didn't farm or even rent the land for farming."

"Why keep it then? Why haven't they sold it off to someone who can use it?" Jax studied the thicket of beautyberry entwined with Carolina Jessamine on the outskirts of the wooded area.

Evie suspected he couldn't identify what he saw, much less notice the place wasn't covered in kudzu, or that the honeysuckle had politely been confined to a stand of wax myrtle. "It's being used."

"For what? Casting spells?" He headed toward the clearing around the pond but stopped when his army boot sank into the soil.

Army boot, interesting. "Something like that." Evie started back down the lane. "Did you let Loretta go off to school?"

He followed her, which was also interesting. Accustomed to being dismissed as an airhead, Evie gave the dogs long leads to sniff the roadside and obligingly allowed Jax to accompany her.

"I talked to Loretta's maternal family in Boston. Their kids always attended boarding school. They're worried about security. But as long as I'm not shipping Loretta back to them, they'll accept my advice. I'm still thinking she needs better protection than you can provide. I have my team devising means of tracking her. I'm not comfortable with the situation." Jax took the mutt's leash and snapped him back into line.

"Her parents are dead and trying to catch her attention." Evie had to draw a line somewhere. "She says her parents called her before they disappeared, said they were coming to Afterthought, and they were selling land here. Why does no one believe her?"

"Because she's a grieving kid in denial. Have you ever met her parents? If they wanted to sell land, they'd call one of those private Realtors who cater to exclusive clients. They would not trudge two hours into the wilderness."

Evie contemplated arguing about Afterthought being wilderness, but it wasn't much of an argument. Charleston's sprawl ended at the county line. "They came here. They're buried here. I need to send them on to the next plane, and I can't do that until you resolve whatever is bothering them. And I'm going to guess that means catching their killers."

Ten

ROARK'S UTILITY VAN WASN'T ANYWHERE TO BE SEEN WHEN JAX arrived back in town. He surrendered the dog's leash to his ghost-busting hostess and stomped down the street to cool his temper and get his bearings better.

She thought the Posts were buried at the pond.

If he didn't ground himself in logic, he'd let Evie and her mad family infiltrate his brain with their weird predictions. He wanted no part in a murder investigation, but he was actually starting to wonder about Loretta's parents. Disappearing in the Bermuda triangle wasn't any more likely for the stiff-necked couple than the Posts visiting Afterthought. He'd simply accepted the firm's assessment and his guardianship and acted accordingly.

Questioning his adoptive father and his partners was not a good career move.

Still, he'd read the Lakeland legal file last night. Stockton and Stockton routinely handled business for large real estate developers. According to the file, the local mayor and some of his cronies owned most of the farmland around the town. They'd been buying it up for decades and had recently formed a development company.

The pond and land surrounding it were on the edge of town and in the center of the development company's holdings. The pond had been privately held for centuries. The Posts had been uninterested in selling until recently.

Apparently, their desire to sell had led the development company to start planning a golf course, "lakeside" homes, tennis courts, and condos. Given the constant expansion of Charleston and Savannah, a quaint tourist town on their outskirts, one with good schools and a golf course, would become a desirable destination.

That no one in Afterthought, population 3237, knew the extent of the development raised suspicion. Even small towns generally required zoning and development meetings. There ought to be talk all over—and protests. People didn't like change. Instead of fighting for their homestead, Evie's family had dismissed the mention as if the development were little more than pie in the sky.

He entered the ancient brick courthouse and looked for anything resembling a register of deeds department. He found it stuck in a corner at the end of a dark corridor. Flickering overhead fluorescents reminded him of elementary school.

The blue-haired clerk behind the counter immediately came to attention at his entrance. Once upon a time, grannies tinted their gray hair with a blue wash. These days, they apparently streaked it with paint, like teenagers.

"I'm interested in buying property and would like to see a zoning map for the town, if you have one?" He'd already looked online. The county website was limited.

"Oh, we don't have anything like that." She smiled brightly. "Afterthought doesn't trample the rights of their citizens. That's what cities do, isn't it?"

Well, no, every town had a right to set up zoning or they'd end up with porn stores next to the high school. "So I could put a cattle ranch on Witch Hill and no one would care?"

"Well, you'd have to own the land, and that won't happen, but otherwise, yes. You could put up fences and barns and graze cattle and start a slaughter shop anywhere you bought property inside the town limits. Probably the county, too, although they do have a zoning commission. We could use any employment that comes our way." She looked at him eagerly, as if hoping she'd given the correct answer. Or might hire her to slaughter cattle.

"Why couldn't I buy Witch Hill? Not that I mean to, of course, I'm just curious." Jax didn't bother with an ingratiating smile. Officious seemed good enough for the clerk.

"Oh, a local family has owned it for centuries. There may be a family cemetery there. The mayor has tried to buy it several times, but it never comes to anything. Nothing but weeds and raccoons up there now." She shrugged her skinny shoulders.

"I'm more interested in an ice cream shop than anything called Witch Hill, but thank you for your time. It's good to know there won't be any problem if I buy the lot I have in mind." He walked out before she could ask him which lot. Loretta had inherited several.

The *family* wouldn't sell Witch Hill. As far as Jax knew, that family was probably Loretta. The mayor and his real estate company wanted the property—but Jax was pretty certain the Malcolms wouldn't want them to have it. Just call it his walnut-sized intuition. He smelled trouble brewing.

"LORETTA POST? YOU WOULDN'T BE JOHNNY'S DAUGHTER, BY ANY chance?" The middle-aged principal leading her down the hall glanced through Loretta's file. "What a delight to have you here!"

"My daddy went to school here?" That would be exciting, Loretta thought. Maybe she could learn something that would help her find him.

"No, but he occasionally visited. A lot of people know your family. You'll do fine here. This is Mrs. Wright's class. You'll like her."

She led Loretta into a schoolroom with twenty or so kids who all stared. Loretta didn't think she looked any different from them, so they must be staring because they didn't know her. She hadn't decided whether she wanted to change that or not. In general, she didn't like kids her age. Their bubbles were pretty small and uninteresting.

"Hello, Loretta, it's good to have you here." The teacher seemed a little younger than the principal. She had a nice smile and long golden hair she wore tied in back. "I hope you'll enjoy being with us. Just take any empty seat. We're studying the planets today. There should be books in the desk."

The books were battered and old and well below the level of her studies, but Loretta obediently opened them when the girl beside her showed the page.

Mrs. Wright was one of the teachers with a good bubble. If Afterthought was the last place her parents had visited, then she needed to meet everyone she could. Maybe she'd find someone who had seen them. Or if they'd been kidnapped, maybe she'd see the person with a black pit.

She might be able to tell Mr. Roark and Mr. Reuben about the black pit, if she found it. She didn't know why they were on the school roof. Maybe they could track her parents from there?

~

"ALL THE DOGGIES ARE WALKED AND ALL THE ERRANDS ARE RUN. I can cover for you. Go have a good gossip with Gertie. Find out what the mayor is up to now." Evie strolled into her mother's shop, checking the shelves to see if anything had sold today. Mid-week, it was unlikely.

"Lottie Shepherd bought the last of the arthritis balm. I'll have to collect some willow bark and ginger and make a new batch. Can you hold the desk long enough for me to walk out to the Hill and gather them?" Not waiting for an answer, Mavis bustled from behind the counter, removing the apron she used when she mixed her concoctions.

"Take an amulet. I was out there this morning and sense unrest. The Magician was there, too. I don't think he was the cause of this disturbance though." Evie picked up a feather duster and started cleaning the merchandise.

"I don't like any of this. Your friends seem nice, but they're stirring up what should be left alone. Now, if they'd stir the mayor to leave town, I'd be a little more appreciative." She dashed out, straightening the pins in her graying bun.

As soon as she left, Evie set down the duster and headed for the small office in back. She wanted to see that official-looking notice. Mavis had ignored the condemnation notices on the trailer park, assuming lawyers would stop the city from evicting her. But the trailer park lawyers hadn't been as determined as the city's.

Now that Evie had a genuine big-city lawyer in the house, for however long, she'd put him to use, if needed. Otherwise, she'd boot him out as soon as reasonably possible. Jax was disturbing *her* peace, if no one else's. How was she going to talk to Loretta's parents if his disbelief blocked them?

Psy followed her, leaping up on the desk and hindering progress. Evie shoved the cat aside to lift the desk blotter and find the clear-address envelope. Mavis didn't use computers, but she didn't use ink or the blotter either. If her mother couldn't address a bill directly, she gave it to Evie to handle. The desk —and probably her habits—simply hadn't changed in Evie's lifetime.

The envelope had been opened, so she figured she wasn't breaking any laws checking the contents: NOTICE OF TAX SALE.

Stomach plummeting, Evie scanned the contents, then frowned. She might be spacey, but she could read. The notice had Mavis's name and the shop's address. It declared a property lot with some incomprehensible number on it was being sold for unpaid back taxes.

Evie knew they paid the taxes on the shop and Val's house every year. She wasn't *that* scatter-brained. She worked hard and saved ahead.

She'd have to take this down to the courthouse and ask what it was about. She just had this uneasy notion that allowing anyone to see her ignorance would give them the upper hand somehow. Mayor Block owned a real estate firm and squeezed money out of every exchange of property in town—but this came from the *county* courthouse.

The shop bell over the door rang. Evie shoved the envelope in the back pocket of her capris and scuttled back to the counter. Studying the shop's contents with a disapproving frown, her nemesis awaited.

"Does anyone still buy crystals?" Jax asked, picking up a particularly fine black agate. "Or these other gewgaws?" He gestured at the New Age displays.

"They're popular with tourists who have nothing better to spend their money on. But Mavis uses the crystals for healing, so yes, people buy them." More regularly than Evie's ghost-busting or detection talents. "Why aren't you on your way back to Savannah? Don't you have work to do?"

"You don't really think I'm leaving my ward with strangers? I'm paid to see to Loretta's safety, and I'm not convinced that you or the school can provide it." He set a cell phone on the counter and opened it to a map. "Do you recognize this parcel?"

Evie looked at him in disbelief. "Parcel? I don't even know what you're talking about much less what you want me to see. It's a map with a bunch of squinchy writing."

"It's a parcel map of Afterthought. If you had anything as reasonable as a computer, I'd send it to you." He made the screen show a wider area. "The town is here." He tapped a bunch of lines.

"I have a computer. I just haven't given you access to it." She moved the image around and decided the little squares might be buildings along Main Street. She scrolled it to the area where Witch Hill ought to be. The squares got a lot larger and more irregular. "What plot of land are we talking about?"

"All this area outside of town. Is all that Witch Hill?" He stabbed his finger on the area she studied.

"Most of it, I suppose. I don't know where boundaries are. There's an old rock wall around the family cemetery. Is that one of the squares?" The paper in her back pocket itched. Parcels, lots. . . "Do those squares have numbers?"

"Not on here but probably in the deed books. Why?" He stuck the phone in his pocket.

Wouldn't it be loverly if all that intense focus was on her and not land? But his steely gaze gave her cold shivers, so she shouldn't admire.

He was a lawyer. She might as well get as much free advice as she could. She produced the crumpled notice and spread it on the counter. "Would that number be to a lot in the deed book? How would I find it?"

"I'm not certain how much of the county is digitalized, so you'd probably have to talk to the blue-haired lady in the deed office." He got his phone out again and took a picture of the notice. "You don't think it's the shop?"

"It shouldn't be the shop. We pay our taxes. The only other thing we pay taxes on is Val's house, and they're paid up. Mavis used to own a lot where the parking lot is now but the city condemned that. They surely can't be charging her taxes on it."

"Let me put R&R on it. I need to know about the plots around Witch Hill, and I should pinpoint Loretta's other holdings as well. If there are any computerized files, they'll find them. The county couldn't send notices without some kind of list." He started for the door.

Evie called after him. "Mayor Block's realty company will have computers. I bet they have copies of every deed ever recorded in town and maybe a few that aren't."

Jax raised a dark eyebrow, then nodded and let himself out.

Evie hoped Loretta brought her ghosts home for lunch. She needed a lot more information than she currently possessed—starting with, where were they buried?

Eleven

"Why the devil are you still in that godforsaken hole?" Stephen Stockton roared in Jax's ear. "Get the kid back into school and get back to work. You'll never make partner by neglecting your clients."

Jax didn't fret too much over the old threat. His adoptive father and boss had the roar of a lion, but he had positioned Jax to take a place in the firm. Jax only needed to build enough cash and credibility for the partnership buy-in. If he kept his nose to the grindstone, he'd be partner by next year.

He knew how to spin this little hiccup so it didn't stand in his way. "I'm establishing security with Loretta's family. Boarding school wasn't working out. I'll be back in the office as soon as we have a system installed." Protecting their clients was Jax's bailiwick.

Land deals and lawsuits were Stephen's. His father knew nothing about security. "You're leaving the kid with family in the middle of a swamp? Have you lost your mind?"

"It's not a swamp. The kid owns half the town. Everyone here will look after her best interests. If you're concerned about her education, I can call in experts and ask what they recommend. She can pay for anything she needs for less than the cost of boarding school. It's not expensive living here." With the phone on speaker, Jax worked his way through the computer files R&R had sent him. Walnut intuition warned not to mention his research into Loretta's property.

"She doesn't need to be anywhere near that damned town! Find her a real school, one that will prepare her for college." The phone slammed—as in actual slammed. Stephen liked the old-fashioned kind that could be heard.

Jax frowned. Why shouldn't Loretta live with a family in a town she owned? He was pretty damned certain Stephen didn't believe in ghosts, so was it Loretta's *family* she shouldn't know?

Since the debacle that had caused him to leave the military, Jax generally avoided defying a direct order, but something about this whole case created an itch between his shoulder blades. He hoped Stephen wouldn't take out his anger on Ariel. She wasn't capable of living anywhere else but the rural mansion they called home.

As if she picked up on his thoughts, his sister hit him with a text message full of numbers and a warning: **WATCH YOUR BACK**.

Swell, just what he needed. Ariel's cryptic messages usually had teeth. She just never explained. He wasn't certain if she couldn't or didn't want to. Numbers spoke to her, not people.

WATCH YOURS he typed back, because his sister lived on their adoptive father's charity. She was over twenty-one and not a child anymore and totally at Stephen's mercy.

Jax shot the numeric part of the message to R&R to translate.

Their parents had died in a car accident when Jax had only been twelve, Ariel, six. He was fairly certain it had been Tricia Stockton who had insisted on adopting them. She'd never had children of her own and had doted on them while she was alive.

After Tricia died of breast cancer, Ariel had simply continued haunting the Stockton mansion, unable and unwilling to leave the only home she remembered. Jax had room in his condo for her, but she refused to move.

He understood. Condos weren't the quiet haven of rural isolation she needed to function.

When Ariel sent nothing more, he returned to digging through the online deed file his team had found. He'd located Evie's wi-fi instructions and had internet now. The county's digitalized deed file didn't seem to include anything prior to 2007. They were a little late in computerizing. Jax was jotting notes when Loretta popped into the bedroom he'd been assigned.

"Your walnut is cracking," she informed him. "Want cookies? Evie said you're buying, so you ought to have some."

Jax rubbed his brow and fought laughing at his cracking walnut. That almost fit his sick humor right now. "Technically, *you're* paying. I set up an account at the grocery that's billed to your bank. Are you sure you don't want to go back to the boarding school? Food was part of the tuition."

She sat cross-legged on his bed to contemplate the question. Evie had tied ribbons in her pigtails before school, but they straggled, undone, now. She chewed on the end of her hair, explaining the frazzled look it developed as the day wore on.

"I'd have to see the numbers, but I'm thinking groceries are a lot cheaper than that school. I don't want to waste my parents' money. They'll yell after I find them."

"You're too old for ten," he retorted, turning back to his computer. He didn't eat sweets, but if it would send the kid away. . . "Bring me a cookie, please."

"Evie says I'm an old soul." Loretta jumped down. "But my dad said I should understand how money works. I don't, really. But I can add." She departed to the kitchen, where she apparently chatted with their hostess.

He should probably hire a nanny as well as a cook. He couldn't expect the scatter-brained genie to properly look after a kid who wasn't hers. Then the nanny could live in this room, and he could go home and back to his job. Huh, maybe he could find a nanny who cooked.

But first he needed to compare this list of parcels with the tax records—

Evie walked in smelling of cinnamon and vanilla and carrying a platter of lemon bars. "I wanted to test these on you first to make certain I'm not poisoning Loretta."

"Good thought. Got coffee?" Unconcerned, he crunched down on the graham cracker crust, and tart lemony sweetness dissolved on his tongue. If he was going to die, this would be the way to go. He studied the yellow square, then decided the tart worked and ate the rest of it.

"Your coffeemaker arrived, but I have no idea what to do with it. It looks like it might eat small children. Have you found those lot numbers yet?" She picked up one of the bars and nibbled.

Curvaceous fairies shouldn't wear tight T-shirts with sparkly rainbows over their breasts. Orange corkscrew curls did not help his spinning senses. "I'm working on them. Did the coffee beans arrive, too?" He shoved the rest of the bar into his mouth and stood up to look for his coffeemaker. She stood between him and caffeine.

She stepped back, apparently reading his *aura* correctly, which, given his level of lust, might be dangerous if such things were real.

"The grocery sent a bag of whatever was probably priciest. Giving a small store carte blanche isn't the best way of keeping costs down." She spun around and returned to the kitchen.

"Are you looking for my parents or just fighting?" Loretta asked, swinging in circles on the stool at the butcher block. "The principal said she knew my father when he was little. Maybe my parents are hiding with friends."

"Why would they be hiding?" Evie filled up an empty milk glass and put away the cookies.

"Because someone is trying to kidnap them? Or they're working on a secret project and don't want anyone to know. Maybe I could put an ad in the newspaper to say I'm here so they'll find me."

"The paper only comes out once a week. I think they already know you're here. Remember, you wanted a psychic. That's me." Evie began cleaning up the baking dishes in the sink.

"You think they're ghosts." The accusation was clear and filled with disappointment.

Jax leaned past Evie to clean out his new coffee pot. "Do ghosts have bubbles?"

That shut them both up, temporarily. He filled the pot and looked for an electrical outlet. While they warbled over the possibility of ghosts, souls, and bubbles, he unplugged an unnecessary old-fashioned clock to plug in the coffee machine.

A pounding on the roof reminded him he was supposed to warn Evie. She was already halfway to the door when he grabbed her. "That's Roark. He's my hardware expert. You're not under attack." Before she could maim him, he set her back down. Shame she wasn't still wearing that halter though.

She grabbed her silky curls and pulled, apparently to control her temper. Jax leaned back against the counter, listening to the wondrous sound of perking coffee, and waited to see which direction the explosion would take.

Instead, she stalked out to the back step and shouted, "When you're done putting holes in my roof, would you take down the Christmas decorations? There are lemon bars in the pantry."

She looked calmer when she returned to the kitchen sink. "Loretta, do you have homework?"

Apparently understanding Evie's tone—or reading her bubble—Loretta climbed down from the stool and headed for the stairs. "I'll need more school supplies. I didn't bring my colors."

Jax found a mug and filled it with delicious brew and waited. *Calm* didn't mean his hostess didn't intend to slice his throat.

"I need to speak with her parents to find out where they're buried." She plunked a dish into the drying rack.

"They're buried at the bottom of the Caribbean. I need to see that Loretta gets a proper education. My boss is breathing fire and wants her out of here." Jax crossed his arms, leaned on the counter, and sipped the elixir of the gods.

She swiveled and flicked soap suds at him. "Loretta needs people who recognize that she's special, people who will help her learn and use her abilities for the good of humankind. An Indigo child is a harbinger of peace and unity—if we surround her with love. You know any schools that can do it better than a small town where everyone knows everyone and looks out for each other?"

"Bull crap. Small towns have proportionately as many jerks as any other place. She needs a proper education and protection against those who want her money."

"No one would know she had money if you'd shut up about it! She's just a kid. Let her be a kid instead of one of the snots trying to show off who has the mostest. She needs time to learn how to be who she is meant to be. What school will teach her to understand her bubbles? She's talking about *souls*, doofus. She sees right into our souls. What would happen if she mentioned them to a teacher or other kids who have no concept of *different*?"

She might end up like Ariel was Jax's first panicky thought.

But that was ridiculous. Ariel was neurodivergent to the extent of social incapacitation. Loretta wasn't anything like Ariel. She was merely precocious. She needed. . . People who didn't laugh at her.

"Souls?" he asked warily. Was she serious? "And why won't she be laughed at here?"

"Souls," Evie affirmed. "She is not making up bubbles. I have never known anyone who can see souls, but I know better than to sneer at what she sees. So does my entire family and half the town. Afterthought has dealt with Malcolms for centuries. They accept that we're different. They might not understand how or why, but they're willing to let me rid them of ghosts and Iddy teach their animals and my mother remedy their ills or read their futures.

You're standing there sneering now. If you can't believe in her, go back where you belong and leave Loretta to us."

He continued sipping his coffee. The grocery's ground coffee was crap. "She cannot earn a living or survive in this world talking about *souls*, or bubbles she's making up from a video game because she wants to be a witch. She needs to learn economics and finance and make the world a better place by putting her money where it does the most good. You are quite obviously not the best choice for that."

She flung a cup at him. Fortunately, it was plastic and bounced off his shoulder. But the suds landed in his coffee, and he scowled.

"*Money does not make the world better.* Her parents are *dead*, not making anything better. The Posts never did anything with their talents except accumulate wealth that's now hanging around Loretta's neck like an albatross. Had they made money and put it back into the community, *then* they might have made the world better, and Loretta could be a normal kid without a pack of jackals on her heels. One only needs enough money for shelter and food, after that, it's a burden."

She pulled the plug on the sink drain and asked, "Who inherits Loretta's money? If you don't believe in ghosts, then you might consider someone really might be trying to kill her."

When he couldn't immediately reply, she cast him a look of disgust and stalked out.

Jax dumped his soapy coffee into the sink and rinsed out the suds. He doubted that Loretta had a will. Chances were good, her fortune would simply be divided among remaining family.

Remaining family—Evie's family as well as the Boston ones?

Twelve

"WILL MR. JACKSON LET ME STAY?" LORETTA ASKED WORRIEDLY when Evie stormed up the stairs to her room.

"We will sue the pants off Mr. Jackson if he doesn't let you stay," she said reassuringly. "Your money, your choice. But what I want to do is take you out to the land your parents might have been selling. Maybe you'll see something there that I don't."

If her parents had died in Afterthought, would the sad ghosts clinging to Loretta slip away if she came close to any earthly remains? Evie could only guess. Ghosts that haunted people were rare, but then, so was Loretta. She wondered if John Post had a Malcolm gift that allowed him to cling to his family, one he'd suppressed all his life.

"You think maybe they're hiding at the pond?" Loretta asked eagerly, flinging aside her textbook.

"Were they the type to go camping?" Evie was pretty certain they weren't, but she waited while Loretta tugged on sturdy shoes.

"Maybe when they were my age?" Loretta bounced up and raced for the stairs.

Well, sure, why not? Everyone was young once.

"What are your parents like?" Maybe talking about them would increase the connection so they'd speak. It wasn't as if Evie had much experience talking to the newly dead. The ghosts around here were usually decades old, if not more.

Loretta shrugged as she opened the front door. "I don't see them a whole lot, just at holidays. They want me to be a doctor or lawyer, so they gave me doctor bags and computer word games and stuff."

"Parents always want the best for their children," Evie said encouragingly. "Given your abilities, I think you'd be great working at the UN. Do your parents know about your bubbles?" She led the way down the street in the direction of the pond. It was probably a half-mile walk. They should have bikes, but she only owned one and the tires were busted.

Loretta shrugged again. "I tried to tell them, but their bubbles are small. They don't understand. I've learned not to tell anyone unless they have big bubbles."

"Hmmm, I wonder if big bubbles might not indicate old souls, ones who've been around and understand more." She explained the concept of old souls as they practically raced down the road. Loretta was in a hurry.

When they reached the pond and woodland, Loretta wrinkled up her nose. "This is it? There isn't anything here."

"Not unless you know how to look." Evie led her down a well-worn path into the oaks. "I'm not an herbalist like my mother, but every plant you see in here has a purpose. See that scraggly bush? In the fall, it will produce a berry that's good for heart ailments. And those sticks? Those will produce the prettiest purple berries in the fall that are good as chemical antifungal agents and better than the drugstore spray for mosquitoes and ticks."

"But you can just go to the store and buy bug spray!" She stomped down the path, eagerly checking behind every bush, as if her parents might have turned into fairies that could hide in shrubbery.

Evie studied the frail ghosts clinging to her. She was pretty certain there were two, but only one seemed to strengthen as they trudged along. "The things in the store have a lot of chemicals in them that might be harmful, if you're sensitive. If they work for you, fine, but if they don't, we have the alternatives here."

"But my parents want to sell this land? Are you sure? Who would buy it?"

Excellent question. "Well, the thing is, I'm not sure this land can be sold." She knew that was partially her wishful thinking, but she picked up on things not said. Her family had little interest in material things. Land was where plants grew—not real estate to be sold. "But you'd have to talk to my mother and aunts about that. It's always been in the family. Here, I'll show you." She lifted a tree branch laden with vines and revealed a faint path to the western edge, away from the pond.

The ghost on Loretta's shoulder didn't want to go this way. He detached and tried to push back the way they came.

"Sorry, Mr. Post. We'll go that way in a second. Just let me show Loretta her ancestors." Evie paused for the ghost to understand she was talking to him.

Loretta shot her a look. "Are you talking to my dad?"

"I think so." Loretta had to learn sometime, but it would be hard without actual bodies. "First, look over by that wall." Evie distracted the child from more questions.

Ancient, lichen-covered rocks formed a low wall concealed by high weeds. It wasn't that Malcolms didn't honor their dead, so much as protect them. Anyone walking through here wouldn't look twice. Evie stepped over the rocks and pushed aside a huge patch of violets to reveal another low, flat stone.

Loretta crouched down to examine it. "It has words on it!"

"And a date. They wrote funny all those years ago, but whoever carved the letters did so in a manner that's kept them clear for centuries." Evie knew the words by heart. It was part of her heritage and that of every Malcolm in the territory.

"Priscilla Malcolm, mother, witch, beloved, 1680-1752. Wow, that's old!"

"She would have been just a little older than you when she was accused of being a witch back in New England. Her family brought her to Afterthought, although I don't think there was a town then. This was our original homestead."

"Your cousin is named after her?" Loretta began inspecting other stones buried under various groundcovers, daffodils, and wild roses.

"My family is weird. They like keeping the old names alive. You can come back here anytime you like. Why don't we take a look at the pond now?"

Obligingly, Loretta abandoned her tombstone search and trailed after Evie. Her ghosts trailed along with her. The stronger one seemed more agitated than usual. Loretta swatted aside vines and branches and aimed directly at the glimmer of water ahead. "If I'd known we had ancestors here before the Revolutionary War, I could have had a better report than anyone else in my class when we had to tell where our families came from."

The ghosts got larger and clearer.

Evie took Loretta's hand when they reached the muddy bank. "Close your eyes. Let me try to hear your parents."

Her pansy blue eyes darkened. "How?"

"Trust me, okay? I don't promise anything, but I need to try. Remember, I can see auras?" Which let her see spirits, but Evie didn't try to explain. She needed Loretta to relax and let go of her fears—and her parents.

Loretta obligingly held Evie's hands and closed her eyes.

"Think about bubbles," Evie suggested softly. "Try to remember your parents' bubbles."

Her own eyes open, Evie watched the lighter shadow detach and shimmer in the afternoon heat. "Now, let go of those bubbles, if you can. Just open your mind and let it go blank. Breathe deeply."

Apparitions didn't usually talk—except inside Evie's head. She'd much rather send them on to the light or the next plane of existence than communicate. The shimmer hesitated uncertainly. "Go," Evie whispered. "Let go. She'll be fine."

"I hear her!" Loretta shouted, unexpectedly. "I think I hear my mom. I think she's angry. I heard a bad word." Her eyes popped open and she looked around eagerly. "She must be close, right?"

The shimmer popped and disappeared. Evie sighed. The bigger, darker shadow grew even more solid. "She was right here, kiddo. She was trying to say goodbye, I'm sure. Did her bubble go away?"

Loretta's eyes darkened and puddled. "No! She's not dead! She was right here. I *heard* her." She jerked her hands from Evie's and began running around, searching under bushes.

Dang, it was so hard to know how to handle these things. Charming, if the last word Loretta heard from her mother was a curse. Evie waited, watching the dark shadow pulsing with more energy as it hesitantly followed Loretta, then lingered nearer Evie when the child roamed further.

"I'm sorry, Mr. Post," she murmured. "I'm doing all I know to do. If there's something you need to tell us, I'm open. We really will look after Loretta as if she's our own. She's in good hands. But it would be nice to know what happened to you."

She thought she heard *Deeds* whispering in her head. *Desk* popped in next. *Look.*

The shadow reattached to Loretta as if channeling her energy.

"What about your dad?" Evie called to her distraught charge. "Did you see his bubble? Hear him? Want to try again?"

"No! I know they're alive. They're not stupid ghosts." Giving up her search, Loretta marched back toward the road. "I'm gonna make Mr. Roark look harder."

The shadow attached to her seemed somehow sadder. Evie tried not to cry since it served no purpose, but her eyes were wet as she followed her newfound cousin down the road. She didn't think there was any doubt that the Posts were dead—and they were in the pond.

There was some possibility that the Posts didn't know that, especially if they'd been killed elsewhere.

～

JAX WAS ON EVIE'S FRONT LAWN, CHECKING THE ANGLE OF THE images beamed from the security cameras to his phone, when Loretta stormed up. He glanced over her head to see Evie trailing dejectedly behind. That the genie wasn't bouncing and smiling or glaring at him spoke volumes, if he could read genie-speak.

"Are you looking for my parents?" the kid demanded as soon as she was in range. "If you're not looking for them, then you can go home. I'll find someone else."

Ooookay. Evie's look of defeat told him things had not gone well on the search of the pond, which was to be expected. Of course, Jax didn't have a better idea. "We're tracing their last known location." That sounded good.

"It wasn't the Gulf," Loretta shouted. "Did you search my daddy's desk?"

Evie's eyebrows skyrocketed.

"The police did," Jax said as reassuringly as he knew how, hoping to calm her down. "The firm hired people to pack up his valuables and put them in storage until you're old enough to know what to do with them. When you're ready, we'll have an estate sales firm sell the furniture and larger items still in the house. I can take you there anytime you like, but it's probably best to wait for a weekend."

He'd been the one to insist that they not sell the house until the kid was ready to understand that her parents would never be there again. He remembered the horrible jolt when he'd learned his home had been sold after his parents died. Selling was the practical thing to do, he knew, but a kid needed time. Still, they couldn't leave the place empty much longer.

"Did the police keep any of his effects or are they all in storage?" Evie asked quietly.

Evie, talking quietly—something serious was happening here. Jax gestured for them to go into the house where half the town couldn't hear them.

"They turned over all they took when they concluded the investigation." Jax let Loretta and Evie enter the Victorian first, then closed the door after they entered. The dusty, cluttered parlor got stuffy without circulation from outside, but he didn't know what was going down here. If Evie was filling the kid's head with ridiculous stories. . . But so far, she hadn't done anything that screamed con artist—beyond acting flaky.

Looking miffed, Loretta stomped back to the kitchen.

"I tried to talk with her ghosts," Evie whispered. "Her father told me to look in his desk for deeds. Loretta may have heard. It's hard to say. She's still not accepting they're dead."

"You got any more of those lemon bars?" Jax asked loudly, following Loretta. He didn't want the kid thinking they were doing anything behind her back.

Not that whispered words about impossible subjects were real secrets. He had to work out why a con artist might want him to look at a desk. Evie didn't seem real interested in the kid's money.

"No sugar before dinner," Evie objected. "We're having lasagna, and you won't be able to eat it if you pig out now. Loretta, have an apple if you're still hungry. Wash your hands first."

"What kind of lasagna?" Loretta asked suspiciously, reaching for an apple. "The school did nasty eggplant stuff."

"No eggplants this time of year. Some spinach, maybe, and a touch of the Shepherd's sausage for spice. Are you done yelling at us? If so, you need to do your homework." Evie entered the pantry, presumably for lasagna ingredients.

"I *heard* them." Loretta glared at both of them. "You can't tell me I didn't."

"I'm not telling you that you didn't. I heard your father. I didn't hear your mother. I told you they were with you." Evie reappeared with jars of canned goods and whole onions.

"They're not ghosts!" Loretta took her apple and stomped upstairs.

"Are, too," Evie whispered. "And your mom has moved on to the next plane."

"Tiffany is gone?" Jax felt like an idiot in asking. Evie and Loretta's argument was so real that they almost had him believing in things that go bump in the night.

"I don't think she was as attached to Loretta as her dad. And I don't know if that has anything to do with love or ability." Evie began chopping an onion. "If I were to hazard a guess, I'd say John Post had some Malcolm ability and used it to latch onto Loretta and his wife. He's been dragging her around with him, but Tiffany simply didn't have his energy or talent. She was a pale shadow of him."

"But you *both* heard someone say to look for deeds in the desk?" Jax had seen Evie's surprise when Loretta mentioned it. That didn't mean she wasn't using Loretta's words to accomplish her own goals, whatever in hell they might be.

"And Mavis saw deeds in her scrying ball. I think John Post is trying to tell us something about Loretta's property. Did you find anything in the deed books?"

The kitchen was filling with onion fumes. Jax poured more coffee just to have a better smell in his nose. "There are no good deed maps showing parcel numbers that we've been able to find. The number on your mother's letter leads to a register entry with a description that seems likely to be out by the pond. It's a really old entry. We're scouring others in the same number pattern and they also appear to be in the same general area. We'd need a surveyor to read the boundaries and map them for us. That doesn't mean those lots haven't been sold off over the years."

"We don't generally sell our property." Evie shrugged and flung the onion in the pan and started on a bell pepper. "The land simply passes down through the family, so if that's recorded, there might be name changes over the years. This house was built by a Malcolm over a century ago. Great-Aunt Val's name is currently on the deed. Val used to live here, but she gave the use of it to me after she moved to Atlanta. She'll have to deliberately leave it to me or the entire family inherits, which happens often. The land out by the pond has most likely been in the family since the first witch moved here in the late

1600s. There may have been additional plots purchased by different families over the centuries, but the main plot with the cemetery probably belongs to all of us. The Posts might have demanded some share of it outright when they left town, but I'd look closely at those deeds. Even sharing that property might take an act of Congress."

"The deeds I've found only go back to 2007 and definitely not the 1600s," he said dryly. "So you don't think the Posts were planning on selling the property?"

"I have no notion of what they thought they might do. I'm just thinking they may have discovered they *couldn't*. Loretta may have inherited everything her parents owned. That doesn't mean she's free to sell it any more than her parents were. The mayor buys and sells real estate for a living. He has been buying up cotton fields between here and the outskirts of Charleston since the beginning of time. He's tried to persuade my family to sell. I'm guessing there's a very good reason they haven't."

"My law firm specializes in deconstructing deed restrictions." Jax hadn't seen any restrictions on the deeds he'd uncovered so far. He just wanted to learn what he could while she was offering insights.

She wasn't quite as flaky as she occasionally seemed—not any more than the rest of her family, anyway. Extended family ownership was an obstacle but not a dead end.

"You don't suppose there's a reason Afterthought doesn't grow much?" The pepper entered the frying pan with the onion.

Jax wondered if there was a metaphor in that. "If you know something, come out and say it."

"I don't *know* anything. I've never been interested enough to ask. You'll need to talk to my mother or my aunts. My grandmother died last year, which may be what triggered the notion the land only belongs to the Posts now. Can you look up wills? Great-grandmother Letitia Post may have left her *share* of the land to her children, but that didn't mean she owned it in its entirety."

"The firm should have a copy of the will. I'll check on it." Jax had a hard time conceiving of such a loose relationship to reality, but after dealing with Evie's family, he could see it happening. "If the ownership of these lots is in question, then who has been paying the taxes?"

"The Posts, one assumes, if they thought the land was theirs. Great-Aunt Val may know. She handles family finances—or her husband's accountants do. But I'm very surprised your law firm isn't aware of the situation." Evie crumbled sausage into the skillet. Her tone was definitely disapproving.

Jax thought he might echo that disapproval. Knowing his adoptive father, it was very possible Stephen did know about any contingencies. That would not necessarily stop him if there was a large development in play. "I'll have to take you to Savannah with me, introduce the partners so you can read their auras. I can't tell when they're lying."

"It's doubtful I can either. If an aura is steeped in lies, then one more hardly makes a difference. And I know you're being facetious. I'm not. Dinner will be ready in an hour. Go away."

Frowning, Jax returned to his vanity-sized desk and computer.

Swamp owned by a dozen heirs in the back of nowhere was essentially worthless and not worth killing over. He saw utterly no reason to believe the Posts had been killed here—yet.

Did he listen to a crazy woman and her family, dig deeper and bring down the wrath of his father—or simply accept that they were flakes and go home?

He couldn't very well leave Loretta in the hands of conspiracy-spouting paranoids.

Of course, it was Loretta who had set them down this path of doubt.

Thirteen

"I WANT TO SEE MY DAD'S DESK," LORETTA DEMANDED THE NEXT morning.

Evie poured milk into her cereal bowl. "Not today, you have school."

"You haven't filed my papers yet. That means you're not my guardian, and you can't tell me what to do." She turned her big pansy eyes to Jax, who was scanning his phone for news. "You're my guardian. Take me to see my house."

"Not today, you have school." He repeated Evie's admonition without lifting his gaze from the phone.

Huh, so he listened sometimes. "Can she go tomorrow? It's Saturday."

Jax shoved the phone in his pocket and grabbed his coffee cup. "If I can have peace and quiet today so I can get my work done, we'll go to Savannah tomorrow, okay?"

Evie wanted to ask what work, but Loretta bounced up and down and cheered, and the moment was lost. He wouldn't tell her anyway.

Besides, she needed time to find an alternate dog walker and someone to hold down the fort in the shop. Saturday was their busiest day, and Mavis had a tendency to drift off and ignore cash customers for more interesting ones.

So after sending Loretta off to school with new school supplies, Evie made her dog-walking rounds. Then, after watering Hank's tomatoes and cleaning the hardware store windows, she pocketed his donation to her retirement fund, and stopped in the shop to give Mavis a break as usual.

"Where do we keep the deeds on this shop and Aunt Val's place?" Evie asked. "In a lockbox? I need to find a more secure place for Loretta's papers, even if they might be forged." Which was why she wasn't filing them—she really didn't want to go to jail.

"Ask Val." Mavis removed her apron and tucked straying gray hands back into her bun. "Now that Letitia is gone, she's the eldest and handles everything. I don't have a lockbox but she might."

Pure Mavis, no material interest whatsoever. Evie got out her feather duster and started on the shelves. "I don't want to put Loretta's papers into anyone else's hands. Guess I'll need to bother Jax about an allowance so we can rent one."

"Put her allowance in the bank, and I think they give you a free box." Mavis bustled out, eager for her morning coffee and the gossip that was an essential element of her success.

Coffee and gossip equated marketing in Afterthought. Pity it didn't reach beyond the county line.

Did she dare stir the dragon of Great-Aunt Val to find out about deeds? Wealthy, drama-prone, and with abilities even Evie didn't understand, Val possessed a strong aura of power that overlay any compassion she might possess. Evie avoided her where possible.

Unable to sit still, she had the shelves dusted and rearranged and new flyers drawn up on her laptop when a disturbance of energy at the door caused her to glance up.

A stocky, nearly bald gentleman in a suit tailored to Mr. Moneybags perfection stood gazing at the shop's eccentric contents—much as Jax had that first day. Evie's internal alarms screamed. As if to confirm her fear, Psy leaped up on the counter and nuzzled her hand.

"May I help you?" she asked as brightly as she could while her heart stuttered, and she wished she had La Chusa to send for help. She scratched Psy's head to reassure both of them.

If she didn't fear ghosts, why was she afraid of this character? Really *twisted* vibrations, she decided, using Loretta's apt terminology. She was almost afraid to open her inner eye.

"I want to speak with Damon." Not toweringly tall but threateningly larger than her, he finally entered the shop, leaving the door open.

"The only Damon I know isn't here." She said that firmly and quite capably, she thought.

His gaze swept over her springy curls and purple cropped T-shirt adorned with a sparkling peace sign. Dismissing her, he looked over her shoulder. "Tell him his father is here."

"Ummm, I just said Mr. Jackson is not here. Can I interest you in a high-quality crystal ball? Or perhaps one of our quartzes? Your chakra could be improved with. . ." Evie took a deep breath, slipped into aura mode, and nearly choked. The man was seriously brown. Shit brown, if she could be so crude. His soul must be suffocating under all that bad attitude.

"Call him, will you? I don't have time for this nonsense." He slapped his hand on the counter and stalked back to the doorway.

"If you know him, you're able to call him yourself." Evie had written down Jax's cell phone number but her rebellious streak raised its head. Slavery had been outlawed for good reason.

He snorted and pulled out a cigar.

"No smoking inside," she warned.

He snipped off the end and applied a match. "Tell Jax I'm waiting."

"Not until you listen to what I'm saying." She'd be enjoying herself except she figured he didn't hear a word she said.

As expected, the jerk didn't turn around or reply.

With nothing better to amuse herself and always curious about how other people's heads worked, Evie slipped into her mother's office. Mavis kept a blazer for when she had to talk to the mayor or his council. Evie had always hated the blazer, but she grasped its purpose—it made her mother look more male and thus, acceptable. The coat was too large, of course, but it was a lovely blue that looked good with her purple T-shirt. She found a hair brush in a drawer, along with some barrettes, and pinned up her unruly curls. She found a black silk scarf she draped around her throat in a facsimile of a tie. Checking the mirror on the back of the door, she decided she looked as masculine as she ever would.

She returned to the front, produced a pad of paper from beneath the counter and a pen from the bank. "You wish to speak with Mr. Damon Jackson, is that correct?" she asked in her deepest, most officious voice.

El Jerko swung around, blew a smoke ring, and regarded her with hostility. "That's what I said."

No, you didn't, but a good office worker wouldn't argue with the boss. Not smiling, Evie wrote down the name. "If you will be so good as to give me his number, I'll give him a call."

As anticipated, he rolled off a number when confronted with the kind of toady he expected. Hiding a grin, Evie jotted down the numbers. Chin high, expression placid, she picked up the landline receiver and poked the numbers in. She got voice mail. "Mr. Jackson, there is a gentleman at the shop who wishes to see you. No, he has not given his name. Very well."

She hung up and continued in her officious voice. "He's otherwise occupied. May I take a message?"

"Dammit, I told you I'm his father! Get him back on the line." He crushed out the cigar and stomped across the old wooden floor.

Ha! Finally got aura-shit's attention.

With exaggerated politeness, Evie poked the numbers again and handed him the receiver. By this point, she'd deduced Jax wasn't answering any call with his father's phone number on it. But then, he wasn't answering her calls either. Or the shop's, anyway, since cell phones were out of her budget.

The old man slammed the receiver down on the voice mail message and pointed at her. "You. Tell him to get that kid back in school and his tail home instantly or his ass is grass." He stormed out, chewing on his cigar.

Whooeee.

That called for a good negativity clearing. Evie lit some sage and switched on the shop's meditative harmonics. A minute later, Loretta walked in, wearing a frown.

"That man who just left has a raisin where his bubble should be. Can I eat my lunch here? It's noisy in the cafeteria." She settled on the windowsill with the lunch bag Evie had prepared for her.

A raisin and a shitty aura and that was Loretta's lawyer and Jax's father? No wonder Jax walked around with his aura battened down. It was a pity she didn't practice black magic. She'd like to plague the old coot with a few toads.

She called the house phone instead of his cell. Jax answered instantly.

"Your father just sprinkled us with goodness and light and left you a message of great wit and wisdom. Would you care to hear?" Evie pried the confining barrette out of her hair.

Jax's rumbly voice muttered an expletive. "What in hell is he doing here? Did he see Loretta?"

"She saw him. She says he has the soul of a raisin. His aura needs a good karmic cleanse."

"I might start believing in your mumbo-jumbo if he wasn't such a super-cilious A-hole that everyone recognizes him for what he is. I'll have Roark follow him, see if he meets with anyone. He didn't come all the way up here just for me." He hung up.

While Evie was still staring at the receiver, trying to work through all those unspoken messages, Mavis bustled in carrying a bag from Gertie's. "I brought lunch, dear. I need to run over and talk to Bill at the bank. I'll be back in a jiffy."

"It would help if you'd explain tax notices to me instead of calling on Bill." Evie rummaged through the bag.

"When you're old enough, dear." Mavis pattered off.

She was twenty-five, for pity's sake. How old was old enough?

"Your mother has a very weird bubble." Loretta munched her sandwich and watched out the window. "Do you think I'll ever learn what the differences mean?"

"I think it takes years of study and paying attention to people. Are you prepared to do that?" That's what Evie had done, but she'd lived here where there weren't many people to study.

Could she take her knowledge into a larger world? Not that anyone would hire her anywhere for her gift. *She* knew she could be useful in ways well beyond reading auras. Convincing others was another matter.

Loretta shrugged. "Not much else to do when you're a kid."

"You could collect recyclables, sell them for cash, and contribute the money to charity. I imagine there are a lot of things you could do."

"Did you do that?" Loretta picked through her bag and found the cookies.

"I did, but I had to use the money to buy book bags and things. I didn't have an allowance." And the shop barely made enough to cover groceries, which was why it was convenient the family owned it outright.

Huh, and having entire families own property made them almost impossible to mortgage. What if taxes came due and no one could pay them?

～

JAX SAT BACK IN THE RIDICULOUSLY UNCOMFORTABLE VANITY chair in Great-Aunt Val's sixties bedroom and studied his computer screen.

He'd spent the better part of his thirty years pleasing Stephen Stockton out of an excess of gratitude for being offered a home and education. He'd always thought his adoptive father a busy but honest and generous man. He'd worked hard to please him. It hadn't been until he'd actually joined the firm that he began to see Stockton's aggressive behavior for what it was.

Admittedly, Jax wasn't an open book either. After returning from service, he'd joined the firm to look into the reason his birth father had been accused of fraud and kicked out. No one would talk to him about it and the files were locked up. Now, if he were made partner. . . To do that, he had to listen to Stephen and return to Savannah, Loretta in tow.

If he continued in his current direction, however, he'd be lucky to keep his job. And Ariel was likely to be booted from the house.

Unfortunately, he couldn't shove facts aside just because he didn't like them. Stephen Stockton wasn't exactly the charitable man a younger Jax had believed.

His cell rang with Roark's number. Grunting, he answered it.

"Stockboy meetin' with da mayor and the CEO of a holdin' company for Lakeland. Mic in lobby of City Hall picked up Stockboy swearin' about you and some chick in a shit shop who gave him the run around. Give your lady a high five from me. He usually don' get riled with clients."

Jax rubbed his temple as he translated Cajun to English and fought back a small smile just imagining the scene between the Space Cadet and Stephen. His adoptive father still lived in a world where women were ornaments. "Evie is not my lady. She's more like a hostile witness. You didn't call me to high five Evie."

"Right. I'm reportin' I got mics all over City Hall—but dey have a sound jammer in the board room. Why would public officials want to block their constituents from hearin' city business?"

"I assume that's a rhetorical question. These deed books you've sent me don't line up. You know that, don't you?"

"All I'm doin' is filmin' anything I get my hands on. *Mais,* you're getting paid da big bucks to interpret. Have you gone through them files from da mayor's real estate company?"

Like Reuben, Roark had a degree from MIT and could talk ivory tower English when he wished. He just had a lot of unaddressed issues.

"The mayor's files are good for tracing the lot numbers, except they're not agreeing with the photos you're sending me of the deed books. I'll need a survey for the big picture of who owns what around the pond. At this point, I'm not entirely sure why I'm looking. John Post is dead. We can't send him to jail if there's any fraud involved."

"You give up now, and we quit," Roark warned. "Even my fried brain can tell you da deed books been shuffled. That tax notice your lady give you is from old books and don't agree with da new tax files online. Reuben's about to pop a gasket. Someone will want to see this."

"But if I'm looking at the new taxpayer list correctly, and this map is right, my client owns all that property," Jax warned in exasperation. "You want to dig up the old files and send a kid to jail? What exactly is your end game here?"

That was a stupid question to ask an anarchist. Roark didn't need a defined goal other than bringing down the Man. Except Jax happened to be the Man in this case. His client, his duty to defend.

"Kid don't need millions anyway. Cover your ass because we got copies." Roark hung up.

Jax believed in loyalty. He was loyal to his adoptive father, the man who'd raised him, put him through school, and given him a place in the firm. He was loyal to his sister and his clients.

Unfortunately, loyalty wasn't his team's strong point. They'd served together in Afghanistan—Jax in the legal division, Roark and Reuben in tech. They'd uncovered graft and blackmail at headquarters. It wasn't exactly as if all of Afghanistan wasn't rife with corruption. Their officers had not been pleased. After the inevitable confrontation, Jax had been ready to go home and had accepted his honorable discharge with a shrug.

Roark and Reuben had been a little less thrilled at being given the brush-off. The result had been ugly. They'd never find a job in their chosen professions with that dishonorable on their records.

So he'd put them to the kind of work that let them direct their energies profitably rather than going to jail. They'd been doing fine uncovering evidence in the criminal fraud cases Jax specialized in.

He rubbed the back of his neck and contemplated his next move on the chessboard of his life.

Ariel pinged him again. He'd given her access to all of the financial accounts Loretta had inherited. Unlike Jax, Ariel enjoyed watching money move around, and the Posts had had enormous investments with multiple brokers.

Her message highlighted and bolded an account he didn't recognize—one in a bank in the Cayman Islands. What the. . .

Shit. There was the reason the Posts were yachting in hurricane season.

Fourteen

Once Mavis returned from the bank, Evie took her mother's retriever for a walk. She needed to clear her leapfrogging brain. She'd never given much thought to the land her family owned. It was just convenient to have a house of her own. Mavis could have lived there, too, but she preferred her own space, and she owned the shop—or maybe only some portion of it? Her mother probably didn't even know.

The woods and pond were used for so many activities that Evie had always looked on them as a kind of public park.

But now that it had been brought to her attention—someone had to own the property and someone had to pay taxes and that tax notice on Mavis's desk was worrisome.

And being fairly certain that Loretta's parents were buried on that land. . . Could she use Loretta's funds to hire dogs to search for them? Loretta would have a conniption.

A yellow road truck parked on the town side of the pond claimed her attention much as a squirrel might claim the dog's. A white van was stopped in front of it. Honey tugged on her leash, drawing Evie onward. After her run-in with Jax's father, she had real bad feelings about those trucks. She didn't want to go forward. She wanted to run home and raise a tar-and-feather party.

But that was childish and irresponsible and the reason she got labeled a flake—she acted on things others couldn't see or hear. So, fine, she'd gather evidence. Trucks weren't ghosts, after all. They had to have drivers who talked.

She wished she had a cell phone so she could take pictures of their license plates, but she didn't even carry a purse or notepad to write the numbers on. The yellow truck had state insignia, but the white van had no markings at all. A state truck signified someone was serious—about *her family's* land?

She jogged along behind Honey, following her down the pond path instead of the woodland one. The town had scraped up a foot-high levee along the lower end of the pond to prevent it from running into the road during storms. Right now, the water level was so low that she didn't even get her shoes muddy after she passed the levee. Her capris didn't protect her too well from the long grasses alongside the path, however.

The men in boots setting up tripods didn't even notice the bluestem they were crushing. The pond was a habitat for birds and deer and other wildlife that fed off the grass.

"Hey, whatchadoin'?" she asked casually as she jogged closer.

She guessed the men in hardhats were the road department employees. The ones in khakis and hiking boots were setting up surveying equipment and probably belonged to the van. All four of them ignored her.

"County expanding the road?" she asked, not giving up. The road was a two lane to nowhere, but one never knew.

None of them seemed inclined to answer that either. This was the South. People *talked* to each other. Just her luck not to find a communicative crew. Maybe they didn't like redheads. Or dogs, since not one stopped to pet Honey, who eagerly pointed her nose in their direction.

"It's my family's land you're standing on," she continued genially. "We've not received any notice of road improvements. Do you have anything official allowing a survey?"

"We're just here to keep the surveyors safe," one of the hardhats answered curtly.

"Umm, wise use of county time, I'm guessing? I'm pretty sure the quail won't attack. Someone here must have written orders allowing the survey. This isn't public property."

The surveyors continued ignoring her. The hard hat produced a clipboard from his truck and shoved it at her. The whereas's and wherefore's were Greek to her. She sought signatures and didn't recognize them. She noted

Titan as the surveyor's name among them and handed it back. "Thank you, sir. But this doesn't say who gave permission to trespass on my family's property."

"Owners had to give permission for us to receive these orders," Hard Hat said laconically.

Now was the time to bring out her half-baked lie detector, even if they thought she was stoned. Opening her inner eye, she saw nothing disturbing in the hardhat's aura. He was just a low-level non-thinker doing his job.

The surveyors. . . Evie swayed trying to interpret the muddy gray over-laying their normal shades—guardedness. They feared they were doing some-thing shady.

Honey barked, dragging her back to the moment. She shook off a shiver. "I think I'll have to ask you to leave unless you produce a letter of permission from my family."

Hard Hat shrugged and shoved his thumb in the direction of the survey-ors. "Ask them."

She raised her voice. "I *am* asking them. Sirs, you are trampling an envi-ronmentally protected area housing endangered species." She didn't think quail or deer were endangered, but she liked to sound not-flaky. "You need to leave *now* or I'm calling the sheriff."

"So, call him." The older, larger of the khaki-wearers continued setting up equipment. He had EMMITT embroidered on the nametag on his shirt.

Evie sighed and addressed the county worker who'd deigned to speak to her. "He doesn't know what he's asking. If you don't have any authority over them, sir, I suggest you put your hands over your ears."

He looked at her as if she were demented. Perhaps she was. She just got perverse pleasure out of irritating authority figures who ignored her. Her diminutive stature, red hair, and genial personality seemed to give the impres-sion that she could be easily dismissed. She needed a T-shirt that said *Go ahead, underestimate me. It should be fun.*

Without further warning, she began screaming.

The two surveyors swung around and glared. The hardhats hastily covered their ears. She escalated an octave. She wasn't that far out of town yet. A car alarm went off and a dog howled.

She wasn't more than five minutes from the courthouse. It might take a little longer than usual. . . She put more energy into pushing with her diaphragm to achieve full range. One of her aunts was an opera singer. She'd taught Evie how to cast her voice to the furthest edges of the theater—and regretted it later. Evie didn't have a musical voice. She just had good lungs.

All four men were swearing by the time she heard the siren. Not one of them packed up to leave. Evie didn't really want them to leave. She wanted to know who they were. Since they wouldn't talk to her. . .

The sheriff's car slammed to a halt behind the road truck. Sheriff Troy climbed out, looking seriously disgruntled. "Why the hell don't you just call like everyone else, Evangeline?"

Evie took a deep breath and allowed silence to descend for half a beat before answering. "Because I don't own a cell phone. And if I did and punched in 911, who would I get? A dispatcher in Charleston? What would I say is my emergency? Trespassers? This way, I cut out the middleman."

Snorting, Troy pushed back his Mounty hat and studied the men who'd at least stopped working. "It's easier to listen to the ladies around here than ignore them, gentlemen. She's right. This is her family's land. You got papers for being here?"

To Evie's surprise, Jax came jogging up the road. Well, she supposed he ought to recognize her scream by now. She waved at him. "Here's my lawyer now. Show him what you've got, fellows."

"Lawyer?" Troy looked over his shoulder and snorted. "Damn, if that don't beat all. You got him trained already?" He returned to sheriff mode and focused an eagle eye on the surveyors. "If the lady says she didn't hire you, you got no business here. We're a small community. We don't cotton to strangers."

Oooo, cue the horror music as the city slickers stumble into the hick town full of witches. Evie grinned in enjoyment as Jax followed this dialogue and raised his bushy dark eyebrows.

The older surveyor scowled and stomped back to the van, probably crushing a quail nest or two in the process.

"There's a reason we stick to paths, gentlemen. The grasses conceal wildlife nests." Now that she had backup, Evie ambled closer. Men with gray overlays didn't drift into town often. She wanted to study them. Jax stepped up right beside her. She cast him a surprised look but then returned to her examination of the surveyors.

Jax's male air of authority had the one named Emmitt handing the paperwork to him. Evie snatched it first. More Greek. She recognized John and Tiffany Post's names though. She couldn't identify the legitimacy of their signatures. And again with the Titan Surveying. She handed it over to Jax, who brilliantly used his smartphone to snap a picture.

Before he could say anything lawyerly, a white Cadillac Escalade pulled up on the far side of the road. Oh, goodie, more fun. Evie stepped behind Jax as Mayor Arthur Block got out of his vehicle and strode over.

"What's happening here, Troy?"

Dressed in an impressively tailored suit that had to be warm in this humidity, the mayor was a few inches shorter than Jax and considerably less muscled. Yet the mayor always behaved in a swaggering manner that had swayed the town into believing he was a leader. Evie figured he had his silver-fox hair professionally blown dry every day to keep it looking fuller than it really was. His swagger didn't impress her.

"Just the usual trespassing disagreement, Mayor. We've got it in hand." The sheriff's genial tone had a surly edge, to Evie's surprise.

While partially hidden by Jax's broad shoulders, Evie slipped into aura mode. She checked the mayor first, but as usual, the dishonest murky pink diluted his red energy and his fifth chakra was muddy blue. The mayor simply was not an honest man, but then, she didn't know many politicians who spoke the whole truth.

She checked the sheriff, and his stress levels were higher than usual.

But she didn't think she saw any killers, not that she'd ever known one. Checking back in, she stepped out from behind Jax just to watch the mayor scowl. Since she'd quit dating his son, she didn't get many opportunities to push His Honor's buttons, so she smiled hugely. "Hey, Mayor, good to see you taking an interest in us for a change."

Apparently having learned her tactics a little too well, Jax grabbed her elbow while handing the clipboard back to the surveyor. "Sorry, this is insufficient. The signers are deceased. My client owns this land, and she hasn't agreed to a survey. You'll need to take this back to your employer and have him update his records."

The mayor's scowl blackened at Jax's words. As the surveyor pulled out his phone and reported back to his employer, the mayor stuck out his hand. "Don't think I've met you. I'm Arthur Block."

Still holding Evie back with one hand, Jax shook with the other. "Jax Jackson of Stockton and Stockton, sir, good to meet you. We have this situation under control, but I thank you for your interest."

Bollocks, Evie thought, watching the mayor's face turn a lovely shade of puce.

"Stockton and Stockton, huh?" The mayor appeared to be stifling a comment or swallowing his tongue before he finally continued. "Good firm. I'll trust you have the matter in hand then." He tipped his head at the sheriff, ignored Evie, and walked back to his hulking monster of a car.

There was some hassling and a few phone calls after that but Evie lost interest. She'd known the trucks were bad news. She now had flimsy evidence of some sort of shenanigans. But she had to rely on Jax to interpret it—and pretty and useful as he might be, he wasn't necessarily on her side. From the mayor's reaction, he thought Jax was on *his* side.

She would have to call Great-Aunt Val and wake the sleeping dragon.

"YOU CAN'T SELL OUR HOUSE IF MY PARENTS ARE NOT DEAD," Loretta insisted from the backseat of the sedan Jax had to rent on Saturday. His Jag didn't have a backseat. "They would be horrified to come home to no house."

Jax ground his molars and waited for the pixie in the passenger seat to reply. Today, Evie had dressed for a visit to the city in purple capris and matching halter top, with a gauzy, multi-colored, transparent shirt as a cover-up. She wore what appeared to be a purple crystal hanging from a silver chain. He didn't ask if it was a magical amulet. He didn't want to hear the answer.

"Jax hasn't sold the house." Evie spoke firmly—unusual for her. "But your parents wouldn't want it to fall apart in their absence, either. If he's to be a cautious guardian of their affairs, he has to weigh the cost of maintaining an empty house against the need to sell it before it falls apart. Houses need to be lived in."

Loretta pouted long enough to hit the interstate into the city. "Then if you're my guardian, we should move into it."

Jax snickered and waited for Evie's patience to fray.

"Do you not like the school in Afterthought? Or being able to walk home for lunch?" She glanced out the window. "Oh, look at those lovely homes! Does yours look like that?"

"No. Mine is boring." Loretta kicked the back of the seat. "I have a pink bedroom. Can I bring stuff from my house to yours?"

"You may bring as much pink as you wish. We should probably pack up your clothes, too. If Jax doesn't provide an allowance soon, you'll be in rags, like me." Evie sounded much too perky after diverting the kid's complaint.

"I don't want pink. I have scrapbooks and a complete set of Harry Potter. I left my clothes at school. Can I get those? I don't want to go back there." Kick, kick, kick.

Jax had a good idea why the Posts sent Loretta to school. "If your parents return, they'll expect to find you at your school."

"No, they won't. *You* sent me there. My dad sent me to a neat school where I didn't have to ride horses."

"You got kicked out of the neat school for telling the teacher she had a raisin for a brain and that you wouldn't share a room with a pious prick. I trust you looked up those words before you used them." Jax steered into the suburban McMansion neighborhood where Loretta had once lived.

It was Evie's turn to chortle. Jax thought it a lot more pleasant to laugh at the kid's foibles than yell. His adoptive father had yelled, teaching Jax to hold his tongue as a child. A silent kid might be easier on a parent's ear, but kids should have rights too. How else would they learn to take their place in society and become responsible citizens? Not by being silent.

He'd never given kids much thought until this past week. He made a lousy guardian.

"The pious prick told me my parents *died*, and she was praying for me! They're not dead." Loretta expressed her indignation with another kick. "And yes, I did too look up the words. After."

"Getting angry because you don't agree with someone isn't practical," said the practical genius in a purple halter top. "This is a pretty neighborhood. The azaleas are gorgeous."

"Everyone has landscapers." Loretta sighed with a ten-year-old's gloom. "I bet my parents have been home and no one told me."

Jax parked the sedan in the driveway of a two-story, many-gabled house of brick and stone. "I changed the locks. Your parents would have to come to me to get in. And I handle all their credit cards and bank accounts. They've not made any charges. What are they living on?"

"Ooo, good point, lawyer-man," Evie murmured before flinging open the door.

Loretta wasn't a dumb kid. She didn't answer but scuffled up the drive, studying the landscape as if she might find her parents hiding in the azaleas.

"This feels cruel," Jax muttered, shoving his hands in his pockets and following behind Evie.

"Life is cruel. She just needs time. I'm getting the impression she didn't really know her parents well, and that might be part of the problem. She misses what she thought she should have had. And now there's no chance that she ever will. That's a tough one for a kid." Evie sniffed the air. "Car exhaust here recently, unless your rental is in bad shape. Oil on the driveway. Landscapers?"

Instead of looking at the oil spot, Jax looked at Evie. The halter made it hard not to notice her ample cleavage. He had to remember her fireplug mother and divert his attention. "Are we playing Sherlock Holmes?"

"This is how I make a living—by noticing what's around me. Ghosts don't generally pop out and say *Hi, how ya doin'*. One has to interpret what one sees." Instead of heading for the front door, she sauntered down the drive, purple-clad hips swaying. "Loretta, don't go inside just yet. Let me take a look around."

She made a *living* at ghost hunting? He didn't think so. At least she'd managed to distract him from the sexual vibrations generated by living with a firecracker. Apparently he'd developed a perverse taste for colorful explosions. Yesterday's operatic screaming had been entertaining—until he'd seen the Posts' signatures on the survey orders and his hackles rose. The papers had been signed right before they'd reportedly disappeared.

Leaving the females to play outside, Jax unlocked the front door. He didn't believe a ghost had told Evie to search the desk so much as instinct had said it was a good place to look. Given yesterday's episode, he wouldn't mind having another go at it again. Hearing Loretta and Evie at the back door, he crossed through the living room and kitchen to let them in.

The door opened before he could reach it.

"Lock's been jimmied," Evie called cheerfully. "You might want to not touch anything until you look for fingerprints."

"The house is full of fingerprints, and we can't identify the ones belonging to the Posts, so that's a waste." Jax studied the lock and cursed juvenile delinquents. "Probably kids, anyway."

"Kids would have trashed the place." Correcting his assumption, Evie ran her hand over a dusty countertop. "When was the last time the cleaning service was here?"

Okay, so he was a lawyer, not a detective. Maybe the door had been like this for months. The notion that someone had just walked in and looked around. . . Made him very uncomfortable.

"First of every month, so three weeks ago." And they would have reported a break-in, dammit.

Feeling a little edgy when a psychic flake was pragmatically examining surfaces for dust and fingerprints instead of exclaiming over the maple and marble kitchen, Jax headed down the hall to John Post's study.

"Then someone was here recently." She pointed out a smear in the dust on a polished mahogany breakfront.

"That's where my mom's silver was kept." Loretta jerked open a door. "It's gone."

"Because it's in storage. That's my job—protecting your assets." Which meant getting Loretta out from under foot while he looked around. "Why don't you run upstairs and start stacking up the things you want to take with you? We'll buy boxes if we need to."

Pansy-blue eyes framed by black plastic glared at him as if he were officially insane. "I want to see my daddy's desk, too."

Evie whistled and sauntered ahead, checking behind doors, apparently hunting for ghosts and goblins. "They even looked behind the mirrors," she called. "Fingerprints all over them."

Crap. "Those were some clumsy crooks." Disgruntled, Jax opened the office door.

The place had definitely been disturbed.

"They tried to be careful, but they were in a hurry. Maybe because someone told them we were coming?" Evie crowded into the doorway beside him. "The desk drawers are almost closed, but the chair's been moved. I can see the dents in the carpet. Not too long ago, either. I smell cigarette smoke, unless Mr. Post smokes?"

His adoptive father smoked, but this didn't smell the same. But now he was drinking in Evie's scent of ylang-ylang and shampoo. Jax wanted to pick her up and turn her around and send her out before she smoked his brain. "Unless they took something, there isn't much point in calling the police. And there wasn't anything here to take."

"My daddy hates cigarettes." Loretta tried to peer between them.

"Any ghosts hovering?" Jax asked dryly, examining the plush carpet for footsteps. One person, it looked like.

"Man's size twelve—a heavy man?" Evie crouched to measure a footprint with her fingers. "Not a ghost."

She gestured for Loretta to enter. "I think you may amplify my abilities, so I need your help. I want you to call up a memory of your father in here, if you can. Close your eyes. I'll take your hands and do my psychic thing, okay?"

With a sigh, Jax got out of their way, crossing the room to study the desk before he touched it. Whoever had been here hadn't bothered with gloves. They'd left smudged prints on the polished mahogany. If Evie could smell the cigarette, they'd just missed running into the bastard.

Using one of the cheap pens scattered on the desk surface, Jax pulled open the middle desk drawer. Post had left his password book in here. Jax had lost all respect for the client's intelligence at that point. He'd changed all the passwords and locked the book in storage, so if the thief was after that, he was out of luck.

"Mr. Post, if you can, will you show us what you want us to see?" Evie spoke in a hypnotic voice that didn't match her normal bubbly one.

Reluctantly, Jax backed away from the desk to watch whatever the hell she was perpetrating now.

She was holding Loretta's hands. The kid had her eyes closed but Evie didn't. She looked over the kid's shoulder, speaking as if she saw someone there. Jax almost snorted at the less-than-dramatic performance, but he occupied himself checking the rest of the drawers.

Evie abruptly dropped Loretta's hands to fumble behind the desk. "Here?" she asked of the air.

While he worked, Jax kept a suspicious eye on her.

A slender side panel of the desk popped open as if she'd sprung a latch. Jax almost swallowed his tongue. Evie swung the mahogany door aside to reveal a document safe.

A *document* safe. He studied the desk's construction and could see nothing that would have revealed the narrow hidden box. How the hell had she known. . . ?

Evie dropped down in a crouch to examine the safe's dial as if she were an expert safe cracker. She looked like a pixie in that gauzy top with the mop of curls in her face.

"Left, ten?" She turned the dial accordingly.

Jax picked up pen and paper and jotted down the numbers. Loretta's eyes had grown wide behind her dark frames. Listening to voices all her own, Evie finished the combination.

The safe opened. Jax realized he was holding his breath when he expelled it in a whoosh.

Evie toppled.

Loretta screamed. Jax leaped to catch Evie before she hit the carpet. She didn't wake.

"Fetch a glass of water," he told Loretta. Anything to keep the kid from screaming more.

Damn, the woman weighed nothing. Well, he'd already discovered that. He just wasn't used to holding her when she wasn't screaming and gouging his eyes out. He settled her into a leather recliner and pushed the button to lift her feet and lower her head. To his immense relief, she began to stir.

He couldn't resist the impulse to brush an orange curl out of her eyes. The damned woman. . .

The kid returned carrying a glass of water and looking anxious, jerking him back to reality. Tears streaked his ward's cheeks. Jax had no idea how to comfort her. Did she finally accept that her father was a ghost?

Did *he*? And that Evie could speak to him? The performance had been credible—but there were far too many variables, and he preferred the logical explanations.

Jax took the water and offered it as Evie moved her head. "Drink," he ordered.

She sniffed and narrowly opened her eyes. "Not brandy?"

Jax wanted to crack up, probably from relief that she was alive and still in this world, but he stifled that impulse too. Loretta ran for the liquor cabinet.

"What just happened here?" he demanded, trying to watch his language with the kid in the room.

Loretta came back empty-handed, looking puzzled and glancing at the safe.

"Mr. Post obligingly showed us what he wants us to see. Why haven't you looked?" Evie struggled to sit up but couldn't figure out how to straighten the recliner.

He'd play along with the ghost scenario for now. "Because you keeled over. Drink this. Maybe you're dehydrated." Jax pushed the button to set the recliner straight again.

She raised her expressive auburn eyebrows and sipped from the glass. "I'm not fond of spectral possession, but Mr. Post was too weak to speak. I hope you wrote those numbers down because I'm *not* repeating that performance."

Loretta appeared torn, glancing from Evie to the desk, and back, then dropping down to examine the safe.

Evie set the glass aside and shoved out of the chair.

"You really want me to believe a ghost told you how to open that safe?" Jax followed behind her, terrified she'd drop like a rock again.

Loretta removed a manila envelope. The safe was too narrow for much else.

"All right, then call me David Copperfield or believe I'm a safe cracker. Take your pick. Can we open this or do we have to do it in front of a judge?" She crouched down beside Loretta to poke at the envelope.

That hadn't been safe cracking. She'd *known* that combination.

Jax would rather believe in ghosts than Evie's involvement in paranoid conspiracy theories. But his training and logic said otherwise. Conspiracies existed, and it was his job to uncover them.

Looked like he wouldn't be leaving Evie alone with Loretta for a while longer.

Fifteen

"THERE ARE RUBBER GLOVES UNDER THE KITCHEN SINK." Officious Lawyer held his arm out to keep anyone from touching the envelope.

Loretta was up and scampering for the kitchen before anyone could tell her to. Maybe Indigo children were particularly obedient, Evie thought—or kept the peace by doing as told. That didn't sound like Loretta.

"I'll make a believer out of her yet." But obviously, she would never make a believer of Jax. He scowled as if she'd committed third-degree burglary.

Sitting down, Evie crossed her legs and studied the ordinary 8x10 mustard-colored envelope. "I'd kind of hoped for gold and jewelry, myself. Would there have been a finder's fee?"

"Immaterial now. How did you get the combination? Did John give it to one of his relatives? You don't need the hocus-pocus with me." As if she hadn't just performed a miracle, Jax returned to searching the desk. He pulled out the drawers, checked the undersides, and inspected them and the interior, presumably for more hiding places.

"Why on earth would I bother with hocus pocus if I had the combination? That's stupid. I'm not stupid, and I'm damned tired of people thinking I am. Where did the liquor go?" Dying to tear into the envelope, Evie turned her always divided attention to the open, empty, liquor cabinet.

"I took the liquor home and credited the value against my bill. The estate sale people can't sell liquor without a license." He slammed a drawer back into the desk.

"Short-sighted of you. One never knows when alcohol will come in handy in a haunted house." Evie smiled at her worried ward as Loretta ran back with rubber gloves. "We'll go upstairs next and gather your books and things."

Loretta plopped down beside her and waited expectantly.

Jax pulled the gloves on over his big hands and unfastened the envelope closure. Several folded, yellowed documents tumbled out.

"My mother saw old deeds," Evie murmured as Jax delicately flattened one document with his gloved hand.

He made no comment on her mother's vision. She peered over his shoulder. Even she could tell the first bundle he opened was a deed. "Is it legal?"

"They're notarized. An exact copy should have been filed with the deed registrar." Jax opened the next. A similar document unfolded.

"Does Loretta own even more property than you knew about?"

"Same properties, if I'm remembering the descriptions correctly. But I think this one. . ." He got out his phone and began scrolling through photos. He held up one for her to see. "This is the county's deed register. Compare the photo with what's on this deed."

Taking a deep breath, Evie gathered her concentration and brought both photo and paper into focus. It didn't take a minute to see the difference. "I'm not a surveyor. I don't know what the lot line description means. But the amount of acreage on the deed I'm holding is considerably less than in the book photo."

"And the register number in the book is a lot older, which means the older, larger lot in the deed book may have been divided or sold. It looks like this deed is newer and represents only a part of the original lot. The book should have a cross-reference number to any newer deeds like this one. I don't know why it's not there."

Jax took a picture of the description, then punched a number on his phone. "Rube, I'm sending you an image. Tell me if you find the deed number anywhere in the registrar's office."

He clicked off and began scrolling through his phone again. "They may be different parcels entirely, even if the location is similar."

Evie had never seen a deed before but, knowing her family, understanding began to sink in. It didn't make good sense just yet. Still, if the smaller plot represented by this yellowing deed was registered *after* the larger one in the book. . . "If these are the deeds John Post inherited from Great-Grandmother Letitia. . . Is it possible she and Great-Aunt Val and their siblings divided the family plot when Letitia married a Post? That could explain the animosity between my family and the Posts."

Loretta looked puzzled and ready to cry. "Does this mean I don't own the town?"

"You never owned the town, kid." Evie knuckled the top of her head. "*Malcolms* own the town. The Posts wanted to but didn't get it all. Or maybe they bought it later, and we haven't uncovered that part yet. But it means nothing to us. Let's go pack your books."

"I can still live with you?" Loretta asked anxiously, glancing at the ancient documents as she stood up.

"You don't have to own *anything* and you can still live with me. You're family. Now show me a birth certificate proving you're the daughter of a politician, and I'll give you back to Jax." Evie stood up and followed Loretta to the door, casting a glance over her shoulder at Jax.

He wasn't listening. He was carefully photographing every page of each document. She didn't know what that meant. She didn't know if she should take possession of those papers—or if she could. She wasn't stupid, but she had a lot to learn, it seemed. But she suspected he was holding her family's future and Loretta's in his hands right now. How far could she trust him?

She hesitated and opened her inner eye. His aura was wider. The angry red had deepened to the red of strong willpower. And oddly, a touch of gold shimmered above his root chakra. His higher self was connecting to his confidence? She'd have to think about that.

They found boxes in the attic and had packed up most of Loretta's outstanding collection of comics, books, and video games when a dramatic mezzo-soprano rose from the downstairs hall.

"Evangeline?"

"Supercalifragilistic," Evie muttered. She'd known this confrontation had to come. She just wasn't ready. "Do you have an emergency ladder in here?"

Loretta looked at her questioningly. "Like a rope? No. Should I have one?"

"Only if you want to escape dragons, especially ones who believe in a scorched earth policy. You may be okay, but we should probably rescue Jax." In resignation, knowing she had to have this conversation, Evie lifted a box of comic books and started for the stairs.

Like a good minion, Loretta carried a box of stuffed toys and followed.

"Who is this man?" Great-Aunt Val demanded imperiously as Evie appeared in the foyer. "And why is he interfering in family affairs?"

"He's my lawyer," Loretta piped helpfully.

Great-Aunt Evangeline Valerie Brindle, Evie's namesake, stood tall and regal beneath the two-story foyer chandelier. Val could be seventy or a hundred. Evie had never tried to work it out. Her aunt's only concession to age was a thin ebony cane with a carved dragon head. She wore her long, gray hair in an elaborate coiffeur and topped with a wide-brimmed hat she was currently unpinning.

She was dressed entirely in purple, like Evie.

"Aunt Val, this is Damon Jackson of Stockton and Stockton, lawyers. Jax, this is my Great-Aunt Valerie Brindle from Atlanta. She's also John Post's aunt. Aunt Val, have you met Loretta, John's daughter?" Evie squeezed Loretta's hand.

Val's presence almost demanded a curtsy. Loretta simply stared, wide-eyed. "I didn't know I had an aunt in Atlanta."

"Because Posts denied our existence, dear. Your father may not have even known about us. But we know all about him." She spun her glare back to Jax. "What are you intending to do with those deeds?"

"What deeds?" Jax asked without revealing his surprise that she knew about their discovery. He'd been debating locking the documents back in the desk, but if someone had already been here looking for them. . . He didn't like the odds.

Evie didn't have a cell phone and couldn't have called her. Was this just another Malcolm fake to test him? Was the whole family nothing but con artists?

Of course they were, centuries of history preceded them.

"The family land is what I wanted to ask you about." Evie interrupted before her aunt could reply. "There is something very odd happening on Witch Hill. And when I ask Mavis, she tells me to ask you. I think we need to sit down and have a conversation about who is responsible for what before my mother loses any more property."

"Your mother has little interest in owning anything." Val sniffed in disapproval. "And we will not be having long conversations about material things. Witch Hill belongs to a trust now, has since Letitia walked off with our backyard. We all contribute to the fund to pay for taxes and improvements. I daresay we should do the same with the rest of our properties. If you have the deeds for the plots once belonging to Letitia, then they belong with the trust as well." She glared at Jax.

"They belong to *Loretta*. And given what we've seen, you might want to look into whoever is handling your trust. I will be happy to help or to recommend a good lawyer." Jax wondered if he could tackle an old lady if she went for the deeds on the desk.

Val's long nose was bony enough to resemble a witch's, except it lacked the traditional hook. Good plastic surgery maybe. Jax kept his poker face on as the old lady looked down said nose at him. When she'd ascertained he had no more to add, she turned to Evie.

"Is he trustworthy?"

"Apparently he has a green walnut for a soul, but his aura has begun to grow. I wouldn't completely trust him yet, but he has potential." Evie grinned at him. "He hasn't called me a lunatic to my face or charged me with safecracking or fraud for finding the deeds. Yet."

Jax supposed that would be the first and natural reaction of most lawyers. She had a point. He was displaying a miraculous amount of patience by playing along with whatever game was afoot.

Astonishingly, the old lady nodded with understanding. "Very well. Should you wish to work with our trust lawyers, you know where to find me. But if you wish to protect Loretta's inheritance, you'll turn those deeds over to the trust. The world is filled with those who believe money buys happiness and land is money. They are ill-informed. Land belongs to Mother Nature. We can only tend it."

Val tapped her hat against her long skirt and turned her attention to Evie. "You are wasting your talents, Evangeline. Expand your mind to a larger sphere." She regarded Loretta dubiously. "Although admittedly, caring for an Indigo may take all you have for a few years. If you don't want to end up like your parents, child, listen to the Malcolm side of your family. We're the earth and sky and water. You need no more than that."

Jax waited for Evie's usual bubbly response, but she did no more than nod. Her fingers were white-knuckled on the box she'd carried down. He took it from her arms and set it on the floor. At least no one was demanding any documents. He really needed to figure out how this family worked. He wasn't about to believe in telepathy.

"Very well, then. Tell your mother we'll see her at the solstice." Returning her hat to her head, the old woman strode out, not using the cane.

Jax followed to close the door. A silver stretch limousine waited at the curb, and a uniformed chauffeur opened the door to assist her inside. "Money can't buy happiness, but it buys cool wheels."

Evie snorted. "She married a theatrical producer who allowed Val's Civil War re-enactors the use of his plantation. Her favorite part is lighting live cannon as she defends her home. I'm convinced she's re-living a former life, the one that came after she was a dragon and torched a few cities."

Jax couldn't help it. After the tension of the last half hour, he laughed.

Loretta giggled.

Evie shrugged and marched back to the study, returning with the deed envelope in her hand. "Even if Val has copies of everything, I want these in a lockbox only Loretta and I can access. And I'm filing those guardianship papers, even if they are fraudulent. Something wicked this way comes, and I'm not trusting your father's law firm to prevent it."

For just a moment, Jax thought she might be on the right track. Which meant he was on the wrong one. He snatched the envelope from her hand and held it over his head. "If you file those guardian papers, my father will have you burned at the stake. Trust me."

Sixteen

Evie clung to the deed papers until Jax drove to a bank he assured her had no connection to his law firm. He reluctantly stayed outside while Evie and Loretta opened a safe deposit box. Unfortunately, they had to use Loretta's credit card to rent it. Evie fumed over that as they drove back to Afterthought.

"No matter what we do, you have control over it." Crossing her arms, she glared out the windshield.

Loretta had nodded off in the backseat with her arms around a magenta teddy bear with a sagging eyeball. That poor kid had stalwartly held up to a very hard day.

"That's because the court appointed me as guardian. And because you have no money," Jax said, just a little snidely.

She scowled. "I need a lawyer. I want those guardianship papers to be *real*. And Loretta should have an allowance to cover clothes and school supplies and bank boxes." With her own degree of spite, she added, "And she needs an allowance for hiring a lawyer."

Instead of laughing at her, Macho Man grudgingly nodded. "I'm starting to think that, too."

Evie figured there ought to be fireworks accompanying that statement. She swiveled to stare at him. The damned man had a square jaw that stuck out just enough to be stubborn and full lips that she wanted to kiss right now.

But he was sitting military straight and keeping his eyes on the road and he was still an uptight bastard.

"You think I'd make a good guardian?" she asked, a shade too tentatively, because she wasn't the least bit certain herself.

"Better than me. I shoved a grieving kid into a strange school and abandoned her because she was just a job to me. I should have known better. I *do* know better. I have a sister and know how hard she took it when our parents died. But I was focused on doing as told, which didn't include getting personally involved with a kid." He glared out the windshield.

Evie took a little peek at his aura and decided it was definitely growing in good directions. But he was still way too angry. There was a story here. "How did your parents die?"

"Car accident, rainy night. My father had just been fired from his job. I was only twelve and didn't understand at the time. I still don't, entirely, which is why I'm working for his old firm."

"Uh-huh, yeah, because that's what one does, right." She wanted to soothe the heartbroken boy he must have been, but her leapfrog mind jumped on the ambiguous statement Jax threw out to divert sympathy. Her eyebrows shot up. The heartbroken boy was seeking revenge. "You're mad at the firm for firing him, right? And you want to find out why he was fired?"

"Impressive deduction. But Stephen Stockton has been good to me and my sister, and I can't believe he'd do anything irresponsible, so there must be more to the story." He left the interstate for the cotton-field-lined two-lane that led to Afterthought. "How did your aunt know we were at the house and had the deeds?"

Evie snorted at the side track. Jax didn't want to reveal the pain that would have helped him understand Loretta. If she was the queen of diversion, he was king. Now that she knew Macho Man hid a heart, she didn't call him on it. "I called her and told her we were going there, and she *knew* Post had his mother's deeds. I assure you, neither of us reads minds, but Val is an impressive actress and chews through ten scenes before breakfast."

"Huh, a con game without a con, weird."

She probably ought to smack him but not while he was driving. So she hit him with words. "And if Stephen Stockton was the cigar-smoking asshat who was in the shop yesterday, he isn't irresponsible so much as. . ." Evie looked for a description Jax might accept. "Concerned only for himself and the bottom line. This is not a bad thing, but over long period, without any benevolent balance—it corrupts the soul. You cannot build a life of plenty for your-self without walking over a few people to get what you want. And if you ignore the plight of others often enough, you get used to crushing souls. And after a while, other people are simply in your way and become expendable. He's rotting on the inside. I bet he has ulcers."

Jax's jaw muscle clenched, but eventually, he gave a curt nod. "Tricia was his conscience. Once she died, he lost interest in anything except the firm. So maybe I've been seeing him through the eyes of the child I once was. He rescued us from foster care, gave us the home we needed, still allows Ariel to live there rent free. I have to respect him, but I don't know if I can trust his ethics anymore."

"Not any more than you trust *me*. I get that." Especially if he thought his parents had been taken from him by treachery—he'd see the world through a prism of cynicism. "Tricia was his wife? Your adoptive mother? Did they adopt you, legally? Can I do that with Loretta?"

"They had no kids, so yeah, they adopted us. Ariel is over twenty-one. He doesn't owe her any support. I guess he's at work so much, he barely realizes she exists. I could set her up elsewhere. She just won't leave. And no, I don't think any court in the world would allow an unemployed, unmarried distant cousin to adopt an heiress."

Charming. And another interesting perspective of the uptight lawyer. Break down a few more of Jax's barriers—and he might almost seem human. But she'd hire a less negative lawyer for Loretta. "Turn down Shady Lane. It's on your right, a mile or two before you reach the pond. I want to see something."

Evie wasn't certain she wanted to know *too* much about Jax. She didn't *want* to like the lawyer who could take Loretta away. But they'd named the shop the Psychic Solutions Agency because sometimes, her family saw solutions others didn't. She didn't think Jax accepted her psychic abilities, but he might appreciate her more practical ones. "Is your sister disabled in some manner?"

"Autism spectrum," he said curtly, slowing down to watch road signs nearly covered by overgrown trees and kudzu. "She has an amazing mathe-matical ability. Our father had it, too, but he was more socially adept, to a point, at least. I suspect the trauma of losing our parents sort of froze Ariel in time. The Stocktons had to hire tutors for her because she couldn't manage school."

"But she can look after herself?" Evie pointed out the road she wanted.

"Pretty much. The house has a daytime housekeeper. Ariel tends to eat at midnight to avoid servants, so she's learned to fend for herself." He swung the sedan down the road she indicated.

As they slowed down, Loretta woke up and rubbed her eyes. "Where are we going?"

"To see your property. When Aunt Val called it the backyard, I knew where she meant. The front yard is the road and pond. The cemetery is where the old farmhouse used to be. On the far side of the hill, out of sight, is the new farmhouse. It's been rented out until recently. Of course, *new* in this case means it wasn't built before the Civil War. I'd guess it was Great-grandmother Letitia's childhood home."

Evie peered through the windshield until she recognized the mailbox on the left. "There. That's the drive. A schoolteacher rented it, but she got married and moved out of town. I haven't heard about anyone else moving in, presumably because the Posts died and no one knew it was here?"

In the backseat, Loretta didn't protest the mention of her parents being dead. She just watched out the window and held her plush toy.

"My father handles the property and investments. He didn't mention rental property." Jax wore his suspicious expression as he reached the drive Evie pointed out.

The house wasn't visible from the road. But as Jax drove down a curved gravel lane, a sprawling bungalow with a long, covered front porch and a single attic gable appeared behind a wilderness of pines and vines. The lawn still looked lush from the winter rains, and the kudzu hadn't run rampant over the shrubbery yet.

"Can we go inside?" Loretta asked.

"No key. It will be empty. But someone needs to rent it soon or it will go to rack and ruin." Evie waited expectantly as Jax studied the brick-and-board cottage.

"There was no mention of a house on this property. I was told this was all undeveloped farmland—and that it extended to the pond." Jax looked grim. "I should have looked for myself but Stephen was handling it and said the firm had buyers."

Buyers? To the cottage? Or the *pond*? Evie kept her surprise to herself. Had the trust agreed to sell after all? She'd known the mayor had been buying up farmland between the town and the county line to the east, but she thought her family had refused his offers. Now that she knew about the trust. . .

"There was more than one deed in that package. Was there only one related to Witch Hill?" Evie feared suspicion might be contagious, but she was beyond certain that something shady was happening. Her family would not sell the hill.

"The others are lots around town of no particular significance. Loretta's money is mostly in investments. Land out here isn't worth a lot." With a slight frown, Jax studied the bungalow.

"Unless someone knows about a big development coming," Evie suggested.

Not understanding the path of Evie's thoughts, Loretta opened the car door. "Maybe my daddy wanted to move back home and that's why they came here? Maybe they're inside?"

"Oh dear, no, I should hope not." But Evie flung open her door and ran after her.

JAX KNEW AN EMPTY HOUSE WHEN HE SAW ONE. HE LET THE females explore while he employed his phone and his time to better use. He ordered Roark and Reuben to Savannah to see if they could break into the Posts' safe as easily as Evie had. He had Ariel send him a spreadsheet of the Posts' bank accounts and transfers between them, including the odd one in the Caymans.

He read through Reuben's comparison of deeds to the registrar's records —it looked as if the Letitia Post property wasn't in the county files, even though the deed Evie had in the deposit box looked genuine. And the land trust didn't show up at all.

He'd suspect Evie's family of making up the trust and everything else, but a worm gnawing at his gut said they'd been nothing but blunt and open from the get-go—if he ignored the psychic drama.

And now he was starting to wonder if he'd been wrong about that, too. The Cayman Island account had been set up at the time the Posts were reportedly sailing in the Gulf—but what if Loretta was right and her parents hadn't been on that yacht and had come to Afterthought instead? And *died here*, as Evie swore.

Just that possibility opened an ugly new path of thought—if it wasn't the Posts, *who had siphoned the money to the Caribbean?*

A lot of people stood to profit from their deaths. Anyone involved with Lakeland Development in any capacity might have an interest in a building boom in Afterthought. All the businesses in town would benefit from an influx of newcomers. Even farmers wanting to sell their land would appreciate higher land prices.

Only people like Evie's family who preferred nature and small-town life would object. And Loretta would certainly prefer to have her parents back than have their money.

As an afterthought—and he used the term ironically—Jax took a picture of the cottage with Evie and Loretta peering in the windows. He sent it to Ariel. Maybe he could inspire her to consider living elsewhere. If there was any possibility that Stephen had become involved in illicit activities, Jax worried about her future staying with him.

He was having a hard time accepting that the man he'd trusted most of his life might be a criminal and that the whacko family living on the thin edge of fraudulent behavior for centuries was the honest part of this scenario. But after Afghanistan. . . He was just jaded enough to not trust anyone.

Loretta trotted back to the car and plopped down on the back seat. "Evie said it's been too long and she can't detect any sign of my parents here. But it can be *my* house when I grow up, can't it?"

"We'll have to rent it out so it doesn't fall apart," he warned. "What about the house back in the city? Should I rent that out too?"

"I like it here. I can make friends here."

Huh, that sounded like acceptance that her parents weren't coming back. Evie's magic wasn't exactly mystical, but good enough with kids who read Harry Potter.

His pixie nemesis slid into the front seat, bringing a breath of fresh air sweetened with honeysuckle. She was carrying a bouquet of blooming vines. "It's hard to make friends in a neighborhood unless you go to school with them. But you're likely to be tired of Afterthought before you graduate. So don't set your heart on living here forever. You'll need to go to college and learn about a wider world."

"Did you go to college?" Loretta asked as Jax started the car and turned it around.

"No money and no scholarship." Evie picked an ant off a blossom.

"Besides, they don't teach what I do there. And I don't think I'd fit very well into a police academy. But I'd like to live in a city for a while. I've run out of ghosts here."

Jax rolled his eyes and figured this was a conversation he could stay out of. He simply couldn't see anyone as naïve as Evie thinking like a criminal mastermind.

Of course, Evie had been the one dragging him down the road of suspicion from day one.

Jax drove into town with every intention of dropping off Evie and Loretta and returning the sedan to the rental company where he'd left his Jag. But his phone pinged as soon as they hit town. Saturday Main Street traffic was too busy to park. He had to pull into the drive of Evie's house so he could read it.

A deputation of Evie's family was waiting for them.

The text from Reuben on his phone read: **WAR ZONE. RUN**

Oh, well, yeah, thanks, friend, Jax thought, watching the army of females through the windshield. At least they weren't carrying battleaxes.

Evie almost flew out the door. "What's wrong? What happened? Where's Mom?"

Huh, the two older women weren't Mavis. He recognized the three younger ones from the séance. Next to scary Aunt Val, this bunch looked like a book club, except maybe for the tall witchy vet called Iddy.

"What's wrong?" Loretta whispered from the backseat.

The kid had had enough trauma. She didn't need more. Jax considered backing out and returning to Savannah. Maybe he could find Loretta a better school. He could introduce her to Ariel—

Before he could put that plan into motion, Loretta launched herself from the backseat so she could hear everything.

The women waved papers at Evie and glared at him. This did not look good.

Evie gathered all the papers in her fist and stalked back to the car. With a sigh of defeat, Jax got out so she could wave them in his face. He snatched the collection from her grip.

"They're auctioning off our pond for back taxes! Val just told us that the trust has been *paying* those taxes, but there's no mention of a trust on these bills." Beneath her mop of curls, Evie's crystal eyes shot light beams that ought to paralyze, at the very least.

"Are you certain this is the Witch Hill property?" Jax scanned the tax notices addressed to individuals, not to any trust. "And this is my fault, how?"

One of the older women roughly resembling Mavis with her graying brown hair and plump curves held up one of his business cards. "Because you work for the same law firm handling the Lakeland Development Company that wants our land."

And they were just realizing that? "I have nothing to do with tax notices or the development company. I'm here solely as Loretta's guardian."

Except he had a pretty good idea how the city had made the notices happen. Explaining this to a bunch of angry women. . .

"Aunt Felicia, give Jax time to—" Evie tried to intervene, but her aunt was too wound up.

Evie's aunt shook her fist under Jax's nose. She appeared to be holding a crystal. "Lakeland Development was partially owned by John Post, and his share is now part of Loretta's inheritance."

The willowy vet approached to hold back the waving arm, but she glared at him as well. "We'll have to sue you and Loretta to stop this auction. Those taxes were *paid*."

Oh, shit. Just as he was starting to trust Evie, he recognized their ploy now. They wanted Loretta to pay their damned taxes—and that would just be the beginning.

He steered Loretta toward the car. "C'mon, kid, we're getting out of here."

Seventeen

Loretta ran.

She didn't want to go with Jax. She didn't want to be blamed for whatever was happening to Evie's family. She just wanted to go home. But seeing the empty house in Savannah. . .

Nothing had been touched since she'd last been there. Her mother *always* put her toys back on the shelf in the closet after she left. Pink Bear would never have been left on her bed. Ever. Which meant her mother hadn't been home since they'd dropped her off at school. Gulping back sobs, she rubbed hard at her eyes, trying not to cry.

Her mom and dad were really and truly gone. Without them, the house was no more than an empty shell. She had no home.

With a runaway tear leaking down her cheek, she dodged down alleys and through backyards where Jax couldn't follow in his car, fighting hard against the sobs trying to escape her chest.

She'd been smart enough to get herself all the way here from Savannah and to create documents even a lawyer couldn't dispute. She was smart enough to figure out where to go next.

But if everyone in her entire family was mad at her. . . She hiccuped and slowed down.

Maybe they were just mad at Jax. Evie didn't seem mad. She needed to think about that.

Thinking helped slow the sobs. Scrubbing at her wet cheek, she reached the highway and darted across, into the grassland around the pond. A path led away from the highway, so she took that. If all this was hers. . . Maybe the path would lead back to the little house they'd seen. That was *her* house. She could live there. She was smart and she was an Indigo, whatever that was. Maybe it meant she was extra-special smart and could live on her own.

It was starting to get dark, and she was hungry. There was no fast food place out here where she could use her credit card. It sucked to be a millionaire with no money and no food.

But she wasn't going back until. . . She didn't know what the *until* was. Until she had time to think things through? Until she'd scared everyone into working together. Adults should work together to solve problems and not shout at each other. Even she knew shouting was stupid. She felt better having a goal. The adults had to stop shouting and listen.

A huge black bird flew over her head, cawing, or whatever one called that rackety noise. There were probably wild animals in the woods. But the woods were on top of the hill. She'd go around and into the *backyard*, where her cottage was. Walking to school from all the way out here might get old. She needed a bike.

Her parents had never bought her one.

Her parents were *gone*.

Tears leaked down her cheeks again. "Parents aren't supposed to die!" she shouted at the sky.

The big bird dropped down to a branch ahead of her, making it bounce. It regarded her with a beady eye.

"Daddy, you said you were coming here! Why? How can grownups just *disappear*?"

Despite the lack of any breeze, a waft of air brushed hair from her face, and Loretta stopped walking to push at it impatiently and look around. The heat of the day was wearing off, but she was still sweaty. If she lived out here by herself, she could jump in the pond and swim anytime she liked. She was a good swimmer.

She shoved her glasses back up her nose and left the path to study the edge of the pond. There was mud beneath the tall grass, and a short mud wall holding in the water. She stooped down to look for animal tracks. Maybe she could take up studying animals if she lived near the woods. These looked like dog prints, though, and lots of people tracks.

The raven flew to the branch of a bush barely large enough to hold it. It cawed at her again.

A hand shoved at her back, and she stumbled into the low wall and hastily righted herself. She could have fallen into the pond! Frightened, she turned around, but no one was there.

The accidents had stopped since she'd moved in with Evie. Had the killer followed her?

Evie said there was no killer, that her father was trying to talk to her.

That had seemed silly when she'd thought him alive. But now? Her father knew she could swim. "Daddy?" She tried to hide her fear. She didn't want him to be dead. But if he was and he was trying to talk to her. . .

The bird cawed and bobbed. The weird waft of air blew her hair into her face again. Her shoulder felt as if a heavy hand was leaning on it.

A little scared, a little excited, she turned in the direction of the blackbird. Raven. Whatever. Idonea's pet could talk, sort of. Could this one? "Is that you, La Chusa? What are you telling me?"

The bird squawked. Something tapped her shoulder—like her daddy used to? Her stomach felt really strange now, and she wasn't hungry anymore.

The bird fluttered up in the air, then dropped to the water's edge where the pond had receded far down the muddy bank. The invisible hand pushed her shoulder again.

"I am not drowning myself in a muddy pond," she said belligerently, crossing her arms.

She should probably go back to Evie and have her explain why the pond was haunted. Except Jax would try to take her away.

The raven squawked, flapped its huge wings, and pecked at the gravel.

For a moment, for a very brief moment, Loretta felt an extreme sadness surround her. The air turned icy, chilling the sweat until she was almost shivering.

She needed Evie. She'd find a way around Jax. . .

The raven flew up carrying a mud-encrusted chain, dropping it at Loretta's feet.

She shivered even more, terrified to look closer. The bird waited expectantly.

Biting her lip, she crouched down and picked up the chain. And screamed. And ran, screaming, back the way she'd come, holding the filthy chain with her mother's dangling pendant.

Evie had almost reached the pond when Loretta burst out of the field, screaming as if a bear were on her heels. Seeing no bear, she simply ran to catch the child, holding her close while her own heart slowed its thumping and Loretta quieted to sobs.

"Your lungs are almost as good as mine, kid," she murmured, stroking Loretta's ratty braid.

Although, it hadn't been Loretta's screams that had brought her here. Knowing Loretta would head this way, she'd had Idonea confirm that La Chusa saw her at the pond.

Evie had never had to take care of anyone but herself, and well, Mavis, sort of. She wasn't certain how this comforting business was supposed to work, but Loretta clung to her, and this just seemed the best thing to do until the child was coherent again.

Jax came thumping up the road after them, probably trying to escape her family. He'd looked as if he'd been pole-axed when Aunt Felicia attacked him. He'd probably thought they were all a bunch of featherheads. Or maniacs. Her family could be pretty overwhelming, and he hadn't seen the worst of them yet.

"You still want to stay with me?" Evie murmured into Loretta's ear.

The girl nodded and clung tighter.

"It's you and me, then. We'll have to turn Jax upside-down." She tried to stand, but Loretta wouldn't let her go. It was then that she realized the child was holding something that rattled down her back.

La Chusa circled them, then flew off, squawking. Jax didn't appear to even be breathing hard as he halted to tower over them.

"What's that?" Zeroing in on whatever was bouncing against Evie's shoulder blades, he reached down to pull it from Loretta's clenched fist.

Evie was pretty certain she heard Loretta whisper, "*Mom's.*"

A chill settled over her. With a sigh, she opened her inner eye to see John Post hovering anxiously, and very transparently, behind Loretta.

"Let her go," Evie murmured to the apparition. "I've got her, honest. Just let her go. We'll find you. We know you're there. Join Tiffany and rest in peace."

Sorrow swept over her. The apparition raised a ghostly hand and brushed at the wisps of hair on Loretta's brow. Loretta glanced up, as if she'd felt it, and looked directly at what she shouldn't be able to see.

"He's there, isn't he? I feel him. He's dead." She rubbed at her eye, then abruptly pushed away. "He wants me to find who killed him!"

Oh dear.

Evie glanced up at Jax, who was cleaning off a pendant and scowling.

"Where did you find this, kid?"

Loretta pointed back the way she'd come. "La Chusa found it. It's my mom's. Daddy gave it to her for her birthday, right before they took me to school and came here."

"Show me." He sounded angry.

"Not now." Evie stood up and took Loretta's hands. "We'll be covered in mosquito bites and Loretta needs to eat. Whatever is back there has been there long enough."

"No, too long. I'll call my team. You take her back to the house." Jax already had his phone out of his pocket. He glared at Evie. "You and your family need to stay out of this. I'm calling in the state cops."

"Sheriff Troy is an honest man. Call him before you call in anyone over his head. He won't tell you that we're nuts. The state cops will listen to him." Evie tugged a reluctant Loretta toward the road. "Come along. Jax will be labeling all of us murderers and demand the police take you away. So let's just leave him to learn otherwise, okay?"

She knew if she looked, Jax's aura would have shriveled back to angry red. He had issues, she understood now. She could help, but he had to ask.

A subdued Loretta clung to her hand and followed her back to town. Evie's heart ached for the bright-eyed kid who'd first confronted her so bravely at the shop. She was no child psychologist. How did she bring out that sparkling Indigo again?

Evie's front room was filled with family noshing on Aunt Felicia's fried chicken and some kind of spinach-cheese thing Priscilla had whipped up. Her cousin catered fancy city functions.

Everyone was arguing as only her family knew how to do—books levitated, birds scattered feathers, crystals glowed, and they'd break out brooms shortly and start whacking each other.

"Psy broke the tea pitcher," Iddy announced when Evie and Loretta entered. "He's acting out. I had to tie Honey outside before she tried to lick up the glass."

"Is the tea still on the floor?" Evie dodged a flying tarot deck and calmly proceeded down the hall toward the kitchen, dragging Loretta.

"We picked up the glass," her sister Gracie called after her. "Didn't think bringing out mops a good idea." Especially since Gracie could levitate them and whack without getting involved.

Entering the kitchen, Evie drew the pocket door from the wall and closed it, shutting out her family. "I am not Val. I cannot take a cane to all their heads." Muttering more or less to herself, she took down the mop from the cellar wall and applied it to the spilled tea.

"They're upset?" Loretta finally spoke while she studied the mess of the kitchen.

"Putting it mildly. Let me finish up here, and we'll rescue the rest of that chicken and take it outside. I'll grab some biscuits and slap tomatoes on them and call them a vegetable."

Given a task, Loretta tip-toed around the spilled tea, found plates, and filled them with chicken from the skillet while Evie cleaned up.

Evie met her on the back porch with glasses of milk, napkins, and biscuit sandwiches. "I can't say I know how you feel, because I don't. So you'll have to tell me in any way that makes sense to you." She petted her mother's retriever and fed him a piece of breast meat she pulled off the bone.

Loretta sat in an ancient lawn chair and kicked her feet against a post. Silently, she nibbled her chicken.

Kicking feet made a statement of sorts. "Life can suck," Evie replied, as if Loretta had spoken. "I never got to know my dad. Mavis drove him off before I was born."

"Where is your mom now?" Loretta asked.

"Wherever her sisters aren't. Probably at the shop. Saturday is when all her clients come in. But she knows what's happening and is plotting. So we probably ought to put a net over her head before she floats away." Evie chewed on her biscuit. She ought to call her mother, but she wasn't in the mood just yet.

Loretta took this statement without question. Smart kid, given the level of shouting in the house behind them. "Yelling isn't logical."

"They know that. But they're like teapots. They have to release the steam before they can cool off. This land thing caught them by surprise, so they don't know who to blame. Jax will straighten them out, eventually." Evie hoped that wasn't a lie. She was placing all her faith in that burgeoning aura of responsibility she'd detected buried under anger.

"After he finds my parents," Loretta concluded, rightly.

"Yeah, he's pretty steamed about that." She had *told* him the Posts were in the pond, but she supposed a lawyer's rational mindset needed evidence before he could ask the county to drain a big mud puddle. Of course, Jax suspected her and her family of all the wrong things, but that couldn't be helped. Logical minds did not accept the paranormal easily.

"I want to stay here." Loretta reaffirmed her goal.

"You will. If you haven't noticed, we're a large family. We know a lot of people. We may not be rich like your parents, or most of us aren't, anyway. But we have lots of friends who know lots of people. It all works out eventually. Once tempers stop flying, anyway."

"Then they need to stop fighting and start thinking." Loretta set her plate on the swing, hopped down, and marched back into the kitchen.

"Oh, goddesses above and beyond, help me." Carrying her plate, Evie followed the Indigo child of Peace just to see what happened. Honey trotted in after them.

Not hesitating, Loretta opened the pocket door and walked straight into the eye of the hurricane. Cards dropped. Birds perched. Honey flopped down by the front door and the Siamese cat joined her. All eyes focused on Loretta.

"Somebody killed my parents," she announced into the silence. "Aunt Val said material things aren't important, that we are the earth and sky and water. Doesn't that mean we can do anything? I want to know why my parents died."

Mavis chose that moment to walk in the front door. Evie expected her to be carrying her crystal ball. Instead, her mother—the one who ignored tax notices and thought bookkeeping involved libraries—carried a businesslike file folder. Ignoring the silence that greeted her, she dropped the folder on the table where the tarot had been before it went flying. "Goodness, I'm hungry. Do I smell fried chicken?"

She tottered off on her heeled sandals.

Gracie, the schoolteacher, was the one who leaned over to pick up the file. Out of all of them, she was the one who had learned to deal with bureaucracy.

Loretta retreated into the shadows, sitting down beside the cat and dog, presumably considering her task to be done.

"Bank transaction numbers." Gracie flipped pages. "Copies of *paid* tax bills! Bring the notices here. Let me compare the deed numbers."

So, that's why Mavis had gone to visit Bill at the bank. It would make sense that the trust bank account would be local. Sometimes, her mother really could be pragmatic. Although she may have promised Bill free palm reading for life.

Evie sat down beside Loretta and allowed Psy to climb into her lap while her family produced tax notices. She wondered if Val had received a notice on this house.

"The numbers aren't the same," Gracie announced in disappointment. "What property has the trust been paying taxes on then?"

Interesting notion that the family owned any property besides the Hill. Evie was guessing that wouldn't be Jax's view. More likely, one property, different bills.

"I think," she addressed the room, "that the past due notices are for the *original* property, before it was put into the trust." And because she thought in paranormal terms and not practical, she added, "Someone has rendered the trust invisible."

Eighteen

Exhausted after spending half the night with Sheriff Troy and the state cops explaining why they needed to cordon off the pond on such flimsy evidence, Jax slept late the next morning. A cat leaping on his back jarred him awake enough to realize daylight poured through the striped cotton curtains.

A dog's cold nose rubbed his hand, and groggily, he opened his eyes. A ragged magenta teddy bear sat on the vanity chair, turned to face the bed, with a postcard attached.

The women must have unloaded Loretta's boxes from the sedan. Evidently, the kid was making a statement with this toy—while leaving his door open. Good thing he didn't sleep naked.

Swinging his legs from the bed, he leaned over and detached the note: *I want to stay here.*

Well, that was clear enough.

Although, if her parents were killed for that land, he couldn't think Loretta safe in Afterthought.

Showered and dressed in khaki shorts and short-sleeve shirt in an attempt to defeat the heat, Jax wandered into the kitchen. Evie was cleaning up enough dishes for an army, and he recalled he was supposed to hire a cook.

Glancing at him, she got out a frying pan. "Eggs, over easy?"

"You're not a short-order cook. I can go to the café." He'd rather not.

He'd rather watch her curls bounce and hear what she had to say after last night's coven convention.

She cracked an egg. "Breakfast is easy. You're on your own for dinner. What did the police say last night?"

"Too dark to search. They'll be out there with search and rescue this morning. You do realize the probability of bodies staying under that mud puddle all winter is slim to none?" He didn't want to ruin her breakfast with details, but he'd seen death. Corpses floated.

"I read up on it last night. I know—unless they were tied down. The water would have been low last September, before the hurricane came through. I don't have enough of a criminal mind to go from there." She got down a clean plate.

"For reasons beyond my understanding, your sheriff is still inclined to believe you. He twisted arms. He wasn't pleased with the notion of wealthy dead landowners dying *again* in his jurisdiction. He's not buying murder. Not sure I am, either. The necklace could have just fallen off or been dropped there. But Troy seems to accept ghostly messages." Jax turned on his coffee machine and popped bread in the toaster.

"I've helped Troy a time or two," she said with a careless shrug. "I can't say I know all the rules of how the spirit world works. I thought ghosts were tied to the place they died. John Post has already broken that one by following Loretta. I have no experience in bodies moved after death. So maybe the Posts died at the lake, but their bodies are elsewhere. I just know that John Post said goodbye to Loretta last night and moved on to the next plane. He accomplished what he set out to do. That was one strong-willed man." She ladled the eggs on a plate and set it on the counter.

John Post came from a line of strong-willed females, Jax thought as he waited for his toast. He supposed it took a strong will to convince people to believe the impossible, the impractical, and the insane. That a sensible man like the sheriff had agreed to have the pond searched based on Evie's word. . . said a scary lot. It wasn't as if Evie's family had money to buy an election.

"I didn't know Post." Jax buttered his toast and took a seat at the counter. He wasn't accustomed to leisurely breakfasts or women cooking for him. He usually grabbed an egg bagel and coffee on the way to work. Watching Evie in her skimpy shirt and tight shorts was far more entertaining. "Even though I'm a fraud investigator, I'm the only one at the firm with a recent background in family law, so they appointed me to guardian duties. I have access to the estate documents and Loretta's funds, which gives me very little insight into his thinking. Post knew how to make money, although I'll make a wild guess that it wasn't in technology."

He shouldn't get used to this family thing. Evie would figure out how to hire another lawyer and have him heaved out soon enough.

"He's the descendant of Malcolms, and we usually aren't much on technology, although I don't know too many male Malcolms. What happens next? They drag the pond?" Evie poured a cup of tea and leaned back against the sink counter to watch him eat.

Movie-star cleavage like that required diaphanous drapery, not T-shirts. Jax focused on his eggs. "Maybe divers. Did you explain to your family about the tax notices?"

"Pretty hard to explain. The bank provided proof that taxes were paid, but they don't appear to be paid on the property the notices were on. It's as if the trust doesn't exist except as a bank account." She sipped her tea and spoke without accusation.

Jax breathed a little easier. He didn't want her blaming him for whatever was happening, like the rest of her family did. "My guess is that the registrar's files have been tampered with. With no computerized records as backup, anyone can tamper with the original deeds. Not sure about the tax list. I'll have to ask for a state audit. My father will fire me."

There, he'd said it. Given that S&S was heavily involved in Lakeland Development, chances were very good that the firm played some role in the deed deception. Jax refused to believe they had anything to do with the deaths of Loretta's parents. That had to be some desperate local, if he wished to believe in ghosts. He didn't want to. He'd rather find out which of the investors was heavily in debt.

"If you get fired, you won't have another chance to find out what happened to your father." She stated it flatly, as if reading his mind.

Evie wasn't a mind reader, he reminded himself. She was just very good at observation and deduction—which could seem magical to the superstitiously inclined. But yeah, he was staying with his father's old firm until he learned what had happened to him—which required that be a partner with access to board files.

"Your family could ask for the audit. I'll recommend a property lawyer with expertise in the area."

Evie wrinkled up her nose. "Since my family is essentially saying that

Loretta's land really isn't hers, I'm guessing we can't use her funds to pay a lawyer. We'll have to consult Aunt Val."

She made that sound as if she'd have to take the yellow brick road and confront the wizard. He could understand her point. Val was the scariest of them all.

"It will be ugly. My firm will fight you, tooth and nail." Jax chewed slowly, while he contemplated the ravages of war. "Chances are good your mayor or town council are involved. They'll join forces with my firm. Crystal balls won't be useful."

"Crystal balls are seldom useful." She shrugged. "It's what people know that we need to tap into. You need to give up on caution and start digging around your office to find out more about your father in case you're fired. And maybe look into the development company while you're at it, although that will almost certainly lead to explosions."

Jax sipped his coffee and pondered a future without his Jag or condo. "And what will you be doing to expedite this confrontation?"

Evie shoved curls out of her face and grimaced. "I need to have a few casual conversations with people at the courthouse about deed books before anyone realizes I'm not an airhead. Perhaps Reuben and Roark could dig into the owners of the development company. None of that will find killers, but it might stop a property war."

She recognized how she came across and used it, of course, Jax realized. That's what charlatans did—except Evie didn't go for the all-knowing seeress character. Apparently town clown worked for her. Underhanded, but practical. *Damn.*

"I'm thinking if the Posts died here, asking questions was the reason. Stay out of the courthouse until the cops have done their work," he advised. "If Troy knows you're not a fool, others suspect it."

She shot him an enigmatic smile. "Nice of you to notice."

That smile struck him where his heart ought to be. He went on as if she'd said nothing. "I have to warn Ariel of impending explosions. If I end up shredding ties with our father, she'll be vulnerable." And Jax would be out of a job. If pissed enough, Stephen could make it difficult for him to find another.

There was a reason he moved cautiously. And a reason to be reluctant to believe Evie's family over his own. He needed more time to investigate.

"If I find evidence that the mayor and his crooks have stolen the official records of our trust deed, I'll call Val and we'll hire lawyers. Consider this fair warning." Beneath her mop of curls, she looked serious—not easy for someone wearing a lime green T-shirt declaring *If the earth was flat cats would have pushed everything off it by now.*

"I just told you it wasn't safe." Jax pushed his plate away.

"And you have vested interest in telling me that. You're not my boss."

Damn. He should have expected that. "Fine then, but don't expect me to come to your rescue. I'm still Loretta's guardian and her well-being comes first. And if I discover you're just trying to blackmail her out of her money, I'll have you all thrown in jail. Where is Loretta? This is Sunday, not a school day."

"We didn't want her hanging around the pond if they're dredging up bodies. Mavis and Aunt Felicity have taken her, my fake guardianship papers, and a note signed by me to her school to reclaim her clothes. You'll have to settle up with the school." She took his plate and dipped it into the dishwater.

Jax rubbed the bridge of his nose. The school was definitely not a good fit if Loretta hated it and could walk away so easily. But the witchy sisters as babysitters. . . Why not? "She needs security if someone killed her parents."

"Yeah, I know." Evie's shoulders slumped as she rinsed and dried the plate. "We're notifying the local school. We'll have eyes on her every minute. We just don't know if any of those eyes are the bad guys."

Jax dragged out his phone and began scrolling through messages. His team reported that they'd found the desk vault but couldn't crack it. That proved nothing. Evie or her family might have located the combination or Loretta gave it to them. But the little things were stacking up. If it was a con, it was the most convincing one he'd ever seen.

But with millions of dollars at stake, he couldn't take chances. For all he knew, Evie's family had dumped the Posts in the lake.

Grimacing, he gave his illegal hacker team the password to the firm's cloud account and told them to start searching for any old files involving his father and copy them into Jax's private account. He warned them there might be other password-protected files that he didn't have access to. He'd already downloaded the ones on Lakeland Development. He'd not found anything suspicious so far.

Like John Post, his father's firm wasn't high on technology. Security was lax, and computerized files were minimal. Which meant a physical search of paper documents was also required.

"I need to go into the office archives and find nearly twenty-year-old files if I'm to look into my father's cases." His life was just a bed of roses these days. "I'd have to be on the board to access board minutes from that period, but I could start with his cases to see if he was into anything shady. Stephen will want to know why I want them."

Evie's eyes widened, and she went spacey for a moment, before returning to ground earth—thankfully with no new reports of ghosts hanging out behind his back. "How long has your firm worked with John Post? Can you say you need birth certificates or old tax returns or anything to give you an excuse for digging around in archival files? If I can help you find out about your father, I'd like to. Can we go in today?"

Damn, wherever her head went when she did that, it paid off. He wanted her to be on his team and not the enemy.

"You can talk to ghosts in files?" he asked sardonically, but he was already working through his phone, checking to see if anyone was in the office on Sunday. "I don't like lying," he added for good measure, because he knew the slippery slope ahead too well.

She leaped over this objection into another fantasy.

"We need a psychometrist." She produced an old-fashioned address book from a drawer and reached for the landline.

"Wait a minute! I can't take just anyone into the firm's vaults." A psychometrist? Jax walked that through his basic Latin, scowled at the result, and looked it up on his phone: *the supposed ability to discover facts about an event or person by touching inanimate objects associated with them.* SUPPOSED being the keyword.

"Cousin Orbis Junior is harmless. He's a well-respected antique dealer in Charleston. You can tell your firm that you found something old and need him to verify authenticity or whatever. But first I'll have to ask him if he can find anything on old papers." She held the receiver, waiting.

"I haven't even talked to Ariel yet!" And talking to Ariel didn't happen often. He'd have to text and warn her he wanted to call. And lie to everyone he knew—the reason he hadn't gone digging through his father's cases before. "Lying only leads to trouble."

She shrugged. "When people don't believe my truth, I learn to speak theirs. We'll just poke around, see what's there. If you find anything, you don't have to act on it until you're ready. In fact, it's usually better to wait a while after you've gone poking before magically producing the evidence." She grinned. "Professional secret."

Damn. He really was working with con artists. He ought to listen and learn, but when she started talking about a difference between her truth and others—reality became ephemeral.

～

As they drove toward the interstate, they passed the pond. It was lined with police cars and vans, marked and unmarked. All Evie knew about forensics was gained from the internet, and that was enough to know she didn't want to be there when they started finding remains.

Should she have tried harder to persuade Mr. Post to explain what had happened? But ghosts often didn't remember the trauma and were obsessed with problems they'd left behind instead, like his stupid property. Well, maybe he was also trying to warn of thieves and protect Loretta. She shouldn't think ill of the dead.

"I'm thinking maybe John Post hadn't realized his grandmother didn't own all of the pond property until after he inherited and became involved with the development company." She sounded out her theory as Jax drove.

"Why do you say that?" He looked grim as he sped down the road a little faster than required. He'd changed into trousers and button-down shirt without a tie and looked like a lawyer again.

She preferred his earlier casual clothes. He had filled out that polo shirt nicely. She cast a glance to bulging biceps and wondered if he was a gym rat. She'd had bad luck with self-centered guys focused on body building. Somehow, she didn't think Jax was of that ilk.

"The ghost mentioned *thieves*. And he led us to the actual deeds. We might never have had proof if he hadn't done that."

"So your scenario is that the development company wanted to buy Witch Hill. They found John or his mother's name on a large parcel and contacted him. Then John handed the deal to his law firm, and it spiraled out of control after that?" Jax tapped his steering wheel as if pondering the improbable.

"The family had offers for the land. We refused them. We've been refusing them for years. I'm guessing Letitia did the same. So, yeah, something like that after John inherited the property. He didn't know the history and had no reason not to sell. And I'm betting that if you look into the owners of the development company, you'll find Mayor Blockhead associated in some way. He always is when it comes to land around Afterthought."

"Observation or deduction?" he asked.

"About the mayor? Observation. He owns a realty company, remember? The only one in town." Evie felt cramped in the little car, almost rubbing shoulders with Jax. She liked men well enough, and Jax had what it took to turn her on. But her relationships never worked out. She was simply too weird, and men couldn't handle it, especially straight shooters like Jax.

What she really wanted was to convince Jax and his law firm that she made a good detective. If she could work with them for a few years, she'd have a basis to apply for a license. So, she could dream. Of course, if Jax blew off his job. . . The Universe never dropped plums in her lap.

"That's a conflict of interest. The mayor shouldn't be able to vote on anything to do with land." Jax hit the gas as soon as they ramped onto I-95.

"It's a small town. Every vote is a conflict of interest in some way. The whole point of being on the council is to influence how the town grows. I'm not pointing fingers, much. I'm just saying the development company is not operating in outer space. It has connections to the council." Living in a fish bowl all her life, she'd had time to observe how human interaction worked, upfront and personal. College couldn't teach the lessons she'd learned.

He gripped the steering wheel tighter. "Lakeland is a consortium of contractors our firm has worked with for decades. Stockton and Stockton is an old, reliable firm, small but well known in business circles. So I'm not ready to buy they'd do anything illegal. But the fact remains, the deed books, the deeds, and the tax notices don't line up."

"And the town, the developers, and presumably, your law firm, stand to benefit. And Loretta, since I'm guessing there's a nice amount of money being paid for her land. The only ones suffering are my family, which might be a motive for skullduggery right there. The town would rather have a barbershop on Main Street than Mom's shop, and my mother and her sisters have been a thorn in the town's side for years." Evie slumped in the seat and tried to pull all her revolving thoughts in line.

"One assumes the conflict between your family and the town goes back longer than that," he said in what sounded like amusement.

"Well, yeah." She huffed a laugh recalling a few memorable town meetings. "The school teaches all the creative arts, plus horticulture, forestry, and carpentry because, over the years, my family browbeat every family in town for educational support. It's a small school with a curriculum wider than that of most cities. Few people here can afford college, so vocational courses make sense."

"Let me guess—to pay for all that, the town had to raise taxes because the tax base is too small to fund all those classes. So the council members—who probably don't have kids in school—want to reduce their own taxes by expanding the tax base with a massive residential anthill on your property—just to get even."

"Yeah, probably," she said gloomily, glaring out the windshield. "They don't consider that Main Street businesses are thriving because the school offers opportunities and educational value. Families don't leave Afterthought the way they do in every other small town in the country. We're a prosperous community with a lot of creative, educated, skilled people who bring money in from outside."

"But those people need a place to live," he argued.

Evie rolled her eyes and gestured at the cotton fields they passed. "You think there's a shortage of land? The pond *floods*. It's a natural basin. Build on that soil and the whole town floods. Our ancestors were not idiots. My family would probably donate the property for a public park if anyone asked, but no, parks cost money instead of making it. Short-sighted."

"And they think you're flakes and can be cheated," he added.

"They're wrong. And even if we can't turn them into toads, we can run them out of town in the next election. So where in heck does this leave us?" Feeling disgruntled but relieved that Jax understood and maybe accepted the problem, Evie watched with interest as they left the 95 for the 16 into downtown Savannah.

"Considering the lower property taxes in your county, the ease of access to Afterthought, and the demand for bedroom communities outside of Charleston and Savannah—that leaves us with a raft of suspects two states wide," he admitted.

"Well, how many are in a position to doctor the registrar's records?" Evie watched as he expertly dodged in and out of traffic, catching turn lanes and driving a zigzag path into a commercial district that wasn't historic downtown. Dang. She'd hoped to see a ghost or two.

"The blue-haired lady at the desk? Anyone else who works there?"

"Emma Blue?" Evie laughed. "She's a lovely, flag-waving fascist, but I'm pretty sure it would never occur to her to change anything, anywhere. Admittedly, she's not fond of my family, but she's unlikely."

"So are my father and John Post. I'll look deeper into Lakeland, see what connections I can find."

"The name on the surveyor papers was Titan, not Lakeland. What does that signify?"

"Titan is just a surveying firm. I'll have to see if they're invested in Lakeland."

He spun down a side street into a warehouse district. "Our archives aren't housed at the office. I think I can get into the storage unit without too much trouble, but there are cameras all over. If anyone is monitoring them, I'll need to explain why I'm digging in old records when I'm supposed to be returning Loretta to school."

Well, double dang. She'd hoped to see where he worked. The big aluminum-sided structure he pulled up to was beyond uninteresting into deadly dull.

She followed Jax out of the car. He inserted a card in a reader, just like a hotel room, and pushed open a security door. Snapping on a switch in the interior revealed metal shelving stacked high with ancient boxes. Evie sighed. "Even Cousin Orbis couldn't find a ghost in here."

"It's a paper graveyard." Jax flipped through a computerized index on the desk at the entrance. "The records of clients dead for decades reside here. I need a roster of my father's clients to know what he was working on when he died. This is a dead end."

"Negativity gets you nowhere. Are there dates on those boxes? Can you find dates around the time of your father's death?" Evie roamed down the first aisle, examining labels, looking for the order of storage.

"There are dates for when they were archived. The section for the year of his death is over on the far right, aisle H, block 3. That doesn't guarantee it contains anything he was working on though."

"Got it." Evie ran her hand over the dusty boxes, reading faded labels. "They're organized alphabetically by client name. So we have about three dozen file boxes in this section starting with Abercrombie and ending with Thomas. Apparently no Vanderbilts or Zacharies died that year."

Jax joined her, crowding close to examine the labels. They were all alone in the semi-dark, and Evie wondered if it were only her hormones jumping.

He seemed pretty focused as he yanked boxes out by their handles and flipped back lids, hunting for something only he understood.

"This one has his name on it." He dropped a box on the floor and started through the next row. "I still have no idea what we're looking for."

"Memories," she sang, sitting down beside the box and pulling out file folders. "Huh, a lot of these papers look as if they're printed from a computer file, so they must have been digitized at some point."

"Reuben and Roark haven't found them online. Twenty years ago, they could have been on disk, for all I know. Stephen still likes his copies in print." He tossed down two more boxes.

"I'll write down client names and addresses and so forth. Maybe you can start there." She'd actually brought a notebook with her to prove she could be organized. She began taking notes.

Jax handed her his phone. "Take pictures of client info and I'll send them to the team."

"Spoilsport." With a sigh, she figured out how the camera worked and snapped the original interview notes from the first box. "Disks." She held up a couple of the old-fashioned square ones.

Jax looked torn but finally nodded. "Put them in your bag. I'll return them after I've uploaded them to our cloud files. Nothing wrong with that."

Evie checked that each disk had a client name, took photos of the labels along with the interview notes, and pocketed the squares.

Several boxes in, she noticed Jax had gone still. She didn't know how she noticed the difference between his usual composed state and this, but she could feel the impact. Glancing up, she watched as he pulled one box out as if it might be a time bomb. She'd already calculated what part of the alphabet the shelf represented before he spoke.

"*John Post* has been a client for a long time." Jax set the box on the floor and lifted the lid as if it would explode in his face.

Nineteen

Surrounded by a warehouse full of dusty paper, Jax had just torn open the Post file box, when his phone vibrated. He never left his phone off, in case Ariel needed to reach him. Reluctantly, he let Evie dig in while he checked his messages.

SEND CAR was all his sister's text said. That was sufficient to escalate his pulse into the red zone. He tried calling but she didn't answer.

"What's wrong? Is Loretta okay?" Apparently picking up on his vibrations, Evie watched him, her crystal eyes wide with anxiety.

He'd dumped a hell of a lot on the genie lately. He hated seeing her natural exuberance crushed. Ruthlessly, he ignored his better instincts to reassure her and punched in Roark's contact number. "My sister."

Not having any life of his own, Roark answered instantly.

Jax knew Evie was listening, but he wasn't whitewashing his urgency. "Ariel needs a car. For her, that's ominous. Can we get someone over there ASAP? Make it look good, black Lincoln, uniform, whatever. Take her to my condo."

"Reuben's scrolling through the list now. We'll get the van out there too, hide nearby in case reinforcements are needed. How dangerous can one old man be? Explosives?"

Jax grimaced at his friend's instant paranoia. "This is *not* a combat zone. Ariel is neurotic and not dangerous to anyone. *Yet.* I suspect it means she's found volatile information and doesn't want to send it from home. It may mean once she passes on her information, that we'll have trouble."

"Which means she suspects she's been hacked or watched, got it. On our way."

Yeah, it probably meant Ariel was more uncomfortable than usual and needed a getaway. Since she hated leaving the house, it had to be uncomfortable. On a Sunday. When Stephen might be home?

Ignoring his own advice not to panic, Jax began flinging boxes back on the shelf.

Evie clung to the Post box. "You have good excuse to want this one. I'll put on a good performance for the cameras. Take it to your office or condo or whatever. You need some idea of what your father was working on, and this ties in with your current case."

He wasn't arguing. He needed to be there for Ariel. He lifted the long box to his shoulder. Evie clung to one of the file folders. As they headed for the door and cameras, she started smacking him with the flimsy cardboard.

"Loretta is mine! I don't care what you find in there, she belongs with us." She ranted and raved as he signed the box out and passed the security cameras to the parking lot, smacking him with vigor.

Jax suspected she was enjoying herself, but she performed the angry woman role as if she had experience.

"Drama runs in the family, I take it." He flung the box into the trunk and handed her into the car.

She crossed her arms and continued her furious act until he'd pulled from the parking lot and was halfway down the street. Then she relaxed and opened the file she'd been hitting him with to read it.

"Drama is useful. People don't believe me if I calmly say, *There's a ghost in your living room*. Or if Mavis sees romance in your future, what fun is it if she just says, *The guy at the desk next to yours wants to boff you*."

"Well, I'd probably walk out on her if she said that to me, but I take your point." He'd work that around in his head some other time. Right now he was focused on Ariel. What the hell had happened?

"Does your sister send messages like that often?" Evie closed the file, apparently unimpressed with whatever she'd seen.

"No. She's pretty independent within her own realm. If she felt physically threatened, she'd probably shoot first and ask questions later. I take that back, she'd just shoot and text me. She does not respond in socially acceptable ways, but she is not helpless or insane." Jax glanced at Evie as he recognized what he was saying. "She might have a bit in common with your family."

Evie laughed curtly. "That's what I was thinking. Poor thing is probably just out of place."

"No, not entirely the same. Your family might be atypical, but you're socially adept and communicate. Ariel does not. She lives inside her head. She has so much happening inside her cranium that she can't deal with what's outside of it. The computer helps. She can communicate without sensory overload, less distraction that way."

Jax thought about his condo, his neighbors shouting greetings, cars and trucks constantly in and out, repairmen coming and going, salesmen knocking. . . Ariel would go mad within half a day.

He was aware of Evie studying him, but he was concentrating on maneuvering around traffic to make it to his place before Ariel did. How long would it take for Roark to send a car out?

"Your anger is still intense, but there's a clear pink emerging. You love your sister and want to protect her but you're still angry—maybe because she's atypical? That your parents left you to deal with her? Those are all perfectly acceptable feelings. Am I annoying you yet?" Laughter tinged her voice.

"You sound like a therapist. You missed your calling." He took the ramp into the residential area where he slept. *Lived* wasn't the right word. He lived to work.

"I'd love to be a therapist, but there isn't any way I can concentrate on textbooks. I'm lousy at school. If I wanted to be a charlatan, I'd hang out a therapist shingle, fake a certificate, and advertise. I'm probably as good at diagnosing as most therapists. Cures might be beyond me though." She studied the shopping centers they passed. "Wow, could you find an area any more yuppie?"

"Everything in one place—coffee shop, pizza, dry cleaner, grocery, drugstore. Convenient." He swung into the condo development. Ariel was really going to hate this anthill.

"Huh, and this is how the other half lives. I'm thinking maybe I don't want to move to the city. Maybe I should run for town council. Or mayor. That might be fun." She peered up at the tall condo structures before he drove down to his basement parking space.

"If you can't focus on textbooks, you definitely can't read legislation. I don't recommend political office." Jax checked his phone and opened the video Roark had sent. "The car has arrived at the house. Ariel is leaving with only her laptop case. Maybe she's planning on returning."

"Maybe she's afraid someone will stop her if she takes a suitcase." Evie climbed out and went around to the trunk.

Right. The file box. Jax shoved his phone back in his pocket and popped the trunk.

He was taking Evangeline Malcolm Carstairs into his home, with a file box of his client's papers. That was wrong on so many levels that he gave up working it out. Shouldering the box, he led her upstairs.

Opening the door to his living room, he felt the cold draft of the air conditioning, unlike the hot and humid room he'd been squatting in these past days. It felt more like an icebox than home. When he bought the condo, he'd called a furniture warehouse and hired someone to pick out the brown leather furniture and accessories. It had seemed practical at the time. Looking at it through Evie's colorful eyes. . . Well, they wouldn't be here long.

He slid the box onto his dining room table. "I probably have cold cuts and cheese in the fridge. Want anything?"

She stood at the window, watching the parking lot. "Cheese is good. Crackers, maybe. Water. If we draw all these drapes and blinds, we can shut out the world a bit. How is she with music? Something low and classical as white noise maybe?"

Remarkably, Evie seemed to understand his sister's needs, probably better than he did. "Atonal. Think monk chanting. Does Pandora have a channel for that?" Jax checked the refrigerator, found a beer, and sorted through the cheese to find something not moldy.

"Not good with tech, remember? Let me do the food, and you handle Pandora whatever." Lowering and closing blinds as she went, she joined him in the kitchen.

"You're trying to pacify me." He leaned against the counter and drank from the last cold beer. He already knew Evie didn't drink anything harder than ice tea. She'd never fit into his wine bar crowd. She was a splotch of bright yellow and orange today—abstract art in his soulless gray kitchen.

She opened his refrigerator and shook her head at the empty shelves. "You need stimulation more than pacification. If I'd beat anyone else with a file folder the way I did you, he'd have ripped it from my hands and swatted me back." She turned and waved a dismissive hand at him. "Pandora, maestro. How soon before your sister arrives?"

He'd been thinking of Evie as an adorable fluff ball. Had she always been this bossy? And damned analytic?

He checked the time on the video. "Ten minutes, depending on traffic. I bought on this side of town so she wouldn't be far. She had panic attacks when she was younger."

Stimulation more than pacification? He doubted he could handle any more stimulation than being pounded on by a file folder, jacked up with fear for his sister, and cooped up in a confined space with a woman who pushed all his buttons. He'd never understand her. Jax returned to the front room to find Pandora on his computer and look for atonal music.

"Why did your sister call for a driver instead of asking you to pick her up?" Evie arrived with a platter of sliced cheese, crackers, and apple slices, setting them next to the file box on his tiny dining table. Without asking permission, she began sorting through the John Post folders.

"Impersonal transportation is the only way Ariel leaves the house. Once driverless cars are on the road, she'll be in heaven. She usually takes taxis because they have that plastic shield between front and back, and she knows every non-talkative driver in the company. Asking me for a car. . . probably means something is wrong that needs my attention. I'll hope Roark found someone professional enough to respect her distance."

He joined her at the box. "I'll give the disks to Reuben. He'll have the equipment to read them."

Evie produced the ones she'd stolen from other boxes. "The file names and whatnot are on your phone. None of the names mean anything to me." She returned to the kitchen. He heard her adding ice cubes to a glass.

"Not even this one?" He pulled out a folder labeled John Post vs. Blue Construction. "Didn't you say the clerk in the property office is called Blue?"

Returning with her water, Evie snatched the file from his hand. "Huh. I thought she made up the name to match her hair. Emma doesn't have a drop of blue in her aura." She didn't skim the file the way he did but studied each piece of paper. "I didn't know she had a brother, Emmitt. Sounds like twins. Also looks like he was in hot water a lot back then."

Jax's phone pinged. He glanced down and hurried to the door. "Ariel is here."

~

ARIEL WAS NOT QUITE AS ETHEREAL AS HER NAME WOULD LEAD
one to believe, Evie discovered. Jax's sister was thin, on the tall side, with long,
straight hair an even darker hue than her brother's, and skin several shades
lighter. She seemed more brittle than waif-like.

Without a word of greeting, she entered, looked for a place to plug in her
laptop, and settled at the dining room table. She didn't give a second glance to
the dusty box or the folders scattered on the surface.

"I'll take those disks down to the guys," Jax murmured, gathering them
up. "Bring Ariel a bottle of water?"

Transcendental meditation music drifted from the speakers. Evie felt right
at home. She found bottles of water and rummaged through the freezer to see
if there was anything edible. Frozen pizzas, of course. She popped one in the
oven.

She handed a bottle to Ariel and took a seat on the far end of the table to
continue reading the Blue file. Ariel absent-mindedly helped herself to the
cheese and typed on her computer. Weird, but not any weirder than Evie's
noisy family.

Eventually, Evie couldn't resist. Settling down behind the file folders, she
opened her inner eye.

Ariel was a rainbow of clear colors—except for a thin line of muddy blue
probably indicating fear. Evie had no way of knowing what she feared, but an
aura that transparent said Ariel could be trusted.

An aura that transparent looked crystalline. Indigo children were the
harbingers of crystal peacemakers. Or maybe she was getting a little too woo-
woo even for her. Still, she liked the concept.

Evie returned to reading about Blue Construction. Looked like Emmitt
—why did that name ring bells?—Blue had a bad habit of borrowing money
for construction jobs he never completed. He took the advance money on a
job, used it to pay down on a loan from a prior job, and then moved on to
another contract. When did he have time to build anything? Apparently he
didn't, since John Post had hired Jax's father to sue for non-performance.
How old could John have been twenty years ago? Barely out of college, she'd
think. Interesting. Stockton and Stockton were the Post family lawyers even
back then?

Evie flipped through the pages of the lawsuit. She didn't have the legalese needed to grasp the details of the courtroom transcripts. It looked like Franklin Jackson—Jax's biological father—of Stockton and Stockton LLC had won the case for his client, John Post, against Blue's construction company. Maybe Loretta's father got rich by suing little companies. The sum was hefty. The bonding company would have had to pay through the nose, then never insured Blue again. Jax's father didn't come off too shoddily either.

Jax's phone began binging. He must have set it on the table when he ran downstairs with the disks. Evie ignored it while she flipped through more pages, trying to focus while the phone pinged and the music fluted.

She felt Ariel's gaze on her and looked up. Jax's sister hastily lowered her eyes to study the binging phone on the table between them. Remembering not to talk, Evie gestured for Ariel to take it.

Ariel grabbed the sleek phone, hit a few buttons, opened up the screen, and began hitting more buttons. Icons. Whatever. Finished, she pushed the screen at Evie.

This just got weirder and weirder. Studying the screen, she saw a bank statement in the name of John and Tiffany Post—one with an address in a place she thought might be an island in the Caribbean. Ariel leaned over and swiped the screen away, hit another button, and brought up another statement. This account was in the name of Stockton and Stockton, care of Damon Jackson, same foreign bank. The opening transaction was an amount nearly equal to the final balance transferred out of the Post statement.

She got a real bad feeling in the pit of her stomach. "Isn't Jax in charge of the Post accounts? Shouldn't the bank statement have the Post's trust name on it and not Stockton's?"

Ariel bobbed her head in what appeared to be a nod of agreement, then crossed her arms over her head and ears and put her cheek down against the table, retreating into her own world.

Evie grabbed the phone and raced out to meet Jax before he could disturb his sister. Men simply emitted noisy vibes with their existence.

She knew these statements made it look as if she should suspect Jax of stealing Loretta's inheritance, but that was pure nonsense. This was a setup if she'd ever seen one, and she'd seen more than one.

She caught him just as he was pushing away from the van. She waved the phone frantically. "Wait!"

Roark saluted her from the open window and turned off the engine. Jax glowered. She shoved the phone at him. "Your sister just showed me this. I assume it's what she wanted to send you earlier. Is she afraid your father may be picking up her messages?"

Jax scrolled back and forth, his face growing pale and grim before handing it to Roark. "The transaction date is Friday, when I didn't return to the office as ordered."

Roark whistled. Reuben emerged from the rear to take the passenger seat. Roark handed the phone over to his partner. "You've been set up, man. Bet that was done from your office computer."

"Any chance we can transfer it back, then empty the entire account into Loretta's investment fund? Then change all her passwords again? I'll make her financial advisor a co-exec so it will take two signatures for a transaction." Jax took his phone back, checked for more messages, and shoved it into his pocket.

Evie hovered, uncertain if she was allowed to say what she was thinking. This didn't involve Loretta so much as Jax. This was his world, his sister, she had no claim. But once Jax had given his orders, she stopped him with a hand on his arm.

"Your sister is terrified. She's as open and transparent as you aren't. The muddy blue streak in her aura is abnormal. She should have no reason to fear, but she's *scared*. I don't think she should go back to your father's house." There, she'd said it. She couldn't do more than that. Persuading Jax to believe her gift simply wasn't in her realm of authority.

Jax ran a hand over his head. "Outside a padded cell, I have nowhere else to take her. Maybe she'll get used to the condo if I stay away."

"She's up there with her head buried under her arms right now. And sending you that bank statement didn't ease her fear." Evie clenched her fingers to prevent running them through her own out-of-control mop. "If it's rural solitude she requires. . ." She shook her head. Sometimes her need to help raced ahead of her ability to do so.

"No people, no traffic, no startling noises." Jax waited for her to finish her sentence.

Evie wrinkled up her nose. "The schoolteacher's house on Shady Lane. It shouldn't be left empty. You can pay rent to Loretta's trust. I don't know if any of the furniture is still there. She'd need household items. . . can Ariel cook for herself?"

"As well as I can with a properly-stocked kitchen." Jax slapped the van's open window. "Can you get that driver back? Will he make an hour drive?"

Already regretting her suggestion, Evie stuck out her hand for his phone. An hour wasn't much time to organize food, furniture, and linens—while quelling her family's curiosity.

Planting Ariel on land a development company wanted to claim was like throwing gasoline on hot charcoal. They'd need strong safety measures.

While Jax worked out his logistics with his team, Evie began calling her family.

Twenty

Scrutinizing the cottage Evie's family had hastily cleaned and arranged for his sister, Jax wished Ariel would allow him to stay with her. But his sister's text had been adamant in wanting a place all to herself. *Ariel* and *adamant* were not words that normally went together. He'd left her at the condo, waiting for a car, while he and Evie had sped ahead in his Jag.

"It would have helped if we knew what she liked to eat," Evie complained from the tiny kitchen, where she was poking around, verifying basic necessities had been provided.

"She eats whatever is available, as long as it's edible. Your family did a fantastic job. They need to pull together an invoice and let me pay them for their time and trouble." Jax examined the pantry. They'd even included some of their homemade jams and canned fruits and vegetables. Ariel ought to be able to figure it out—if she didn't go comatose from over-stimulation.

"Does she have that meditation music on any device? The place lacks anything resembling electronic equipment. And there won't be any internet until the cable is turned on." With her hair and clothes rumpled and dusty from the warehouse and arranging the cottage, Evie appeared oddly more grounded than usual.

Once he got to know her, her first impression of ditziness wore off.

"She can hide under that stack of quilts if there are too many unfamiliar noises. She's had over twenty years and lots of therapy to teach her how to neutralize overstimulation. Everything is difficult for her, so I try to help, but we're not magicians. We cannot provide sanctuary in a box." Jax checked out the window to see how his team was faring on installing security.

"I've asked Priscilla to stop by." She nervously checked the linen closet. "I can't claim to understand what Pris sees in other people's minds, but maybe she can make a connection we can't. I want your sister to not hate it here."

"What difference does it make to you?" he asked callously, because she was making *him* nervous with her flitting about, throwing up concerns he couldn't fix.

Evie threw a pillow at his head. "Because caring for others is what people ought to do. Although that seems to have been bred out of those of you raised in rarified atmospheres."

"I care for Ariel." He just couldn't fix his sister. Jax flung the pillow back.

A black Lincoln slowly trundled around the bend in the lane, so he didn't finish the stupid argument. Good thing, because he didn't have a defense in mind. Ariel was about the only person he cared about. He wanted to please Stephen, but that was more about himself than his boss.

Hearing the car, Evie headed for the kitchen. "I'll go out the back. Ask your guys to pick me up down the lane, please."

The house echoed emptily the instant she closed the door. Sharing space with Evie's energy ought to be exhausting, but her absence left him hollow, as if she filled up his empty spaces.

He sent his team after Evie, wincing as the dust rolled up from their van to coat the shiny black car approaching. He'd have to tip the driver well.

After paying off the limo, Jax waited outside on the porch while Ariel inspected what he hoped would be her new home. The cottage didn't begin to compare to the sprawling luxury she'd been living in—or even the comfort of the condo she'd rejected.

He heard her footsteps on the wooden floors recede and return. When he heard nothing more and she didn't invite him in, he winced. Silence could mean anything. He didn't possess interpretative powers.

A moment later, his phone pinged.

THANK YOU appeared on his message screen. He really wanted to go in and verify that she was okay, but she would have invited him if she wanted a visit. She'd obviously had as much stimulation as she could manage, so he resisted doing more than sending her a heart emoji.

Needing a bag to punch or a hole to dig after this emotionally taxing day, Jax reluctantly drove back toward the craziness of Evie's household. He could almost relate to Ariel's plight. The sight of official cars still parked at the pond gave him an excuse to pull over the Jag.

Sheriff Troy met him halfway. "Divers found rags and some foot bones. We're bringing in a bulldozer. We won't have ID without DNA. As Loretta's guardian, you need to sign the paperwork to see if she's a match."

Shit, damn, friggin' hell. What could he tell Loretta? *How* would he tell her? He was a lawyer, good with paperwork, not with kids. He needed Evie. Loretta needed Evie, just as they'd told him. Repeating a litany of obscenities, he drove into town and parked in Evie's empty drive.

Entering through the back door, Jax found Mavis and her sister, Felicia, in the kitchen, concocting dinner. They ignored him. He tracked Evie to the dining room, where she was unburying the table from accumulated junk. At sight of him, she set everything down and unexpectedly hugged his waist.

Caught off guard, Jax hugged her back. It had been a long time since anyone had offered sympathy or support. He hadn't realized how much he needed a human touch. And then her round curves and honeysuckle scent aroused more primal urges, and he began enjoying the closeness a little too much. He kissed the top of her head. She hugged him tighter, and she definitely registered as female.

Wisely, she pushed away and returned to setting the table. "How's Ariel?"

The hug had oddly eased his escalating tension, despite raising expectations that shouldn't be raised. "She sends her thanks. That's all I know. The guys are hooking her security to my phone as well as the security company's and their own equipment. If she runs screaming into the night, we'll know about it."

He took the silverware and began distributing it around the table. "You heard about the bones?"

"I did. That's why the crows are gathering." She nodded toward the kitchen. "If there are bodies, the state will want to call it accidental."

"Of course. I'll remind them that someone went to a great deal of trouble to prove the Posts died elsewhere. They won't like that."

"Have to prove it's them first. That could take weeks. Loretta will go berserk. We need to give her answers. I hate sounding like a therapist, but she needs closure."

Jax knew she was right. "I'm trying, but we don't have much to go on other than the Lakeland development. Fraudulent deeds are one thing, murder quite another. In my experience, most major development companies have the ability to acquire land without killing anyone."

His nerves were a ragged edge. He didn't know what to worry about first —Loretta and Evie's safety? The cause of his father's death? Scratch his job. He needed to verify his world was safe.

"Where did you put your father's file box? I know that's ancient information probably unrelated to what we're doing, but the stuff in there makes me feel. . . itchy." Evie dug out napkins and condiments from the sideboard.

"The whole damned situation makes me itchy." Jax didn't have time to say more.

Loretta bounced down the stairs, followed by Mavis and Felicia with dinner. The cat and dog trailed in after the smells, and a brief knock at the door indicated more guests arriving. Evie set additional plates and silverware on the sideboard.

In moments, Jax was surrounded by so much angry estrogen that he couldn't breathe. Deciding the women could tell Loretta whatever version of truth they thought best, he grabbed a plate, filled it with what looked like collards, rice, beans, and sausage, and took it out on the covered back porch.

Sheriff Troy joined him there not much later, carrying bottles of beer and his plate, with a generous helping of cornbread.

"Thought you might need this." Troy dropped a frosty bottle next to Jax. "They're good people, but not man-friendly."

"I'm guessing there's a reason for that." Now that Jax thought about it, there didn't seem to be any men in the family.

Troy shrugged and slugged his beer before answering. "Not too many have the guts to handle them. And the ones with guts tend to have dangerous occupations and get themselves killed."

"So Loretta's great-grandmother leaving town after marrying was probably a self-defense tactic, kept her family out of her marriage. Makes sense." Jax dug into beans and rice tastier than the frou-frou stacks of unknown components he'd consumed in five-star restaurants.

"Letitia would have come back here if it hadn't worked. The women always come back to family. Mavis was in Charleston when she married. Came back with just Grace and Evie in tow." Troy dug into his food.

Jax sipped his beer. "And you're telling me this why?"

"Thought you might like to know that Evie's father hired your father's firm to handle the divorce, and that he's in the construction business, and once worked for the mayor. It isn't just small towns that are small worlds."

Shit. The mayor would be just the sort of client Stephen would cultivate because of these sorts of connections. And the mayor obviously knew the firm. Maybe S&S wasn't as upright as he'd always believed.

Jax sipped his beer while he processed this new information. "Whatever's going down, I'm on the side of the law, first. Loretta's welfare is next. That's how it has to be."

"Women won't look it at that way. Tigers defend their cubs, tooth and nail." Troy cleaned up his plate with a slice of cornbread, then stood up. "You got your head on straight. Keep it that way."

Jax figured he could do that, if he kept his head on his shoulders. Evie's hug had knocked him sideways.

AFTER EVERYONE LEFT AND LORETTA HAD BEEN TUCKED INTO BED upstairs with her books for company, Evie poured herself some ice tea and debated sitting on the porch until her room cooled off.

Seeing a light under Jax's door, she tapped lightly. When he grunted with what she took as permission to enter, she opened it. "Would you like some tea?"

He held up a half-empty glass to show he'd helped himself.

"Did the sheriff provide any more illumination?" She leaned against the doorjamb. Jax was back in casual clothes, and she wasn't averse to admiring the scenery. Hugging him earlier had probably been a mistake, but his aura had been so dismal, she'd thought he needed it. Revving her hormones had not been her intention, but they were on full throttle from just watching him.

"He warned me that your family are tigers, and I could get my head bit off. Oh, and your father is in construction and knows the mayor." He shot her an inquisitive look from beneath heavy eyebrows.

"He's no more than a sperm donor as far as I'm concerned. He's never been part of my life." Evie had resented that when she'd been younger. She understood more over the years, as she'd watched her aunts wash recalcitrant men out of their hair, as the song went.

Apparently not too interested in her absent father, he returned to tapping at his keyboard. "Does your family always gather here to eat? I need to provide a grocery allowance, and I'm not sure how much to cover."

"It's why Val left the house to me. I don't have a regular job, I can cook, and this is the best place for gathering. The house has been the heart of the family since before Letitia married a Post."

He nodded, sat back, and sipped his drink. "Looking through my biological father's files, it seems he handled a lot of small lawsuits like that twenty-year-old one against Blue Construction. I don't have all the data, of course, but between the names we took down today and records online, it looks like construction and mining lawsuits were his specialty."

"Can't be a lot of money in that. Most contractors I know operate on debt and half don't have bond insurance." Evie lowered herself to the floor, not daring to get closer.

He scoffed. "How many contractors do you know?"

"I've been working since I was a little kid. I'm good at juggling lots of tasks. I'm curious. If you haven't noticed, I also listen well. If I have to hire anyone to fix this house, I know who can do the job right, and who's skating on thin ice and can't be trusted."

"And you read their auras." He hit a few more keys, apparently employing a search engine.

"That, too. Probably the reason I turned out so curious. If I see someone with an unusual aura, I want to know more. I'm better with people than computers."

"If I give you a printout of all the names and companies I've found so far in my father's old files, will you be able to remember ones you've heard about?"

"You have a printer?" Evie studied his laptop setup on Aunt Val's vanity and shook her head in amazement. Even as she asked, he was printing a page from a tiny machine on the floor. "You need to set up in the library."

"You have a library?" He pulled the sheet from the machine and held it out.

She reached over and grabbed it. "The room with the books all over the floor. Val never had shelves installed. But there's an old library table."

"Right, and probably a desk chair from the fifties. Better than that basket chair in your front room, I suppose." He stretched his back and rubbed it. "Check the names you recognize." He flung her a pen.

"These are all from your father's files? Their addresses are all over the

Southeast," she complained. "Just because I know a George Thompson here in South Carolina doesn't mean he's the one in Florida."

"We can work that out later. Just tell me if any of them sound familiar."

"Why do you want to know if I recognize the contractors your father took to court?" Evie check marked several names.

"Bear with me. Franklin Jackson didn't always take the lead in these suits. Most belong to my adoptive father, Stephen Stockton. But for some reason, my biological father had those files in his office when he died. Some of the cases had been closed years earlier. All settled for substantial sums. Lots of rotten construction companies around twenty or thirty years ago."

"I hope they had good insurance." She started to hand the sheet back, but he already had another one printing. Wide-eyed, she waited for it. "More?"

"Lakeland investors. Match the names to the ones you see on your sheet. Sometimes, it helps to touch and see everything physically."

Evie whistled as she compared the papers. "Every contractor I checked is on the Lakeland list. How big is Lakeland anyway?"

"It's registered as a corporate cooperative—some fine legal maneuvering there. Basically, they've gathered all the contractors needed to rapidly throw up an entire development. That way, they have dedicated contractors who can hit the ground running as soon as the first bulldozer moves in. My suspicion is that everyone in that firm has invested in buying the land as their share in the business. If Mayor Block owns all those sheep farms surrounding your land, he stands to make a substantial killing."

Titan Surveyors wasn't on the old list from his father's files. Emmitt Blue was. She'd not heard of Titan before she'd met Emmitt at the lake, but they were on the Lakeland list.

"Do all these companies know they'll be buying the land by any means necessary? I'm not liking the looks of this, and I only understand about half of what you're implying. Stephen Stockton is listed as an investor. Your adoptive father is not a contractor. I guess he brings his legal services to the table?" Evie watched Jax's aura as she handed back the papers.

It was still red but not as tightly controlled. He was reaching explosive. She thought that, for a change, she wasn't the reason.

"And he could be bringing the land in Loretta's inheritance to the table." He looked grim. "How did the kid take the news about needing her DNA to identify bones?"

"She was interested in the process, but I found her crying in her room.

Her aura is almost the exact opposite of yours. She's open, caring, honest, generous, communicative, and more clairvoyant than her bubble-detector indicates. I think she enhances our gifts, allowing me to see her father even when he was disconnected from his remains. I don't think she's crying for herself so much as for her parents, who may have suffered and will never grow old. I'm pretty sure she'll do whatever it takes to find their killers, so DNA is no problem."

Jax wrinkled his nose, presumably at her woo-woo description, but he didn't argue with her conclusion. "I want to believe if those are their remains in the lake, that they accidentally drowned at an inconvenient moment. It's bad enough that we're looking at fraud in the deed books. Imagining a killer on the loose. . . seems far-fetched."

"We might never know." Evie wanted to leave it that way, too, but if the town harbored a killer. . . he might strike again. She changed the subject. "What about Ariel's belongings? Does someone need to fetch them?"

"Roark and Reuben are watching Stephen's house. They have keys. Once the coast is clear, they'll take in boxes and carry out everything in her room except the furniture." He rubbed his brow. "I have no idea if that's the right thing to do or not."

"If Ariel is afraid of your father for some reason, her departure might set him off," Evie concluded. "Or will he even notice?"

"If he's looking to control me, he'll notice eventually. I need to figure out why my staying here is agitating him. I don't think anyone else could have known passwords to transfer that Cayman account into my name and set me up for a fall. He's the one with the Post trust passwords—unless we've been hacked. Why would he do that?" He spun around to his computer and typed a message.

Evie reluctantly returned to her feet. He had work to do, and she only knew enough to be dangerous. But she was the intuitive, not Jax, and her deduction skills shouldn't be ignored. "Do you know anything about check kiting?"

He continued typing. "Where did you pick up that term?"

"I worked for an accountant once. I'm trying to recall how it worked."

"Writing a check without funds, depositing it in another account, withdrawing the cash before the bank realizes the check is no good. Doesn't happen much anymore with stricter banking laws."

"Is there another term for it when we're talking borrowing from Peter to pay Paul with other people's accounts?"

He spun around to stare. "Construction companies do it all the time—we talked about that. It's illegal, especially if you don't perform the work. That's why John Post sued Blue Construction."

"But what if you *do* perform the work? You have a large debt, win a lawsuit, use the client's proceeds to pay your own debt, pay the client with the proceeds from the next suit. . ."

"And you're always one lawsuit behind, so if you lose one or more suits, there are no proceeds to pay the clients you've robbed. Illegal as hell." His mouth tightened in a grim line. "What are you telling me?"

"I think there was a reason your biological father had years' worth of miscellaneous construction company files in his desk and that they all got filed away when he died."

Evie hated to hit a good man when he was already down, but she had to protect Loretta. She sure hoped she was right in judging Jax as a good man.

Twenty-one

JAX WATCHED EVIE HUG A SADLY SUBDUED LORETTA BEFORE sending her off to school on Monday. After the visit to her old school, the kid now had a closet full of pricey clothes but chose to wear jeans and a T-shirt, presumably like the other kids in her public school. A Harry Potter doll stuck out of her backpack.

"Should I hire a therapist?" he asked anxiously once the kid was on her way. "This all has to be hard on her." The death of their parents had hit Ariel with a double whammy from which she'd never recovered, even with counseling.

"I asked. She refused. Loretta is strong in ways it's hard to understand. I think she needs to feel helpful. Give her a task, and we can hope she'll perk up." Evie returned to scrubbing pans.

Huh. Jax eyed Evie busily scrubbing pans—the task she'd chosen to stay useful? After following up on the bombshell she'd exploded last night, he'd found enough ammo to destroy his mental blocks about looking into the firm's and Stephen's finances.

Insanely, it seemed he had accepted that Evie's abnormal talents and skills had relevance. Which meant Stephen could be in deep shit. If they were both wrong. . . he'd accept the punishment.

Right or wrong, she shouldn't be scrubbing pans. Picking up his phone, he finally remembered to punch in a text to his secretary to locate a cook for

Loretta. He could add chauffeur to the kid's employees, and it would still be cheaper than that exorbitant school.

If he got fired, he wouldn't be able to pay a secretary or his team.

"How good would you be at selling real estate?" he asked, trying to think of a better means of employing Evie's people skills.

"Truly awful," she replied without giving it a second thought. "I couldn't pass the licensing test, couldn't do the paperwork, and frankly, I'd not be able to sell a balloon to a kid. It's not in me to hold back vital information like *The balloon is gonna pop, kid, and if you don't pay attention, it's gonna fly off.*"

"But you admit to playing with the truth all the time. That's all sales is— telling people what they want to hear. And you'd be particularly adept at knowing what they want." He thought. He still didn't have a good grasp on how she leaped to her conclusions, but scarily, she hadn't been too far wrong yet. If there were bodies actually in the lake. . . He'd have to decide if she had paranormal information or if she knew a murderer.

"I do drama to make people *understand* the truth." She gestured at the kitchen and spoke in a clipped, professional voice. "And here is the kitchen, my friends. Dating back to the turn of the last century, the plumbing and electricity were recently updated in the 1960s, probably to the tune of the Beatles. You can imagine Beetlejuice dancing over the kitchen counter as you pry off half a century of linoleum and sand genuine walnut floorboards."

Jax snickered. "You'd have a lot of happy customers—eventually. But I guess you wouldn't be good at producing videos and websites. The business has gone high-tech these days."

She shoved pans back in their proper places. "I learned to use Val's computers. If I could afford a phone, I'd learn that too. I'm not completely challenged. Technology simply isn't who I am. If I'm looking at a phone screen, I'm not noticing your expression or your aura or that you used a dash of aftershave this morning and you're wearing your lawyer clothes. I could let you head out to confront Emma Blue and the mayor without giving you a head's up and suggesting you take me along as a diversion. If I want to be oblivious, then a career in real estate involving technology would make sense."

"I may be wearing these clothes because I'm returning to my office," he reminded her, even though she'd totally nailed his itinerary for the morning.

"You didn't pack your computer or a bag of any sort. You have your walking shoes on and not your fancy polished office ones. I have to perform my dog walking duties right now, so unless you're checking out the pond first, I can't accompany you to the courthouse or city hall until later. Not that you meant to ask me anyway. Have you heard from Ariel?" She removed the apron saying *Many have eaten here, few have died,* and tossed it over a chair to dry.

"I don't expect anything more exciting at the courthouse than working through rolls of microfiche. Now that I know what to look for, I'll gather copies of the conflicting deeds and confront Stephen—after my team assures me that all Loretta's accounts are safely under lock and key, and he can't blackmail me."

Jax scowled at his interfering hostess. Underneath her apron, she wore emerald green and yellow in an outfit little better than a swimsuit. It was hot and he appreciated the view, but so would every other male in town. "There is nothing we can do about Loretta's parents. That's police business."

She beamed sunnily. "Of course it is. I'll just have a word with Sheriff Troy when I take his pug out later. Have fun with the microfiche."

"It was much easier when the only women in my life shared my bed and nothing else," Jax muttered, refilling his coffee cup and leaving her to taunt the town in short shorts barely covering a bodacious booty.

Carrying his coffee in a travel mug, Jax strolled downtown in the relative coolness of early morning. The place was small enough that Evie's house could be considered the suburbs, even though she was only a few blocks from the main drag. Since his goal was on the far end of Afterthought, he had a pleasant walk past her mother's shop, the café, the hardware store, a flower garden in an empty lot, a tearoom, and a line of offices for the lawyers and other businesses associated with the courthouse. The other side of the street wasn't much better.

But for city dwellers looking for cheap housing and safe streets, Afterthought would look idyllic.

Knowing the location of the registrar's office now, Jax entered the back door of the courthouse and went right in. Emma Blue looked up a little warily but pushed her glasses up her nose and glanced at another customer.

Jax studied the big older man leaning against the counter as if doing no more than passing time. He didn't recognize the face, but judging by the jeans, work boots, and company shirt, he was with a construction firm. The name Titan was imprinted on the back of his work shirt.

Emma came to the counter to greet Jax. "You found the property you want to build your ice cream shop on?"

He'd forgotten that convenient story. He suspected she knew who he was by now, but he nodded as if agreeing. "That's not why I'm here today, sorry. I need to look up a few deeds, if you can direct me to the right files?" He showed her the deed numbers, not the deeds.

She whistled. "Those are oldies. If you're lucky, they'll be on microfiche. Some of those files were too old to even film. Come on back, and I'll show you the drawers and the machine." She glanced back at the other man. "Emmitt, I'll see what I can do when I have a minute."

Emmitt, her brother? Was this the Emmitt Blue who owned the construction firm his father had sued decades ago? Jax tried not to look too startled but surreptitiously watched the other man as he removed himself from the counter and lumbered out. What kind of favors could a clerk in the registrar's office perform for someone who worked at—or owned?—a construction company? Although, wasn't Titan the name on the surveyor's work orders? Bells chimed.

He texted Roark with the name Emmitt Blue and Titan, then settled in with headache-inducing piles of film.

LORETTA WAS HAPPILY FINISHING UP HER BOOK REPORT ON *THE Sorcerer's Stone* when the principal entered the classroom, looking worried. She handed a folded note to Mrs. Wright, stopped a moment to listen to Loretta's report, smiled, and departed.

The principal's bubble was transparent, but there had been a *worried* aspect to it. Or maybe she thought that because the lines on her forehead had been troubled. Whichever, Loretta was already anxious by the time Mrs. Wright gestured her over to her desk.

"Here's a hall pass for the principal's office. Your guardian is waiting for you." Mrs. Wright looked as cheerful and unconcerned as always.

Mrs. Wright thought Loretta's guardian was Evie. The principal might be concerned that the person in her office *wasn't* Evie. Why would Jax come looking for her?

Loretta stopped at her locker in the hallway and picked up her backpack. If she had to run, she wanted her books and Harry Potter. She donned a ball cap she'd found on Evie's hall tree. No one checked her hall pass as she slipped outside and past the principal's windows. She tried to see in but the angle and sun and blinds were all wrong. She didn't see Jax's Jag but a long black sedan sat in the bus parking zone.

She could walk back to Evie's, but anyone could find her there. She didn't think she wanted to be found until she knew who was looking.

Climbing had always been a useful tool. Skirting around the school building, she found what she needed. With the help of an overturned bucket, she reached the lowest branch of a tree that overhung the flat school roof. It was only a one-story building, so that was an easy climb. Once up there, she ran around the edge until she saw the parking lot. The car was still there. No one was out looking for her yet.

She wished she had a phone to call Evie, but then, Evie didn't have a phone either. She was probably out by the pond walking dogs. Loretta decided Jax had to buy them phones once she came down.

She shouldn't be so suspicious, but her parents were *dead*. Both of them, at once, and probably not on their yacht. She knew Evie thought they'd been killed. That was pretty awful scary, so Loretta didn't plan on taking any chances. Harry Potter got in trouble when he did dumb things like trusting people. More scared than the first time she'd run away, she sought one of the cameras Jax's team had to have installed up here.

Right over the entrance, of course, just below the roof line. Leaning way over, Loretta turned the camera up and made an awful face into it. Then she pointed down at the entrance. She didn't think they'd bother with microphones way up here, so she didn't bother trying to explain.

Confident she had done all she could, she sat with her back to the wall, dug into her backpack, and found her lunch. She didn't want to die hungry.

It didn't take five minutes for Roark's van to roar into the parking lot. She recognized the noisy muffler. Munching an apple, feeling a smidgeon better, she leaned over and saw the sheriff's car following the van. Huh, had the guys been speeding or had they actually called for help? When Roark and Reuben jumped out of the van, she waved.

They saw her at once. It felt like a ton of bricks had been lifted from her shoulders, and she hastily wiped away her tears. She could be brave, if needed, but she really liked not being alone.

Reuben ran for the back of the school before the sheriff could climb out of his car. To Loretta's delight and concern, she saw Jax jogging down the street. He only needed a camouflage uniform to look like a military commando on TV. So if it wasn't Jax in the office, who was it?

Reuben strode up behind her. "This ain't Bubble Witch, girl. Whacha doin'?"

"This ain't the ghetto, boy, whacha think I'm doin'?" She liked Reuben, but he needed to get over himself.

"You don't call nobody who looks like me *boy*, got it?" He watched over the edge with her, not sounding particularly peeved. A man wearing a bone in his topknot ought to be scary, but he wasn't.

"Sorry, but you called me *girl*, so it seemed fair. I didn't think it safe to meet anyone driving that car and calling himself my guardian. Who is it, do you know?"

"Yeah, that's Jax's adoptive dad. Want to hear the fireworks?" He flicked on his phone just as a pudgy balding man stomped out of the school.

Reuben apparently alerted Roark that he was with her, because his partner climbed back in the van, out of the line of fire as Jax confronted his father. Loretta knotted her fingers into fists, hoping she hadn't caused a whole lot of trouble. She liked Jax, even if he didn't believe in bubbles.

Reuben put the phone on speaker and let her listen. These guys had mics everywhere.

"What the hell do you think you're doing, Damon?" The older man pulled a cigar out of the handkerchief pocket of his coat. "This damned school can't even find the kid. She needs to be in a place with security. And where the hell is Ariel? She didn't run off on her own."

"Loretta *is* in a place with security. That's why you can't find her." Jax wasn't even breathing hard. He snatched the cigar from his father's hand, flung it on the parking lot, and ground it with his shoe. "Doctor says you have to cut these out. And Ariel did run on her own. She caught a taxi. What did you do to scare her?"

"I didn't do *anything*! What the fuck is the matter with you these days? I'm trying to take care of the kid and your sister and you, whether you want to believe it or not. Have I ever done anything to convince you that I'd do otherwise?"

"His bubble is too far away for me to see," Loretta said with regret. "But it was pretty small when I saw him last time, and he's using bad words. Is he a bad man?"

"If bubbles are souls, he's too rich to have one." Reuben shrugged and sat on the roof's edge where anyone could see him.

Loretta pondered being rich in money but poor in bubbles as Jax and his father fought.

"To start with, wanting to take Loretta out of a school she loves and put her in one she hates is not *taking care* of her in my lexicon. I don't know what you did to scare Ariel, but transferring Loretta's funds to the Caymans, then putting them in my name scares *me*."

Reuben whistled. "Jax got more guts than sense."

Loretta swelled with pride just a little bit that Jax used his guts to protect *her*.

"I did it to keep all of you safe!" Stockton shouted.

Then without explaining, he stalked off to the long black car.

Very weird. Now that the danger was over, Loretta handed Reuben his phone and headed for the tree. "I want a phone too. You won't always be around to lend me one."

"They're tools of the devil, kid. You'll have to ask Jax." He climbed over the edge first and helped her down.

Jax met her at the bottom of the tree, caught her in his arms, and gave her a big hug. "When the guys sent me that photo of you grimacing into the roof camera, I turned gray. Don't ever do that again."

Wiggling a little in happiness that he held her just like a dad should, Loretta glanced dubiously at his buzz cut. "Your hair isn't long enough to see gray. Are you going bald?"

"I am not bald, unless you cause me to lose my graying hairs. Now promise me next time that you'll talk to a teacher instead of running off! They've all been told to watch out for you." He hugged her again and set her back down.

"Then they should have called Evie before they called me out of the class-room." Loretta looked at him accusingly. "We need phones."

To her absolute and utter amazement, Jax gestured at Reuben. "See that they get phones or I'll be both bald *and* gray."

Then taking her hand, Jax dragged her back toward school. "No cookies for you when you get home. When I tell Evie what you did, she's likely to rope you to a post."

Loretta almost skipped beside him. It was almost like having parents again.

Twenty-Two

"WHY ARE YOU LETTING THEM DIG UP THE LAKE?" A MALE VOICE roared into Evie's ear.

She scratched Psy's head, held out the shop's old-fashioned phone receiver so she could contemplate it, and tried to recall the name behind the voice. It took a moment, but high school eventually returned to her. "Toby? After all these years, you finally call to yell at me?"

"The cops are digging up the lake! That's a delicate ecosystem out there! You have to stop them. That's the last place gopher frogs have been seen this far west of the coast. They're endangered!"

"Well, the *pond* and all of Witch Hill are endangered if your father has his way. Go yell at him. I can't stop the cops." Evie spun on the counter stool and admired the rainbows of light dancing on the walls through the crystals she'd hung on the front window. She had to unwind the other way to prevent running out of cord. "Or call the governor and have him stop them, although I don't recommend it. I just laid a pair of ghosts to rest out there, and they're likely to come back and haunt me if their bodies aren't found."

"Just get your family over there protesting in all their craziness. I'll call journalists. Let me know when you're—"

She remembered why they didn't make a good couple. "Don't you dare hang up on me, Toby. I'm not a naïve teenager you can order around anymore. Frogs are *not* more important than murder investigations. My family is not any crazier than your father is greedy and selfish. And you can start your own danged protest march. I prefer to nail your underhanded pig of a father to a wall for trying to steal my family's land." With wicked delight, she slammed the receiver down. She could really get into slamming phones. Who needed a stupid cell phone?

He rang right back, of course. She didn't answer.

Tobias Block had been the coolest kid in school. He'd had a motorcycle the instant he'd turned sixteen. Long blond hair, shoulders twice as wide as his hips, football star, rich, the works—and he'd dated her for about all of two seconds after she'd turned sixteen and grown big boobs. Then he'd gone to college and she'd never heard from him again.

He'd been her first taste of male conceit. Not necessarily the last, but the first was the one that counted. And the troubling part was—Toby was actually a good guy, if his aura was to be believed.

And then Jax with the angry killer aura strolled in, and she was pretty sure he was a good guy too. He eyed her with interest as she answered the blaring phone by removing the receiver and letting it dangle on the far side of the counter with Toby's voice still barking orders.

"New means of talking to ghosts?"

"Old boyfriend. He says they're digging up the pond and endangering the gopher frog. I don't suppose the cops care?" She didn't want to hurt the frogs, but she couldn't abandon the Posts either. Life never happened in black and white. One was always left choosing the paler shade of gray.

"Old boyfriend?" With a malicious look in his eye, Jax picked up the receiver and spoke into it. "If you had any brains, you'd hire a lawyer to protect the frogs. I'll send you my fee schedule, if you like. Nonprofits get a special discount." He handed the phone back to her. "He hung up."

Evie laughed. "That's what he does best. Have you talked to your sister this morning? Pris says she established a link with her and doesn't sense any disturbance. She didn't try to go in. Did your team fetch her clothes?"

"As far as I'm aware, Ariel is fine and well supplied with clothes. It's Loretta you should be asking about. Your gossip network must not be working. Did you stuff Mavis in a trash barrel? Shoot the raven? Do you need a cell phone to keep up? The kid thinks you do." Obviously enjoying himself, he set the window crystals swinging.

The rainbow collision almost did her in. Annoyed, she came out from behind the counter to stop the spinning. "I've been out walking the dogs and keeping an eye on the pond. They gave up on divers, and they're trashing the low end with heavy equipment. I hope the frogs move to the other side. What did I miss?"

After Jax explained Loretta's flight, and his consequent confrontation with his adoptive father and boss, Evie covered her mouth and returned to circling on the counter school, contemplating the implications. She opened her inner eye as she did so, but she really didn't need to verify that he was both furious and confused.

"Can he fire you? Does this mean Ariel can't go home?" She wanted to run to Loretta, but it sounded like the kid had handled the situation with intelligence. Evie thought her maternal instincts might need a little work if she thought it was okay to escape to a rooftop, though.

"Stephen can probably ask that I be fired, but the other partners will want evidence of wrongdoing, and he can't easily provide it now that I've switched out that Cayman account. But insubordination is a hanging offense, so I'm walking a fine line. I'm going next door to grab lunch. Want me to bring something back?"

She had his number now. Jax brushed off the fight as if it were nothing, but he was seething. Cooling him off wouldn't be easy.

"Bring me a milkshake. Gertie can't poison that. What do you plan to do about Loretta?" Her fingernails bit into her palm as she waited for an answer.

"Buy phones for both of you, I guess. I'd rather ship her off somewhere safe, but she'd only run away again. She needs to be sent to her room without cookies. The sight of her up on that roof. . . I'll get the milkshake." He strode off without finishing that loaded statement.

Evie feared they'd taken two steps back to where she'd plotted her own team to counteract his. They needed to work together but not if he kept rejecting what she could bring to the table. Jax was hardheaded and refused to accept the paranormal, because it only led to conjecture and theory, not hard evidence. She was starting to see the fallacy in believing she could be a detective.

She might call in Orbis Jr., but what good would it do to know twenty-year-old papers held trauma or anxiety or whatever? She'd learned all the spectral Posts had to offer, and that wasn't enough. Auras might tell her of potential villains, but they didn't stand up in court. How did one find a killer and a thief? She didn't even know if they were the same person, although it would make sense that anyone who stole deeds and land might want to remove people owning that land.

And how did that tie into Jax's adoptive father finagling Loretta's accounts? And warning him to stay away and take Loretta with him? Surely Stockton wasn't a killer! He was too old and set in his ways.

Becoming a detective was definitely not a good idea. She just wanted a real job, one where she commanded a little respect for her abilities, such as they were.

Apparently sensing her distress, Psy leaped into her lap and batted her hand to scratch him. Once his itch had been satisfied, he climbed on the counter, curled around the crystal ball, and uttered a commanding *Maaavvv*.

"Mavis? You want me to call my mother to read my future? Not happening, old boy." Evie spun some more. Crystal rainbows bounced around the room. "I need cold, hard evidence, not theories."

Lakeland Development needed the land at Witch Hill.

Someone had removed the deed owned by the family trust from the registrar's office, apparently along with the trust tax payments. That returned all the deeds to their original owners from decades ago. If tax notices had been sent to dead relations—they'd been returned to the courthouse.

The county now wanted to auction off the individual plots for back taxes —which would put Witch Hill in the developer's hands. All that had to happen at the courthouse. The mix-up could have been a computer glitch. Evie was fairly certain it wasn't.

If she blotted out all the other complications of contractors and lawyers and bank accounts, the problem boiled down to land. Could the *city* mayor order the trust deeds removed from *county* files? Mayor Blockhead had invested all his real estate in Lakeland and stood to gain from buying Witch Hill, so yeah, if there was a will, there was probably a way.

She didn't like to think Toby's father could kill, but after the mayor condemned a trailer park for a pharmacy that never got built, she could see him committing fraud to get what he wanted. The mayor had grandiose dreams of turning Afterthought into a suburban oasis where he could buy and sell houses for the rest of his life. So he was her main suspect.

When Jax returned with her milkshake, Evie had her laptop set up on the counter. "Explain how this deed thing works. We know we have the original deed for Letitia's small share of the family land from John Post's desk. But the deed transferring all the other lots into the trust isn't recorded at the registrar's office?"

"Right. I'll guess Val holds the original trust deed. We need that and the trust agreement if we go to court." He set the carry-out bag on the counter and produced sandwiches and fries. "I checked the microfiche this morning. The deed numbers on the tax notices are for the original individual plots in the name of folks I'll guess are long dead. I assume your family never bothered with probate courts and changing titles or anything normal people do? Until the trust came along, anyway."

"We simply know who owns what." Evie waved a dismissive hand. "Knowing my family, they've owned Witch Hill since the 1600s. Maybe no one had pieces of paper. I never saw tax notices in my mother's name except the ones for her property in the trailer park and the shop. They had her name on them because she bought them. I doubt that Witch Hill was ever in her name, but it was quite possible she simply went down to the courthouse and handed them a check every year for her family's plot on the Hill."

"Without probate, any notices would have been addressed to corpses but presumably delivered to the address on the deed. Except no one lives out there anymore." He dug into his sandwich.

"But these new notices were addressed to each of us individually. What happens to the tax payments the bank made in the name of the trust?" Evie tried a fry and deemed it acceptable.

"No record of the trust deeds in the registrar's office, remember? You didn't let me finish." He grabbed a fry while he organized his words. "My team hacked the mayor's realty company's files. There is no particularly good reason for a normal realty company to keep deeds. That's for the mortgage company's records. But for reasons unknown, the mayor has compiled neat spreadsheets of lot numbers, addresses, last known owners—not corpses— and deed numbers. He does *not* include the trust as owner of the Witch Hill lots. It's as if there is an alternate filing system, possibly adapted to your family's weird way of not doing business."

"Because the mayor liked knowing who owned what." Evie sipped her milkshake and pondered that. "He kept a private city file instead of the public county one."

"Nailed it." Jax yanked a bite off his sandwich as if starved.

"The tax notices came from the *mayor's office* and not the county then. They're fraudulent?" Evie stroked Psy, who sniffed her fries with disdain.

"Probably." Jax gulped from his soft drink before explaining. "Someone had to hide the trust deeds at the county office. I don't think the county can send notices from that old film, so there are computer files somewhere of city lots. If the county is using the mayor's spreadsheet, then that seems the reasonable place to start investigating."

"Are we saying the county registrar is in on the mayor's scheme? I suppose that's possible. All that crew over there is pretty tight with the town council. It's a real small county, after all. And now that I think of it, the current registrar is related to the mayor's wife. She's probably Toby's aunt."

Jax circled his finger to indicate that she wait until he finished chewing. After he'd had another swallow of drink, he corrected her. "*Anyone* with access to the registrar's office has access to those files. You cannot eliminate Emma Blue. And her brother was in the office today. He works for Titan Surveying."

"Out of Charleston. I looked them up after the run-in the other day." Evie spun her stool and sipped, her thoughts leaping like gopher frogs. "We may need to have a come-to-Jesus meeting with Mr. Blue. Except my family prefers Witch Hill under a full moon. When's the next full moon?"

The phone rang before she could look it up. Jax's phone rang at the same time. Stomach sinking, Evie reached for the receiver while Jax checked his.

"They're digging the bodies out of the lake bottom," Iddy informed her without greeting. "La Chusa says there are two."

Jax hadn't known the Posts well and was relieved when the sheriff told him the bodies weren't in any shape for identification other than through DNA and dental records. He gave them the dentist's name in Savannah that he had found in John's bank accounts. The sheriff wouldn't give him any other information, so Jax left Evie to handle Loretta while he sought out his team.

Evie had *known* there were bodies in the pond. He either started believing in ghosts or that Evie had known about their deaths. He couldn't cope with the idea of Evie being a killer. Not reporting what she'd seen. . . That was a better possibility than ghosts but didn't make sense.

An urgent message from Ariel had him cruising the lane to the rental property where Ariel was settling in. The guys had parked themselves in the woods surrounding the cottage. Reuben hailed him from the charcoal grill they'd set up. "Got any cold beers, by any chance?"

Knowing his men, Jax opened the trunk and removed a cooler of beer. "Does Ariel know you're out here?"

"We got a system, man." Roark swung down from the back of the van. "We text *Hi* when we arrive and *Bye* when we leave. She sends us a wave emoji."

"And what do you use for plumbing facilities?" Jax wasn't certain he wanted to know. These men had lived rough in mountains surrounded by enemy guns. They could survive anywhere.

"Dude, we use yours when you're not there. And Evie's weird cousin has a place just down the road. She's never home and lets us use the house if we leave her food. Better than scavenging from villagers." Reuben flipped a burger.

"You have no right calling any kettle black." As far as Jax was concerned, all Evie's cousins were weird. "Which cousin?"

Roark jerked his thumb toward the house. "The bébé wit da striped hair sunning herself in your sister's front yard. Ariel say she's allowed. I reckon they've got some freaky mental thing happening, y'know?"

"Ariel isn't psychic." But he should have guessed that Evie's family would figure out how to connect with his sister. He hoped that meant she might develop a support system here. "There have to be phones involved. Did the cable get set up with wi-fi?"

Jax popped a beer for himself. He didn't feel right keeping beer in Evie's refrigerator since the women so obviously didn't drink it. With Loretta in the house, maybe that was a good thing. Heck if he knew about parenting.

He'd have to return to his own place soon. He had to risk leaving both Loretta *and* Ariel in the hands of Evie and her family so he could go back to work. Leaving Loretta anywhere was a lot harder now that he knew her. And Ariel. . . He took another drink.

"Your sis hid in da bathroom while they installed cable. She been sending us all sorts of entertainin' info ever since. Tell us when you ready to hear about your old man." Roark took a pull on his beer and eyed Jax with jaded eyes.

Half-past never would be a good start, but Jax couldn't hide his head in the sand. As much as he didn't want to believe it, Stephen was complicit in this land deal beyond handling the legal paperwork. Had John Post told him about the deed showing he only owned a portion of the land? "Get together with Evie and keep your theories straight. Right now, we have a killer to catch. They've found two bodies in the lake. I want to know what the sheriff knows. Can you do that?"

"We've been doing that." Reuben slid a burger on a bun and handed it to Roark with a scold. "And dude, leave the boss alone. He doesn't want to be bringing down his dad just yet. It's uncool."

Mostly, Jax wanted Loretta safe from a killer, and he didn't think that was out-of-shape Stephen. Killing required physical activity. "So what are they finding in the lake?"

"Dat ain't no lake, man." Roark loaded up his burger with every condiment they'd brought out, then covered it in red pepper. "That barely qualifies as a pond. Judgin' from where they found da grave, look like it wasn't more than a mud puddle before the hurricane last fall."

"Evie said it's mostly runoff. There may be a small natural spring since she says it never completely dries up. You're saying someone dug a grave in the mud?" Jax leaned against his Jag and sipped his beer, picturing the pond as a puddle. "So drowning is out of the picture."

"Most definitely. Someone use one of them little landscape dozers to dig a grave. Da hurricane put 'em six foot under—for a while, leastways. Forensics don't have cause of death yet." Roark bit into his mile-high concoction and let the ketchup ooze down his fingers.

"Remind me never to invite you to dinner anywhere civilized." Jax knew R&R had multiple degrees and the sophistication to sit at any table. He could insult their manners without a qualm.

He wanted to wander up the lane and talk to Evie's cousin about Ariel, but he wasn't certain he'd understand the answers. "I assume we're narrowing the time of death to just before the hurricane hit. And the suspect has access to a landscape dozer, which could be almost any contractor in the whole damned Lakeland company."

"Also assuming Evie is right and the bodies are the Posts," Reuben reminded him. "You want a burger?"

"No, I just ate, thanks." Sipping his beer, Jax paced. "Based on the necklace Loretta found, I think we're safe in Evie's prediction. Loretta said she talked to her parents right after she returned to school the first week of September." Jax checked his phone calendar. "The Posts always called Loretta on Sundays. Last year, that would have been September 6th."

"I looked it up and da hurricane hit here September 10. That gives four days when nobody heard from them because dey was supposed to be on a yacht. Cops checked all that back when they went missing." Roark slugged back his beer.

Jax worked through his phone notes. "The Cayman Island account was set up September 9th. The yacht was discovered in the Caribbean on September 15th. Everyone assumed it turned over in the hurricane." Jax did a quick web search. "Except the hurricane hit the Caymans on the 6th, the same day they were talking to Loretta. If they left right then, the Posts had to sail *through* the hurricane to reach the Caymans by the 9th to set up an account. So they theoretically arrived safe, and the yacht turned over well after the hurricane had passed. They could have hit big swells in the aftermath on their return, I suppose, except their bodies are here."

Roark swallowed and followed up with the next logical question. "But if we assume they buried in a pond, then who set up da account?"

"Don't think you can set up a foreign account by internet." Reuben loaded up his bread, lost in problem solving. "Somebody who knew they were already dead had to have gone down there in their yacht, posed as Post, set up the account, then ditched the yacht at sea."

"Establishing a different time and place of death." Roark nodded as he stabbed an onion to add to the mess in his hands. "And a killer most likely had da Posts identification."

"So the Posts could have been in Afterthought on Sunday the 6th and got themselves killed pretty quickly. It would take time for their killer to drive to the coast, prep the yacht, and cruise down to the islands in a hurricane." Jax didn't own a yacht and didn't know how long that would take. But Stephen had a yacht and would know. He shoved that thought aside for later. "Or more likely, someone was down there already, setting things up—in anticipation of killing them? And the yacht was just tossed out later."

"Dat's premeditated," Roark said grimly. "I get having an argument, somet'ing happening, and they get offed. But luring them here to kill them and steal their money as well as da land? We're looking at someone who's done dis before."

That's why Jax had shoved all thoughts of Stephen to one side.

Jax's parents had skidded off the road one stormy night, possibly right after presenting evidence that Stephen had been robbing Peter to pay Paul, as Evie put it—because he knew that's what Ariel wanted to tell him. He'd already added up the numbers and checked the accounts.

Stephen Stockton had been running a Ponzi scheme for decades.

Twenty-three

AFTER EVIE HAD EXPLAINED TO HER FAMILY THEIR THEORIES about what *may* have happened with the deeds to Witch Hill, and who might be involved in the fraud, the mood inside Psychic Solutions grew grim.

"So we're trusting Jax to tell us the truth?" Pris twirled a curly strip of purple hair on her finger, indicating doubt. She'd arrived late, dusty and disheveled. "Ariel trusts him. I haven't quite got a strong line on her character, but her thoughts are crystal clear."

"Crystal peacemaker," Evie murmured from her perch on the windowsill. She'd prefer spinning on the counter stool but Mavis was behind the counter, laying out her tarot deck.

"What in heck does that mean?" Gracie asked irritably. "Someone has killed two people and is stealing our land. That's not sounding peaceful."

"Well, there has to be war before anyone can make peace." Iddy rubbed noses with the Siamese, then set him loose to prowl. "This sounds like war to me."

"If someone killed poor John Post over his land, then they might go after Loretta as well. And possibly us." Aunt Felicia studied the tarot spread her sister had laid out. "Swords, it's almost all swords. That can't be good."

"Upright five." Mavis tapped a lead card. "Winning at all cost. I played this with the mayor in mind. The Magician is in here, but he's surrounded by hostile swords. Dangerous."

Evie yanked at her curls and glared out the window, understanding some of Jax's frustration. "We already knew all that. We're simply merging what we know and feel about the people involved. And that's not *enough*. We need concrete evidence." If nothing else, Jax had taught her that.

Psy leaped up on the counter, knocking the cards askew. Mavis glared at the cat, who maneuvered the cover off her scrying ball. "It gives me headaches, cat. Why don't you tell Iddy what you've seen?"

Psy sat and superciliously licked his paw.

"He's agreeing with Evie." Iddy removed the cat from the counter. "I never heard a cat actually *think* about anything except his next meal or sunspot or whatever creature comfort he prefers. But Psy seems to be understanding Evie."

"Sweet," Evie said with dejection. "The cat I feed likes me, news flash. Can you tell what the mayor is doing right now? Or the sheriff? We don't even know for certain that the bodies belong to Loretta's parents." Although she was pretty certain they were. She just wanted solid facts before setting off on any woo-woo course. Not that she knew what action to take.

Her inability to accomplish anything was the reason she got no respect.

The room fell silent as Mavis caved to Psy's demand and focused on her scrying ball. "I see men gathering at the pond. I recognize the mayor and the sheriff, not sure about the others. They're arguing. There's a man with surveying equipment. And a fat old guy yelling. There may be others but they're not coming in as strong. There's fear as well as anger. And *Tobias*?"

Of course, Tobias would be there with his froggie protestors. The gathering was predictable.

"I wish you could tell us how much time we had," Evie said gloomily. "Sounds like a party and we should prepare."

"Soon." Mavis dropped the velvet cloth over the ball again. "When the vision is that strong, the parties involved are decided, and it's happening pretty soon. How do we prepare?"

"Excellent question. Depends on what we're preparing for. Catching a killer?" Evie realized that's what she really wanted. Jax could handle deeds and courtrooms and lawsuits. She didn't care who played what silly paper game. She wanted the killer who had taken Loretta's parents away too soon and left her an orphan.

She heard the protests rising around the room. Her family had grown lazy and soft these last years, while times were good. Confronted with an ugly future, they wanted to bury their heads in the sand and pretend someone else would take care of it—just as Mavis had. Remembering what had happened when they hadn't fought back then, Evie resisted the family's tendency to trust.

"Sage, ladies," Evie decided. Without auras or spirits to guide her, she had to fall back on known mayhem. A good old-fashioned mob had shaken loose rusty screws in the past. "Brooms. Hard to see torches in daylight, but rain is moving in. It will be dark early. Iddy, can you send La Chusa to tell us when the gathering starts?"

"She's already there. Someone is tinkering with the police tape, if I'm correctly seeing what she's sending. Do you have extra broom grass here or do I have time to go home?" Iddy wrinkled her nose as she glanced down at her jeans and wrinkled work shirt. "I'm not at my most impressive."

Her cousin *got it*. Evie grinned.

Before she could answer, Mavis took command. "Hats, at least. We need to be quick, before Loretta is out of school. I can bring the sage and extra broom for anyone who needs it. We should go home and prepare, then gather in force here. That will set off the gossip and give the trespassers time to worry."

"Cool. We haven't done a march since I was a kid." Gracie gathered up her purse. "This is totally worth using my half-day off. Here, in half an hour?"

"I hate hats," Evie muttered.

"More attractive than skin cancer," her mother admonished, bustling about, gathering sage and whatever other dried herbs she'd decided on.

"Warts. Witches should have *warts*." With a sigh, Evie stood up, wondering what one wore to a witch parade. She'd heard about them, but she hadn't participated in the one Gracie remembered.

"Those artists who painted witches with warts probably meant to symbolize the pustules from bubonic plague, which was the evil of their time." Unconcerned, Mavis headed up the stairs to her apartment.

Evie had set this insane plan in motion. She'd have to make the best of it, she decided as she jogged back to her house. Jax would take one look and run far, far away once he saw her family in action. That was probably for the best. She and Loretta needed to learn to deal with each other without outside interference.

But the niggling voice in the back of her head said she *wanted* to work with Jax. Since that wasn't happening. . .

What would a good witch wear to an execution?

Might depend on whether it was hers or a killer's.

TROUBLE. POND.

Leave it to Ariel to text incomplete sentences but use punctuation. How was she seeing the pond from this side of the hill? Better not to ask.

STAY INSIDE he texted back, just because he needed to acknowledge her warning. It wasn't as if Ariel would leave the house.

He showed his phone to R&R and climbed into his Jag. "You might want to monitor the pond, if you have the equipment. If nothing else, the TV news will pay for the video on the gruesome discovery of two bodies."

Roark laughed. "Don' go getting' yourself whacked. We'd be in jail in a week wit'out you."

"Evie's family will put you up. They just won't pay you." Jax whipped his car around in the lane and roared off.

He was a lawyer these days. Even in the service, he'd been a lawyer. He was trained to fight, sure, but he preferred courtroom brawls. It wasn't as if he *wanted* to investigate trouble—except Evie was most likely at the bottom of whatever was brewing. He didn't expect her to knit baby booties after hearing about the bodies. She'd had time to notify her entire family of their suspicions. He was probably lucky they weren't on the roof of city hall, hacking their way into the mayor's office.

He'd examine why he should care some other time. For right now, he listened to his fear. It had saved lives before.

Out by the pond, he pulled the Jag up behind the mayor's Escalade. His father's Lincoln was parked on the other side of the road, headed out of town. If nothing else, his father's presence indicated trouble for *himself*. He hoped that's what Ariel meant.

A Titan surveying van was parked way off the road, nearly hidden in the underbrush the cops had stomped on. The bodies had been carried off an hour ago. The black-and-whites had left with them, but the sheriff's car remained. What now? Surely not more bodies.

As he climbed out, Jax heard a mob of chanting voices. For a moment, he wondered if Evie's insane reaction had been to start a protest march—and then he remembered the gopher frogs. Right. He'd looked up the old boyfriend—the mayor's son had worked fast.

Not ready to let down his guard, Jax strolled over to check out the entertainment. He wasn't sure why his father had stopped to watch a frog protest march, but maybe they could verbally beat each other up some more, and he might learn something.

The once quiet pond path had been churned into a sea of dust and crushed grass, until it reached the edge, where a dozer had dug a muddy trench. The protestors circled in the trampled mud, avoiding the long grasses where the quails nested. Tobias had only summoned about a dozen of his pals, but they had their signs and chants already prepared and in action.

Police tape fluttered in the breeze, ignored by all. Jax shoved his hands in his back pockets and contemplated the scene from the slight rise he stood on. His cynical mind wondered if evidence was being trampled and if it was being done deliberately. Could Toby be protecting his father the way Jax was avoiding implicating Stephen?

The sheriff appeared to be arguing with the big burly man Jax had identified as the surveyor, Emmitt Blue. The mayor and Stephen were acting buddy-buddy off to one side with a couple of other men who might be town or Lakeland officials. A heated discussion appeared to be in progress. Jax wished he could be a little bird on their shoulders, then checked the sky for the raven. Sure enough, it circled, but he was pretty certain birds couldn't translate human finances. Would it pick up on fear?

And why the devil was he believing a raven did anything except fly over its territory?

A few more pickup trucks arrived. Maybe the drivers were the town council, out to investigate the damage done to property the town wanted to take back for non-payment of taxes. Not seeing any reason to descend from his safe lookout, Jax checked the road back to town—

And swallowed a hoot of laughter. In full witch's regalia, or a Malcolm facsimile thereof, a parade marched toward the pond. Against the darkened clouds, they almost created an ominous sight. He hoped Roark was filming this.

Grinning, Jax jogged down the path just to hear what the women had come to say.

He saw Evie first. She was wearing what was obviously a slinky-fitting

186

Halloween costume of Morticia Addams, except Evie was shorter and curvier. So she'd whacked off the trailing hem to form a jagged edge above her ankles. Not that anyone would notice anything beyond the curves spilling out of her low-cut neckline. At least she was wearing sturdy sandals instead of going barefoot.

Jax studied the abomination hiding her colorful curls. It looked like a fedora with the brim turned down to hide her face. She'd trimmed it with a black-and-green scarf that blew in the rising wind.

None of the others were quite so dramatically clothed. He didn't recognize most of them. He noted a few red-hat ladies with their garishly decorated bonnets, but mostly, there were a lot of black outfits. It looked like several old men were wearing black funeral suits with top hats. Several women had wrapped gauzy scarf ties around old-fashioned, wide-brimmed garden hats. That's when Jax noticed their other accessories—handfuls of dried weeds and broom straw tied to tree branches.

Besides the human factor, numerous dogs, and a cat in a carry-all over Evie's shoulder accompanied them, while the raven and a hawk flew overhead. He wouldn't doubt the presence of rabbits and possums, and he was pretty sure there were a few goats.

The broom parade numbers were greater than the Malcolms he knew and way exceeded that of the protestors. In their wake followed a stream of townspeople, presumably out of curiosity. Gossip was the lifeblood of a small town —and Evie's family knew it. Their drama was setting the mayor up for a fall. Jax had learned a few things about Evie's family since coming to town. Those costumes had nothing to do with being witches or fools and everything to do with commanding attention.

Ignoring the chanting protestors and arguing men, Jax left his post to meet the parade.

Evie looked wary but defiant. "You can't stop us. We're going to throw our deeds in the mayor's face in front of half the town. For once, I want a little respect for who we are and what we can do."

Jax wanted to kiss her, but he thought that might detract from the show. Instead, he replied in exasperation. "You keep telling me you get no respect, but take a good look around. Every one of these people here respects you enough to listen to you, even Sheriff Troy and the mayor. That's why they're huddled over there, arguing instead of laughing their heads off right now. People who *know* you, *respect* what you can do—and I speak that from experience. Your real talent is allowing judgmental strangers to underestimate you."

She frowned. "That's because I hate it when people think I'm a half-wit because of my looks."

"But people who believe you're harmless say things that they wouldn't say in front of anyone else. Go wave a broom under my father's nose and tell him you know everything he's hidden for years. He doesn't know you and he'll dismiss you, but watch the sheriff perk up and pay attention."

"You should be a trial attorney. You're as much into drama as we are." Evie said that with derision but quit scowling and directed her mob toward the officials warily watching their approach. "I'll just channel Val, shall I?"

Jax grinned. "You're too short, but she's a good role model."

She smacked him with her broom and marched into the trampled field, waving the stick high to direct her troops.

Twenty-four

THE SOPHISTICATED CITY LAWYER THOUGHT SHE WAS
respected. Evie almost snorted at Jax's odd delusion. But it put the puff in her
consequence to know a man of experience and intelligence believed it for even
a minute—especially when she looked like a midget Morticia the Clown. She
could hope he'd understand what she was about to do next and wouldn't flee
back to the city.

"Light your brooms, folks," she called to her troops. "And circle the
wagons."

She pointed at the city and Lakeland officials gathered by the pond. Not
all of her parade was female. They were an equal opportunity assembly.
Women weren't the only ones in town with grievances to air.

"Evangeline Carstairs, what the hell do you think you're doing?" Sheriff
Troy shouted, approaching despite her eccentric Praetorian guards waving
fiery brooms.

The thunderclouds were darker now, and the wind whipping the flames
created a nicely sensational effect.

"Holding a meeting to re-consecrate our property, Sheriff. We're here to
cast out evil." Evie shot a significant look at his fellow officials, who had
stopped arguing to glare at the interruption.

"It's not their property, Troy," the mayor predictably shouted. "John Post sold it six months ago. The permits have all been filed for the construction to begin."

Evie idly waved her smoking broom grass. The scent of sage was refreshing over the stench of bullshit. Now that her parade just about had the officials surrounded, she closed the net, walking past the sheriff until she was face-to-face with Toby's red-faced father, Mayor Blockhead. She tried not to look at Jax, who stood to one side, observing. She didn't want to see his laughter at her methods.

"Those *permits* were obtained over two dead bodies." She didn't raise her voice, forcing the men to shut up and lean in to listen. The stupid hat itched her head, but it probably prevented her from lighting her hair on fire. "The Posts *knew* they didn't own our pond *or* the hill. Who did they try to explain that to?"

"We have the deeds, young lady." The mayor looked as if he was about to have a stroke. "The Posts signed the sale papers for their lot, all fair and square. And tax notices have gone out on the remainder. You still have a few days to pay the taxes, but the land isn't worth what's owed. Let it go, Evie. The town needs development, not a mosquito-infested pond."

"You can't buy what wasn't theirs to sell. The Posts only owned the back hill. The pond and all the rest of our land are in a trust that would take all of us to sell, and *we paid our taxes*!" Evie cried over the rising wind.

Before the mayor could reply, the raven dropped on his neatly coiffed blond hair and flew away with his toupee. Block clutched his balding head and screamed obscenities.

"Someone hand the mayor a hat," Mavis taunted from her position near the pond, safely surrounded by Toby's protestors. Looking gobsmacked, the frog supporters forgot their chants and watched the raven fly away with the mayor's ragged patch of pride.

Tobias strode in and handed his father his ball cap. The mayor threw it in the mud and stomped on it.

Another time, Evie would call him on his rudeness, but she was trying to stay focused. "You still haven't answered a simple question, Mr. Mayor. *Who did the Posts talk to when they came to town?*"

"They *didn't* come to town!" the mayor screamed, obviously rattled out of his usual smarmy charm. He turned around to the other town officials caught in Evie's circle. "Let's go to city hall where we can discuss this without interruption."

Evie pointed out the obvious—the trench. "There's evidence that they most certainly were here."

Aunt Felicia stepped up with copies of all the documents they'd gathered. "We're much happier holding this meeting on their grave, so their spirits may see justice done." She slapped the mayor's nose with the papers. "The land is in a trust and these tax notices are fraudulent."

The day grew darker by the minute. Evie rather enjoyed the effect—and the cool wind. Her cheap polyester costume didn't breathe and was suffocating her.

The Posts had died here. Just because the mayor denied knowing of their presence, didn't mean no one knew about their visit. That person wasn't necessarily the mayor or Jax's father or any of the council. She had no *evidence*. She hated going blank when surrounded by tension, but she needed to see who was lying—

The mayor's aura glowed red with fury, with an overlay of gray that indicated deception and confusion but not necessarily guilt. Maybe he really didn't know the Posts had been here.

Jax's father puffed furiously on his cigar, obscuring his aura to some extent. But she saw the colors of guilt—except they didn't come with overtones of violence. Had the Posts died accidentally? Dammit, she didn't know *anything*. But Stephen Stockton knew more than he was saying.

She'd lose her hold on the gathering if she didn't shake herself back to reality. Closing her inner eye, she glared at Jax's father. "The Posts must have called you about the land. You're their lawyer. What did they say?"

She deliberately didn't look in Jax's direction but prayed he wouldn't interfere.

The older man belligerently bit down on his cigar, narrowed his eyes, then spoke curtly. "They were upset the last time I spoke with them. They wanted to talk with someone at Lakeland Development. I gave them a number. That was it. That's all I know, just as I told the police." He turned to the mayor and gestured toward the road. "Let's get out of here before it pours."

Evie's family circle closed in tighter. The mayor would have to shove them aside to leave.

Jax's voice rang out. "Sheriff, did the cops call Lakeland and find out who the Posts talked to?"

"Don't think so," Troy called back, producing his cell phone. "Anyone got Lakeland's number?"

"Evie, Honey says one of them is getting away." Her cousin Iddy pointed toward the opposite side of the circle from where Evie stood. Her cousin was holding the retriever's leash to keep the dog from taking chase.

Evie stood on tiptoe and found an older, bulky man in a work shirt heading for the survey van. A couple of black-clad men from her group followed on his heels. The circle tightened, closing the gap left behind, bringing her spooky congregation even closer to the men they'd surrounded.

Looking like a super-hero with his black T-shirt clinging to sculpted pecs, Jax took it upon himself to intervene on her behalf. He jogged over and reached the van first. Crossing his arms, he leaned against the driver's door. Evie heard him ask, "Busy man, Emmitt? Got someplace to go?"

Emmitt? Of course, *Emmitt Blue*, the Titan surveyor she'd chased away from the pond. Emmitt Blue, the contractor Jax's real father and John Post had sued decades ago for not finishing his jobs. Emmitt, whose twin sister worked in the deed registrar's office. . .

Her instincts tingled, and not in a good way.

Jax didn't budge from the van even though the Titan guy stood half a foot taller and half a ton heavier. "You wouldn't happen to own a landscape dozer, would you?"

"His son does. That's what we were talking about," the sheriff shouted over the wind as he punched in a number from a business card someone had handed him. "He pushed up that flood wall by the highway last fall."

Ranting about interfering witches, the balding mayor shoved his way out of the circle at the weakest link. Grannie Satterwhite staggered sideways. Pris caught the old lady before she fell, but the circle had been breached. Shrugging, Stockton trailed in the mayor's wake.

Evie's dubious hold on her suspects was fading fast. What would Miss Marple do? Throw out another vague clue and hope for the best, of course. "Mr. Stockton, did you know the mayor keeps a separate set of city deed books different from the county registrar's office?"

Jax's father halted and turned to glare at her.

Over by the van, Emmitt Blue grabbed Jax, apparently intending to lift him from the van. Blue was taller and heavier. The men from her group were elderly and not fighters. They simply waved their flaming brooms in agitation.

Torn between rushing to help Jax or holding the mayor, Evie swallowed and tried to focus on what she'd come to do—communicate.

"It's hard to perform a proper title search when a bunch of the county deeds has gone missing," she told Stockton and anyone who would listen. "Without that legal backup, that makes any tax notices coming from the mayor's office suspect." She'd probably get sued for slander. It wasn't as if the mayor would admit guilt.

"I know where he keeps his files," Toby announced, bless his pea-pickin' heart. "I'll send them to you. *Stop the frog depredation!*" He raised his sign for any cameras on site.

Right. He was practically standing on the Posts' watery grave and taking out his righteous indignation on his father. Despite his Hollywood-star looks, Toby had a very young soul.

The mayor didn't halt.

Easily distracted, Evie caught the action over in the back corner. While Emmitt Blue attempted to dislodge Jax from his truck door, Jax planted his right fist in the bully's soft gut. The uptight, by-the-book lawyer had just assaulted a man—because Evie wanted Blue halted?

The surveyor grunted and bent over. A swing of Jax's left fist connected with a stubbly jaw, and Blue went down with a thud, in a cloud of dust.

Evie tried not to gape or swallow her tongue. Would Jax be arrested? Lose his license? She glanced at the sheriff, who was looking irritated as he spoke into his phone, with his back toward the fight. She had to bring this gathering under control before someone got hurt.

"We are avoiding violence, gentlemen," Gracie admonished as the older men from the circle sat down on the unconscious surveyor. "This is a consecration ceremony, remember?"

"Separate set of books?" Jax's father stopped following the mayor and eyed Evie with suspicion. "Got proof?"

AT THE SOUND OF HIS FATHER'S VOICE, JAX SWUNG BACK TO EVIE. Stephen had escaped her circle, but he wasn't following the mayor. Hope soared that the man he'd trusted all his life would actually explain himself and clear his name.

"Look at the papers Evie's family is trying to show you," Jax called.

Instinct and training said he ought to tie up Blue, but assault and battery charges were bad enough without adding illegal imprisonment. He wasn't a police officer. "Their land is owned by a trust. They have the deeds, proof of taxes paid, and can sue anyone touching this pond."

He strode back toward Evie's circle and his frowning father, leaving Blue in charge of a couple of old codgers. He didn't like Blue but knocking him cold because he was trying to leave this weird scene wouldn't stand up well in court.

The sheriff was still on the phone. Evie's aunt waved the papers she'd been smacking the mayor with. Jax took the stack from her and sorted through them to show Stephen the dates on the deeds. Maybe this could all be settled rationally—except for the deaths of the Posts and the bank account in the Caymans.

From the road, a child cried, "His bubble is black and twisted!"

Startled, Jax swung to see Loretta running toward him, pointing over his shoulder. Her cry chilled him straight to the bone. The kid didn't need to be here to see this. He was already heading toward her before Evie's operatic screech carried over the rolling thunder. "Blue's fourth chakra is almost black. Get her out of the way!"

Not sparing time to look, Jax dived for his ward's small frame, taking her down to the ground in a roll that slammed his shoulder but protected her from whatever in hell Evie was shrieking about. He didn't question Evie's shouts when it came to Loretta.

Training set in. Running anywhere, anytime provided too big a target. Hiding in the terrain was safest. He tugged his ward into a stand of grass while she fought to watch.

Where was Evie? Did he need to go after her too? Heart racing, Jax held a struggling Loretta and peered up through the tall weeds. Stephen glared in his direction as if he were crazed. No one else but Evie was shrieking.

"Her bubble is a silver knife," Loretta sobbed in his arms. "I don't know what that means."

And somehow, Jax knew the kid meant Evie, even though he couldn't see her. He pulled out his cell phone, hit speed dial, and ordered, "Get armed and get down here now."

"Done, boss. Get the kid behind the flood wall. We're coming in."

Jax heard an engine gun and shouted over his shoulder, "Evie, get your ass over here where I can see you."

Keeping his head low, carrying Loretta, he tumbled behind the crumbling pile of mud that might once have served to keep the road from flooding. Overhead, lightning cracked—fitting.

Running from a danger he couldn't see, Evie dived behind the wall with him. Jax almost expired in relief—which proved he'd lost his mind. He wanted to grab and hold her as he had Loretta, but that wouldn't be conducive to clear thinking.

"Blue," she explained breathlessly. "No one is paying him any attention, but he knocked the Shepherd brothers off, and he's getting into his van. His aura is black and vicious. I'm afraid he may have a weapon in there. Now I know what a real killer looks like." She scooped Loretta from his arms and hugged her, keeping her back toward the danger and protecting the kid as he'd been doing.

Just last week, Jax would have laughed off a warning based on a black *aura*. Now, he had mental images of AK-15s gunning down an unarmed populace. He swore and lifted his head above the wall to find the van. Evie's family was scattering for the hills or the road, instinctively dividing to provide confusing targets. The town council simply looked bewildered at their abrupt departure. Seeing no threats, they were casually trailing back to their trucks.

The sheriff, blessedly, was shoving a protesting Stephen toward the road and his official vehicle.

Before they reached it, the Titan van shot from the shrubbery, a rifle protruding from the driver's window.

"Sheriff, down!" Jax shouted, just as the rifle barked. The sheriff and Stephen both went down. He couldn't tell if they'd been hit.

Evie placed two fingers in her mouth and emitted a piercing whistle.

A hail of flaming brooms rained down around the speeding van, causing it to bounce and swerve erratically. Hadn't he just seen the women running for the hills with their torches?

"How the hell did they do that?" Jax muttered as the rifle's next shot went awry.

"Gracie's talent isn't always useless. We owe her a fat steak. She'll be drained."

He didn't have time to question as his team's armored van roared into the field. So much for the frogs and quail. One expert shot from Professor Sharpshooter Reuben, and the Titan vehicle spun out, crashing into an old dogwood tree and snapping it like a twig. Like good soldiers, his guys were out of the van, armed, and racing for the enemy.

"Oh, they're not twisted anymore," Loretta breathed happily, peering over Jax's shoulder. "Roark has silver in his bubble! They're like knights with swords."

Dark knights with rusty swords, maybe, but Jax didn't argue the point. As Blue leaped from the disabled truck's cab, Reuben and Roark grabbed him, flung him to the ground, and disarmed him.

"They owed me!" Blue roared while struggling helplessly. "They all owe me!"

Thunder crashed and the first patter of rain hit the dust. Jax shuddered, fearing who Blue thought owed him. But that would come out later.

"You did it, babe," Jax said into Evie's ear over the roar of the storm. "You caught a killer."

He lifted Loretta in one arm and Evie in the other and rushed them toward the sheriff and Stephen, while his team kept their guns trained on the murderous surveyor.

Twenty-five

"I OUGHT TO SEND YOU TO BED WITHOUT SUPPER," EVIE SCOLDED, drying Loretta's hair after they'd both had a good shower. "You should have gone straight home after school."

She was still thoroughly shaken by the past hour's mayhem. People could have *died* out there. As it was, Jax's father had been wounded. But Jax and Loretta were safe because Jax had believed their weird warnings. He'd listened to black bubbles and fourth chakras and taken defensive action. That might take time to process.

"I *did* come home. There was no one here, not even Psy." Loretta tugged on her robe and sounded piteous. "I thought you'd all left me."

"You're such a liar." Evie hugged her anyway. "You know perfectly well that we wouldn't leave you. You just got curious."

"You could have been killed!" she wailed, flinging her skinny arms around Evie's neck.

That had been Evie's reaction, only in reverse—Loretta could have died in a hail of gunfire! She'd never come that close to death before. She hugged the kid back, reaffirming they were both living.

"I'll try not to die just so I can harass you for the rest of your life, but even if I did get killed, I'd come back to haunt you. And you have lots of cousins and aunts to annoy you the way I do. Dying really isn't bad. It's just graduating to the next level." Evie had never been inclined toward motherhood, but

197

she had to admit that hugs were reassuring, even if the child turned her hair gray.

"Well, don't graduate until I'm ready to go with you." Loretta indignantly pushed away. "Where's Jax?"

"With his father. He got hurt and they took him to the hospital." That could have been Jax or any of her family. It gave her cold shivers thinking about it, so she tried hard not to. It was hard to remain detached when facing death. She was trying to reassure herself as well as Loretta.

Evie took a comb to her ward's damp hair and began plaiting it into a single braid.

"Will they put the man with the black bubble in jail?"

"Definitely, if only for shooting at us. But I think they'll learn more now that everyone knows he's a very bad man." Evie wished she had bothered to examine Blue's aura, but he was such a bit player. . . It didn't make good sense. She hoped the sheriff got a confession.

"Supper's ready," Mavis called up the stairs. "There's so many of us, you'll go hungry if you don't come right down."

Evie sighed and tied a ribbon in Loretta's braid. "Do me a favor and distract them, will you? I'll tell you all about it later."

Loretta narrowed her eyes. "You'll tell me the whole story, even the bad parts?"

"Certainly not. Bluebirds and pumpkin coaches for you. I don't want you having nightmares. I need my beauty sleep." Evie dropped a gauzy tea dress on Loretta's bed. "Wear that, and I'll find you a tiara to go with it."

Loretta grimaced. Before she started on a tirade, Evie slipped back to her room. She'd yanked on jeans and T-shirt after her shower with just this escape in mind. And she'd grabbed clean clothes for Jax and stuffed them in a tote. Mr. Uptight Lawyer had gone straight to the hospital from the field, covered in mud and ticks, no doubt.

Opening her window, she climbed onto the porch roof with the tote over her shoulder. In half a minute, she was in her favorite tree branch and scampering to the ground. The thundershower had ended but the needles had her soaked.

She doubted Mavis would even notice her absence. Checking back to be certain Loretta hadn't followed, she raced out to the street where Jax's team waited.

Sometimes, all it took was free food and a shower to command loyalty. Good thing, since she couldn't pay.

"Take me to the palace, Jeeves," she commanded as the sliding door opened and Reuben helped her inside.

"Did you bring food?" Roark started the engine while eyeing her tote. "I could eat a cow."

"Cows are full of methane and manure. We'll make Jax buy us lobster. I've never had lobster." Evie studied the van's interior in the dim light. "Spooky."

"Well designed," Reuben countered. "All the requisite equipment for the well-prepared spy, plus sleeping quarters. And refrigeration." He opened a small panel in the cabinets lining the walls and produced a can of soft drink.

"Just big enough for hot dogs and beer," she said in admiration. "Generator?"

"Of course, plus solar panels on the roof. All we need are more clients."

"Especially if Jax gets axed from da firm," Roark said from the driver's seat. "This little episode today ain't nuttin' on da evidence he has against daddy-boy."

"Oh shoot, I was afraid of that. Have you worked with his firm long enough to get your detective licenses?" Sitting cross-legged in the narrow space between equipment, Evie took a handful of granola Reuben offered.

"We're not likely to get licenses for anything with our discharges," Reuben scoffed. "And who else would hire us?"

"Smart people with money. Jax will figure it out." She hoped. He'd been in a pretty grim mood when he'd taken off after the ambulance. "Does he know we're on our way?"

"Probably. Ariel's yanking his chains. Now there's a spooky lady." Roark swung the van into the hospital parking lot. "Sheriff posted a guard outside daddy's room. Jax is telling him it's a bodyguard."

"Stockton can't be that dumb." Evie leaned over the front seat to look for Jax's Jag. It was still here. "Blue is locked up, right?"

"Yup, and spilling everything he knows. If he's going down as a killer, he's taking everyone with him. Sheriff's radio is easy to hack. They're rounding up suspects right and left. Mayor won't like being charged with fraud on those tax notices. Whether or not he knew about the Posts, he had to have known about the land being in a trust. His son has already turned his computer over to the cops." While Roark parked, Reuben handed her a mic. "Here, stick this in your pocket. We'll hear fine and be ready if you need us."

"You're not coming in?" Evie studied Jax's friends with surprise.

"Stockton don't like us. We'll hear more if it's just you and Jax. And we can be ready if he spills more that needs looking into."

"Wow, now I'm a spy, too. Jax will be so happy." Cheerfully, Evie jumped down and marched off to the hospital entrance.

She had no particularly good reason to float on air, except that Jax had listened to her crazy and stopped the criminals. Her family might still need to sue everyone in the universe over their property. Jax would almost certainly be fired from his firm. A whole lot of hell was building in the mayor's office, and the ash would inevitably fall on her family. But she had no doubt that they'd caught a killer because Jax had *listened*.

She thought maybe it was confidence buoying her into the hospital and up the stairs.

Looking wiped, Jax sat in a recliner beside his father's bed, his head back and his eyes closed. She admired the dark stubble on his sculpted jaw. He was still covered in mud and grass. It was a good look on him, but it was a wonder the hospital had allowed him entrance.

Stephen Stockton seemed to be sleeping. He didn't appear quite so mean with an IV pumping into his arm and an oxygen mask over his face.

As Evie dropped the tote full of clothes next to Jax's chair, the phone in his lap lit up with a message. Given that the text was only three words, she figured it was from his sister, so she picked it up. **ASK ABOUT FATHER**

Evie grimaced. She assumed Ariel meant their biological father. That might be another nasty tale above and beyond the current one yet to be told. Without compunction, she texted back: **FEED R&R**

She loved the silence following a text. She was about to check and see if the hospital still kept patient charts on paper like in old TV shows, when Jax stirred and opened his eyes. He had such lovely warm gray eyes, although they clouded a bit at sight of her. Figures. Before she could comment, his phone lit with another text. **WILL DO**

"Will do what?" Sitting up, he scrolled through the messages.

"Ariel and I are communicating. You owe your team lobster. They're patiently sitting out there waiting for orders while starving." Belatedly, she recalled they were probably listening to every word. Oh well. "I brought clothes." She dropped the bag in his lap before he could complain.

"I think I need a shower before I work this out." He grabbed the clothes and abandoned her to the patient while he closed the door on the bathroom.

Intense, single-minded, ruthless when needed. . . She really didn't need a man like Jax around.

He may have lost his job because of her.

She studied Stephen Stockton's aura, but it was weak and as muddy as ever. He wasn't a person she would ever like. But Jax had respected him for a reason. She supposed she ought to learn why.

She pressed the button that raised the head of his bed. "I can tell you're awake, you know. I'm weird like that."

Stockton scowled beneath the plastic.

"When you go to jail for aiding and abetting a murderer, you need to promote Jax to partner so he can cover your financial tracks." Evie sat down on the end of the bed and smiled as if she didn't have a care in the world.

Only she could see the black cloud of denial and guilt rotting Stockton's soul.

When Jax emerged from the shower, Evie was sitting beside the bed, offering a spoonful of gruel to his father while a nurse kept an eye on them. The oxygen mask had been removed, and his father looked as if he'd chew nails if offered.

Jax didn't aim for the door but glared at the ridiculous scenario. "Good to know I'm not needed. I'll just head out for some of that lobster I assume the guys are chowing down on."

The nurse took one look and scuttled out.

"I want lobster, too. I've never had it. But it would be rude to eat in front of your father, so sit down and the two of you start talking, *now*." Evie scraped up the last of the clumpy broth and shoved it at Stephen's mouth—opened to protest.

"Or what, you'll scream?" Jax took the bowl from her, set it on the tray, then bodily removed her from the bedside chair to deposit her in the recliner. As he well knew, Evie weighed nothing. And for a change, she didn't fight.

"Or I'll kick you out of the house and sue for guardianship because a jackass shouldn't be allowed near a bright child like Loretta. Your father has information that will put a lot of people behind bars, but you have to get him out of his predicament before he'll talk."

Jax rubbed his head. He needed a haircut. He tried to process what she wasn't saying. "What in hell did the two of you talk about while I was taking a damned shower?"

Instead of answering him, Evie turned to his father. "We have evidence, Mr. Stockton. Jax and Ariel are just like their real father, very focused, do-it-by-the-book sorts. They have enough paperwork to keep the district attorney busy for a lifetime. Do you really want it all aired in court?" Looking like a cherubic pixie in damp jeans, she curled her legs up in the recliner, leaned back, and waited.

"Can't you put a lid on her?" Stephen asked petulantly. "I can make this all go away without involving anyone."

Ah, now Jax was starting to see the light. He turned the bedside chair around and straddled it. "Nope, not happening. I'm finishing up what my father started. Evie's right. Ariel and I have sorted it all out, how you paid off your debts and bought your partnership with the proceeds from that first big lawsuit you won. When the client came after you for the money, you used the escrow from the next case to pay him off. It's been going on for decades with no one the wiser, until recently, right? The cases aren't coming as frequently these days and demands are piling up. You have clients threatening to sue for non-payment, don't you? All you needed was a little extra cash from this development deal to buy some time. *You think I'll sit on that?*"

"There's no reason for you to get involved." Stephen winced as he shifted in bed.

Jax knew he was supposed to feel sympathy, but his adoptive father had only been grazed by the bullet. It was the mild heart attack and emphysema that had landed him in this bed—all brought on by his incessant smoking. "You have the information to lock up a killer for life. You'll probably go to jail as an accessory. And you don't want me to get *involved*? Loretta's parents died because of you and your shady partners!"

Stephen looked gray and old in his wrinkled hospital gown, with his thinning hair disheveled instead of in its usual hair-sprayed glory. His tobacco-stained hand reached for a pocket that wasn't there. "When John Post first came to me, he said his mother owned all that land and wanted to know what it was worth. I had no reason to doubt him. I made a few phone calls, learned the town wanted it for development."

He took a sip of water and stalled. Jax waited him out, not helping.

Grimacing, Stephen continued. "It was a simple business deal, bringing the right people together. I figured I could make Post and a lot of other people a bundle. My loudest debtors are contractors, easily held off with a dangling carrot. They were all gung-ho. I called in a few more and helped them put together Lakeland. They quit yelling for my head and started planning the development."

"And then Post discovered he didn't own the land after all," Jax added when Stephen didn't continue.

He nodded wearily. "I'm not sure what set him off, but he got spooked."

Jax was starting to believe *spooked* might be the reality and not a euphemism. If he believed Evie, her great-grandmother probably came back as a ghost to haunt him for selling the family land.

Stephen continued shakily. "John got his hands on some deed and asked Titan to tell him what it covered. The others had put up considerable stakes to buy the property on his promise to sell. We had cash in hand. But John wouldn't formalize the sale until he knew what he was selling."

"He visited Afterthought as a child." Evie spoke up quietly. "He recognized Witch Hill."

Stephen shrugged. "He thought he owned it all. After all the planning we'd done—someone told him he didn't. So he went there to talk to Emmitt and have him walk off the property. This is all on that chicken-shit surveyor. Emmitt panicked and called me when he saw John's deed. He's in debt up to his ears. This job would stave off creditors and put his company at the top of the list with big contractors, kind of a gift that keeps on giving. He kept raving about the deed not being the right one, that there had to be more."

Jax rubbed his nose and tried not to look at Evie. "So Emmitt conspired with the mayor to steal all the lots with an older deed and tried to get the Posts to agree?"

"I don't know what happened. All I ever knew was that Emmitt called and said the Posts had agreed to sell and were vacationing in the islands, waiting for the proceeds. I wanted proof. We argued. Emmitt pulled out the high card when he said he and the other investors would sue me and the firm for non-performance if I didn't sign off on the deal. I already had the Posts' signatures on the agreement-to-sell documents. I'd just been holding off while John satisfied his curiosity."

"But he didn't call you and say sell?"

"No, and I couldn't reach him if he was sailing. I needed my commission on the land sale to pay off my more pressing debts. Emmitt provided a title search and deed. When I received a message with the name of the bank where the proceeds should be deposited, I set up a cash transfer from Lakeland. After today, I'm guessing Emmitt must have stolen John's ID and e-mail and gone down to establish an account in the Caymans. I thought I was transferring the funds to John." Stephen fumbled for the water on the side table.

Jax held the cup for him while his soul crumbled. He'd been living a lie of privilege for years. He'd believed Stephen was there to take care of Ariel in the wealthy privacy and comfort she needed. If he'd taken her away sooner, would Stephen have sold the house, paid his debts, and not been in the grip of a greedy killer?

"But after you knew the Posts had disappeared and were most likely dead, you didn't do anything," Evie said matter-of-factly. "You could have reported it all to the police, but you didn't."

"I was trying to save my firm!" Stockton protested. "I was trying to protect Jax and Ariel. Once I realized the land sale money was in an account no one knew about but me and Blue, I changed the passwords and locked it up. I didn't know what else to do. Emmitt was the surveyor and claimed the deed was fine. The other investors thought they'd paid for the land. They had no suspicion of hanky-panky. I was the one Emmitt had threatened. I was the only one who was suspicious. They were busy organizing the start-up."

Jax closed his eyes and wished he could close his ears to what would come next, but his lawyer's mind already knew what had happened.

Stephen continued. "I thought I could use the funds to pay off my clients, get that monkey off my back, and then I could let the police know about my suspicions."

"That's theft, pure and simple. And then you tried to pin it on me by transferring your stolen gains to my name!" Jax tried not to shout but he was sitting on a mound of lies and couldn't shovel fast enough.

"That's just what was left after I paid the escrow funds to their owners." Stockton pushed the cup away and looked exhausted. "I wanted you to get Loretta away from this damned town before I did anything, but you wouldn't do it. I figured I could clear it all up later, but I needed something to hold over you to make you leave, so you wouldn't get involved. I taught you to listen to me, but you've not been the same since you came home from the service."

"You can brainwash a child but not a man," Evie said. "Jax may be loyal to a fault, but he has the ability to keep an open mind and question orders. I assume he got that from his father and not you."

"Evie, not now," Jax said wearily. It had been a long day. He knew he wasn't processing everything as sharply as he should. He just didn't think he could handle more. The funds in the Caribbean would have to go back to Lakeland's investors. He didn't know how much extra he'd need to replace what Stephen had stolen from them to pay his debts. He hoped there might be some means of paying people back and covering all this up—but not withholding evidence on a murder. That was one step too far.

"Yes, now," Evie said more sharply than he'd ever heard her speak. "Your father died after this man had him fired—for discovering his Ponzi scheme. You have no reason to be loyal to a thief and fraud."

"I had nothing to do with Franklin Jackson being fired! I didn't know he was uncovering my trail until afterward," Stephen protested, regaining some color. "The partners discovered your father was not who he said he was. I don't know what he was after, but his name wasn't Jackson, it was *Ives*, and he was from California, not Georgia. The credentials he gave us were stolen."

Jax flung the water glass against the far wall.

Twenty-six

BY THE TIME EVIE REACHED JAX'S TEAM, JAX HAD SPED OFF IN HIS Jag. Reuben offered her the last of the lobster Ariel had delivered to the truck. Evie was hungry enough to eat but upset enough not to enjoy it.

"Beans and rice are more my style." She folded up the container. "I guess the fun is all over, huh?"

She'd known Jax would have to go back to his real life. She just hadn't expected it to be so abruptly. But he'd been poleaxed. She certainly couldn't blame him for his reaction. His father hadn't been his father? Had used an alias?

"Did we ever tell you why Jax left the service?" Roark slowed down as they approached Witch Hill.

"Something about fraud in high places. There seems to be a lot of that going around." Evie studied what she could see of the pond. The thunderstorm had partially filled it but not enough to hide the broken grasses. Water seeped across the road from the break in the small embankment. She thought she heard a frog though.

"Way more fraud than us poor people will ever understand," Roark agreed. "But this involved selling military equipment for drugs and cash. We were arming the enemy so headquarters could buy whiskey and women and keep the troops high. Jax was in headquarters, in the legal department, when he received our report. He took the evidence to the highest command since our officers were involved. Next day, the MPs came in and found drugs in our tent. They had a witness who swore me and Rube sold him arms. They threw us to the locals, who staked us out in a desert hellhole where we baked. It took him a while to find out, but when he did Jax literally went ballistic."

Reuben rummaged in the restaurant bag and found a box of cookies. He offered them to her. "Because he had friends in high places, they wanted to keep him quiet. They offered him a tour of duty in some cushy place, thought he'd take the payoff rather than protect a couple of insubordinate scumbags like us. We were already classified as renegades with so many black marks against our names that we weren't ever getting out easy anyway."

"Jax recorded every bribe they offered," Roark said in satisfaction. "Then he took troops out to the desert hellhole and blew out the walls. He threatened our command with his recordings if they didn't send us home. He resigned his commission, sent all his evidence to DC, and came home with nothing to show for himself. He'd had high hopes of rising in the ranks and going into the diplomatic corps. Instead, because of us, he had to settle for a position under the daddy he tried to escape."

"And he's going right back to that firm now to put all the pieces back together again." With a sigh, Evie bit into the cookie—decadent chocolate chunky.

"That's the way we figure it, except with your mic, we heard what Stockton said. Jax will need us to find out about his real daddy. Give him time. He'll come around."

His real daddy—Jax wasn't actually Jackson, he was an *Ives*. Could Stockton be telling the truth? There wasn't any good reason why he shouldn't.

The house was dark and quiet when they returned. Jax's room had been emptied; his laptop and suitcase were gone. Reuben and Roark insisted on returning to their camp near Ariel, not knowing how much Jax had passed on to his sister, if anything.

Upstairs, Loretta was sleeping in Evie's bed. At least Jax had left Loretta to her, although once he had time to think about it, he might decide otherwise. By reading the denial in his stepfather's aura, she'd pushed too hard and brought disaster down on his head.

She didn't think she could have done anything else. She had to believe she'd been given this weird gift for a reason.

Changing into her nightgown and curling up beside the child who'd chosen her dubious protection, Evie vowed to earn the confidence Loretta had placed in her.

And that had to start with giving her security.

～

A WEEK LATER, EVIE HAD MADE A FEW STEPS TOWARD KEEPING that vow. Even though Jax didn't return, Ariel stayed. Roark and Reuben hung around, playing Bubble Witch with Loretta enough for them to develop a routine. Kids needed routines and people they trusted.

That wasn't enough. Loretta needed more than simple routine.

Evie was furious with Jax for not answering emails or calls. She was about ready to consider filing the fake guardianship papers when she picked up an envelope at the post office with the Stockton firm's return address.

"He's probably suing me for child endangerment," she told Honey as she walked the dog back to the shop. "Respect" poured from the café's speakers, but Evie didn't feel like dancing to it.

Respect wasn't enough anymore. She had plans. She just needed Jax to remember she existed. She'd thought she'd developed a rapport—with a military lawyer. What had she been thinking?

It was Saturday and the shop was busy. Loretta was arranging a shipment of Harry Potter books in the window. Evie unleashed Honey, pried open the envelope, and breathed a sigh of relief.

"He's not suing us," she announced.

Mavis glanced up from her customer and nodded happily, as if she knew what Evie was talking about. Loretta gave her a critical look.

Evie waved the enclosed check. "We need to open your bank account, tadpole. Want to buy a bike?"

Beneath the black-framed glasses, a grin spread across her ward's thin face. She jumped down from the window set. "We can both have bikes?"

Good kid. She didn't ask *how much* but if she could *share* her money. Evie gave her a hug.

"The letter says it's for your daily expenses, upkeep, and includes an allowance for your caretaker, which would be me, for now." She'd probably have to sue for a more formal arrangement. She'd save her *allowance* to hire another lawyer.

"Can we go to the bank now? Mr. Wright has Gummy Bears." Loretta turned politely to Mavis. "Will that be okay? Do you still need my help?"

Mavis winked at Evie. "You've done a brilliant job and deserve the rest of the day off. Hank has some nice bikes."

An hour later, they were peddling out of town on their new, used bikes. The fake guardianship papers would soon be safely locked up in their new lockbox, and Evie was ready to carry out her plans. Maybe. Somehow.

"Do you think Ariel will let us visit?" her Indigo child asked. "She must get lonely."

"I don't think she understands lonely quite the way we do. If you've never had friends or much family, it's hard to miss them." Admiring the dogwoods blooming in the woods, Evie wondered if Ariel was enjoying the view on the other side.

Someone had scraped up the mess at the pond and rebuilt the earthwork. One by one, rocks had started accumulating in an impromptu memorial where the bodies of the Posts had been found. Evie had checked with the mortuary, and a funeral had been arranged, presumably by Jax. If Loretta's parents were cremated, there would be room to bury them in the family cemetery. She'd made certain a name plaque had been ordered.

"But Ariel emails you sometimes, doesn't she? Isn't she our friend now?" Loretta's balance on the bike wasn't practiced, but she pedaled earnestly.

"As much as she can be right now. The guys made sure she had a connection to the security cameras so she can see us when we visit. We could bring a picnic out here someday." Evie steered the bike across the empty highway to the side road behind the Hill.

"Will Roark and Reuben be there? Can we visit them?" Loretta pedaled a little more vigorously.

"Let's see if we can surprise them." Probably not a good idea, but Evie still didn't have a cell phone.

As if reading her mind, Loretta added, "We can get phones now!"

"Don't like it, but you may be right. If you text me twenty times a day, I may drown mine, though, so be careful."

The kid made a rude noise. "Then I'll text you forty times a day. Is that enough?"

Evie laughed as they turned down the woody lane to Ariel's house—Loretta's actually. "You're too smart. Fifty, and it's a deal."

The van was parked in its usual spot. The late April day was hot, so the guys had stripped off their shirts. Evie caught a glimpse of gleaming muscles, lean abs, and serious scars before they yanked on their tops.

"New bikes," Reuben crowed. "Now we'll have to find another hiding place."

"I've got one, if you're interested." Evie hadn't meant to break the news so fast, but the opening worked. "I've been thinking about it all week, but I don't have any way to reach you."

Roark stretched inside the van and pulled out a business card. "That's a lie. But to keep you from repeating it, here's all our info. And one for the bubble witch."

Loretta grinned and tucked the card in her shorts pockets. "Should I wear pink to be a bubble witch?"

"You get to make your own rules." Evie climbed off the bike and accepted a cold drink. "Take us back to town and let me show you something. See if you're interested."

"I take it you haven't heard from Jax either?" Roark pulled her aside while Reuben and Loretta loaded the bikes in the van.

"He had the firm send a check for Loretta, that's it. I'm guessing you're keeping up?"

"He knows us, so he's blocked us from everything at the office. We're just picking up what's happening at the sheriff's office. Stockton is out on bond. Billy Boy Blue is behind bars and spilling everything." He looked down at Evie, probably saw her grim expression, and nodded. "Blue claims it was an accident. He was showing the Posts the lot lines, and they somehow fell in the pond, and he doesn't swim and yadda yadda. They're waiting on an autopsy."

"Which will probably show shovel blows to the back of the head. That part is going around already. The coroner is a drunk who talks. What about the mayor?"

"He lawyered up, not with Stockton, obviously. It will take a while to unravel the truth with all the finger pointing. But it looks like Emmitt hoodwinked his sister into letting him mess in the files. He knew he wouldn't get paid unless that whole property sold, and he was desperate."

"Jax won't let them have Witch Hill, will he?" she asked anxiously. "I was hoping he'd be on our side and not use the land to reach some plea deal."

"Loyal and honest to a fault, remember?" His phone pinged, and he held the message up for Evie to see. **SULKING**.

The message included a stock image of a handsome man scowling at an open book.

"Ariel can hear us?" Evie grabbed the phone and typed: **JACKASS BROTHER**

A big grin emoticon flashed back.

Feeling a little better, Evie climbed into the back of the van as Roark took the driver's seat.

"Ariel don't always turn da sound on, but our cameras have mics. She's gettin' pretty bumptious with her own place." The Cajun backed the van out. "Jax been paying us to pick up her groceries and whatnot."

"Don't know how much longer he can do that," Reuben said over the sound of bubbles popping as he and Loretta worked their game console. "Firm's still paying him, I guess. Stockton's put his mansion up for sale. Won't cover all the embezzled money or his legal fees. It's gonna get uglier before it gets better."

"Jax is paid to be my guardian," Loretta said cheerfully. "He won't go broke. Can I make everyone my guardian?"

Evie knuckled her head. "Not your problem. Your problem is fixing us all sandwiches while I show the guys what I showed you the other day."

Loretta bounced and forgot the game. "It's sooooo cool! And spooky and nasty and disgusting."

"Oh yeah, that sounds like a winner. We going to the house? I'm ready for food." Reuben put the game away as Roark turned the van up the drive.

"You're always ready for food. Lucky for you, Loretta's allowance can feed an army. I think Jax is under the delusion that we'd hire a cook and a maid. His secretary never found us one." Evie jumped out to help take down their bicycles and wheel them to the carriage house.

"Y'know, with a little fixin' up, dis place would make a great studio or somet'ing. You could rent it out." Roark pried open the double doors and admired the century-old woodwork.

"I could own a car and need a garage someday," Evie objected. "I just need to earn a living."

"Don't we all?"

While Loretta ran up the back steps to the kitchen, Evie lured Jax's friends to what she hoped would be the treasure chest that would keep them around. Her plans needed people a lot more experienced than she was.

She handed them old brooms and pointed at the angled cellar doors below the back porch. "Originally a root cellar and tornado shelter."

In her great aunt's time, the doors had been painted in a psychedelic rainbow, but the paint had long since faded and peeled, revealing the gray wood beneath. "Your assignment, should you choose to accept it." She ceremoniously yanked open the rusty lock that hadn't worked in years.

She let the men go down first, wielding the brooms like swords. She had no intention of cleaning out spiders if it wasn't necessary.

"Oh man, an original *PacMan pinball*," Reuben crowed as he annihilated cobwebs. The nerd was good with weapons. "There's a whole arcade down here!"

Entering the dim cellar and flipping the switch for the fluorescents, Roark just whistled.

Evie sat on the concrete block steps. "Museum territory. It's either use it or sell it. What do you think?"

They weren't even listening.

"Man, is that an original Apple? Does it work?" Reuben spoke in tones of awe, settling into a space-age gamer chair in front of the ancient computer, checking the wires.

"Val's first husband liked to play. This was way before I was born, as I think you can tell."

"Look at dis futon, man!" Roark cried, examining a moth-eaten faux leopard fur couch. "Clean it up and it would sell in Vegas."

Evie snorted. "Good eye, hotshot. I think that's where he was from. And the showgirls may be why he's Val's *first* husband. She likes her drama but she doesn't share her men. The disco ball appears to be shattered by shotgun pellets." She glanced at the mirrored ball on the ceiling.

"Billiard tables never grow old. *Laissez les bons temps rouler*!" Roark discarded the futon for the pool table, running his hand over the felt. "How did you keep out mold?"

"Val isn't poor. The place has good ventilation, natural air-conditioning from being underground, and a dehumidifying system. You just have to talk to the spiders. What do you think?" She waited for them to get a clue.

Reuben swung the cobweb-coated gaming chair to face her. Roark hefted a custom-made pool cue, cleaning it reverently with the front of his extra-large shirt.

"What do we think about what?" Reuben asked suspiciously.

Evie sighed. Men, the very definition of clueless. "We need work, right? And the two of you will roast in that oven if you try living in your van in summer. So I figure you'll be moving on unless I make an offer you can't refuse. I don't have any money. I can't pay you a salary while I look for clients. I just figure we're all smart enough to market our little success story into a few more jobs."

"Market?" The muscle-bound Cajun set down the cue.

"Offer?" Reuben flicked the switch on the Apple. The screen lit up. His scarred, dark face lit up with it.

"We probably can't call it the Psychics Solution Agency, since you're not psychic. We'll need a better name. We're not detectives, so we have to say Solutions, not detective agency. We'll solve problems in our own unique ways." Evie tried to sound cheerful and confident, as if the answer was obvious. "And while we're building the business, you can live down here and use it as an office."

Loretta came down carrying a basket of food. "Are you staying? Does the Apple work? Do you like peanut butter?"

"You're not eating down here until we clean up this slum," Reuben warned, pointing at the door. "Outside with you, kid."

Evie's heart warmed. She thought that answered her question.

Roark picked up a cue and hit a ball in a pocket. Yep. She'd read their auras right.

The boys needed a home.

Twenty-seven

Jax signed the final paperwork making Evangeline Malcolm Carstairs co-guardian of Loretta Aurora Post. His secretary had prepared the formal document Evie could use to show to schools and doctors that proved she was Loretta's legal representative. If she wanted to start adoption procedures, she'd need to hire her own lawyer.

Thinking of Evie conjured colorful images that filled him with regrets he couldn't afford.

He handed the paperwork back to his secretary.

He'd forced the firm to allow him to remove all of Loretta's fortune out of Stephen's hands and into his control, with the investment broker and bankers as countersignatures. After verifying all was well, he closed his laptop, dropped it into his briefcase, and walked out of his adoptive father's firm.

At his condo, he paid the movers who were hauling his personal belongings to storage. He gave his keys to the real estate agent who would be handling the sale. He wanted no obligations hanging over his head.

He'd already deposited the funds for the Jag. He handed over the keys to the new owner with only a little pain. The XKE had been his pride and joy, but it wasn't practical for a cross-country trip involving suitcases and office equipment. The sale price had allowed him to buy a sturdy Subaru with a bundle of cash left over.

He'd need the cash. Without a salary, his savings would soon be gone, and there was still Ariel to provide for. He was hoping the executor's fees for Loretta's trust would cover his sister's rent and expenses. The Jag cash and his savings were all he had to live on for now.

Heaving his briefcase into the back of the Subaru, he called up images on his phone and suffered a twist of sorrow. Loretta and Evie had bought phones and tortured him with messages. There was Loretta laughing as she biked down Evie's driveway. Loretta could never catch Evie sitting still, so she was a cheerful blur of bouncing curls and outrageous costumes against the backdrop of her house and the shop. There was an image of the two of them, along with his team, having a picnic in Ariel's front yard, taken by Ariel from her windows. He had hopes his sister was in good hands.

There had been a brief moment in time when he'd thought maybe he could unwind, escape the rat race, enjoy having friends and a loving family. . . but he, of all people, knew the futility of dreams.

Just before he climbed into the driver's seat, another message popped up, this one with an image of Evie standing between Reuben and Roark, in front of a sign reading SENSIBLE SOLUTIONS AGENCY.

The message was followed up with a link to the Charleston newspaper with an article on how the agency had solved the murder of the Posts and uncovered scandal in the mayor's office.

His heart twisted along with his gut. He closed the phone without replying.

Until he knew who he was, he couldn't look back. He could only look forward. He'd already determined his destination. He plugged Los Angeles into his phone's GPS and started the engine.

JAX'S STORY IS NEXT! YOU DIDN'T REALLY THINK EVIE AND HIS team would let him drive away alone, did you?

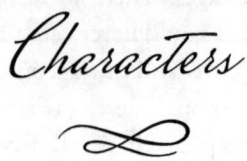

Characters

MALCOLM FAMILY

Evangeline Serena Malcolm Carstairs—Mavis's younger daughter
Mavis Malcolm Carstairs—Evie's mother; owns Psychic Solutions Agency
Gracie— Mavis's elder daughter; school teacher with daughter—**Aster**, age 6;
Great Aunt Evangeline Valerie Brindle—Aunt Val, Civil War re-enactor; lives in Atlanta;
Idonea (Iddy)—Evie's veterinarian cousin
Priscilla—Evie's cousin
Great-grandmother Letitia Malcolm—deceased, Great-Aunt Val's sister, married Evan Post
Aunt Felicia—Mavis's sister; Iddy's mother
Aunt Ellen—Mavis's sister; Pris's mother
Loretta Aurora Post—daughter of John and Tiffany Post; age 10
John and Tiffany Post—Loretta's parents
Cousin Orbis Jr—antique dealer

BOOK ONE:

Damon Jackson (Jax)— lawyer; parents, deceased
Stephen David Stockton—Damon's adoptive father; partner in Stockton and Stockton LLC
Ariel Jackson—Jax's sister
Roark LeBlanc—Jax's Cajun hacker friend
Reuben Thompson—Roark's business partner; doctorate in engineering

TOWNSPEOPLE

Mayor Arthur Block—son Tobias
Gertie—elderly owner of Oldies Café
Sheriff Troy—sheriff of Afterthought
Mrs. Satterwhite—Evie's elderly neighbor
Bill Wright—bank president
Alice Wright—Loretta's teacher; Bill's wife
Tobias Block—mayor's son, ecologist
Remy—owns business shop store
Emma Blue—clerk in city hall deed office
Emmitt Blue—surveyor; Emma's brother

The Indigo Solution
Patricia Rice

Published by Rice Enterprises, Dana Point, CA, an affiliate of Book View Café Publishing Cooperative

Book View Café
304 S. Jones Blvd. Suite #2906
Las Vegas NV 89107

About the Author

With several million books in print and *New York Times* and *USA Today's* bestseller lists under her belt, former CPA Patricia Rice is one of romance's hottest authors. Her emotionally-charged contemporary and historical romances have won numerous awards, including the *RT Book Reviews* Reviewers Choice and Career Achievement Awards. Her books have been honored as Romance Writers of America RITA® finalists in the historical, regency and contemporary categories.

A firm believer in happily-ever-after, Patricia Rice is married to her high school sweetheart and has two children. A native of Kentucky and New York, a past resident of North Carolina and Missouri, she currently resides in Southern California, and now does accounting only for herself.

Also by Patricia Rice

The World of Magic:

The Unexpected Magic Series

MAGIC IN THE STARS

WHISPER OF MAGIC

THEORY OF MAGIC

AURA OF MAGIC

CHEMISTRY OF MAGIC

NO PERFECT MAGIC

The Magical Malcolms Series

MERELY MAGIC

MUST BE MAGIC

THE TROUBLE WITH MAGIC

THIS MAGIC MOMENT

MUCH ADO ABOUT MAGIC

MAGIC MAN

The California Malcolms Series

THE LURE OF SONG AND MAGIC

TROUBLE WITH AIR AND MAGIC

THE RISK OF LOVE AND MAGIC

Crystal Magic

SAPPHIRE NIGHTS

TOPAZ DREAMS

CRYSTAL VISION

WEDDING GEMS

AZURE SECRETS

About Book View Café

Book View Café Publishing Cooperative (BVC) is an author-owned cooperative of professional writers, publishing in a variety of genres including fantasy, romance, mystery, and science fiction — with 90% of the proceeds going to the authors. Since its debut in 2008, BVC has gained a reputation for producing high-quality ebooks. BVC's ebooks are DRM-free and are distributed around the world. The cooperative is now bringing that same quality to its print editions.

BVC authors include New York Times and USA Today bestsellers as well as winners and nominees of many prestigious awards.

www.ingramcontent.com/pod-product-compliance
Lightning Source LLC
Chambersburg PA
CBHW070530100726
47907CB00004B/1064